FLESH AND BLOOD

Patricia Springer

Pinnacle Books
Kensington Publishing Corp.
http://www.pinnaclebooks.com

Some names have been changed to protect the privacy of individuals connected to this story.

PINNACLE BOOKS are published by

Kensington Publishing Corp.
850 Third Avenue
New York, NY 10022

Copyright © 1997 by Patricia Springer

All rights reserved. No part of this book may be reproduced in any form or by any means without the prior written consent of the Publisher, excepting brief quotes used in reviews.

If you purchased this book without a cover, you should be aware that this book is stolen property. It was reported as "unsold and destroyed" to the Publisher and neither the Author nor the Publisher has received any payment for this "stripped book."

Pinnacle and the P logo Reg. U.S. Pat. & TM Off.

First Printing: December, 1997
10　9　8　7　6　5　4　3　2　1

Printed in the United States of America

To my parents, Leonard and Nellie Greer,
for all their loving support throughout the years.

ACKNOWLEDGMENTS

I have been fortunate to have had the cooperation and support of many people in the writing of this book. I wish to thank Detectives Jim Patterson and Chris Frosch, Sergeants David Nabors, Lamar Evans, and Dean Poos, and Lieutenants Grant Jack and Matt Walling of the Rowlett Police Department. Their honesty and sincerity is greatly appreciated. I also wish to thank Paramedic Eric Zimmerman of the Rowlett Fire Department for allowing me to get a glimpse into the emotional impact this case has made on the men and women who fought to save the lives of Devon and Damon Routier. My thanks also to Sandra Halsey, court reporter for Criminal District Court No. 3, Shaun Rabb of Fox 4 KDFW television, Randy Coffey of KRLD radio, Diana Howard, Susie McDaniel, and Martha Cammack.

A special thanks goes to LaRee Bryant for pushing me to succeed, and to Karen Haas for her patience.

AUTHOR'S NOTE

Flesh and Blood is an account of a true crime. The crime and events thereafter have been carefully reconstructed from court records, news coverage, and personal interviews. Some scenes have been dramatically recreated in order to portray more effectively the personalities of those involved.

I regret that Darin and Darlie Routier, although offered the opportunity several times, refused to participate in the telling of this story.

FAMILY MEMBERS

ROUTIER FAMILY
Darin - 28 years old
Darlie - 26 years old
Sons: Devon - 6 years old
      Damon - 5 years old
      Drake - 8 months old
Dog: Domain

DARIN'S FAMILY
Father: Leonard Routier
Mother: Sarilda Routier
Brother: Deon Routier
  Wife: Dana Routier
  Son: Dylan Routier
  Mother-in-law: Lou Ann Brown
Sister: Arenda
Aunt: Sandy Aitken

DARLIE'S FAMILY
Mother: Darlie (Mauk, Peck, Stahl) Kee
      aka: Mama Darlie
Father: Larry Peck
Stepfather: Denny Stahl
Stepfather: Bob Kee
Sisters: Dana - 16 years old
      Danelle - 14 years old
Aunts: Sherry Moses
      Lou Ann Black

Prologue

Ebony darkness shrouded the thriving city of Rowlett, Texas. Only an occasional breeze from the neighboring lake relieved the heavy June heat, rustling leaves, stirring the petals of carefully landscaped flowerbeds, and eliciting a random bark here and there from neighborhood dogs. Secure in the safety and serenity of their homes, the residents of the small Dallas bedroomcommunity slept peacefully.

Except in the big two-story house on Eagle Drive.

Inside the red-brick and white-columned Georgian-style residence, the strobe-like lighting of an oversized television screen flickered in the large first-floor family room, illuminating the innocent faces of the two young boys sleeping on rumpled pallets, and the young mother who had earlier made her own bed on the nearby sofa. Upstairs slept their father and their baby brother.

Into their tranquillity crept evil.

Silently, carefully . . . deadly.

Chapter One

The crash of broken glass followed by a piercing scream jerked Darin Routier from a sound sleep. His first thought was of his eight-month-old son who had been put to bed in the crib across the master bedroom. But it wasn't Drake. Undisturbed, the baby still slept soundly.

Another scream rang out.

"Devon! Devon! Oh my God Devon!" His wife's voice pierced his consciousness.

Downstairs, Darin thought, as he grabbed his glasses from the nightstand and ran for the stairs, nude.

Adrenaline pumping, the 28-year-old father bounded down the staircase and stopped abruptly at the bottom. Disoriented from the sudden disruption of his sleep, he stared questioningly at his wife Darlie who stood at the junction of the shadow-filled family room and the brightly-lit kitchen, shouting into the cordless telephone.

"My husband just ran downstairs. He's helping me . . . but they're dying . . . oh my God . . . they're dead," Darlie screamed hysterically.

Darin's head snapped toward the family room where

the boys had earlier fallen asleep on pallets. Clad only in Power Ranger shorts, Devon, the oldest of the three Routier boys, lay motionless on the carpet. Overturned nearby was the large glass-topped coffee table.

The table must have fallen on Devon. "Oh my God!" Darin shouted. Blocking out Darlie's screams, not even noticing Damon, the five-year-old sprawled on the floor across the room, he rushed to his oldest son.

Two large gaping wounds marred the slender chest of six-year-old Devon Routier. There was little blood, just the frightening sight of exposed tender flesh.

Darin quickly glanced at the round glass tabletop. It rested on its edge, an overturned silk floral arrangement beside it. *No broken glass,* Darin noted questioningly. *How did Devon get cut?* He touched his son's face. The boy looked so strange. *What's happening? What's wrong?* Darin agonized.

There was no time to wonder how the boy received the terrible wounds in his chest. Desperate, Darin set to work. Seven years of first aid and CPR training came flooding back to him. He slapped the boy's face to see if he would look at him. No response. He lowered his ear to Devon's open mouth. No breath. He pressed two fingers to the boy's neck hoping . . . praying for a pulse. There was none. He swiftly wiped the boy's mouth to clear any obstruction, placed the heel of his right hand on the middle of Devon's breastbone and began compressions.

The nearby television continued to play in hushed tones as Darin counted out a cadence.

"One and two and three and . . ." Darin tallied 15 compressions, one full cycle. He leaned forward, covered Devon's nose with one hand, blew two breaths into the boy's mouth, and watched his tiny chest for results. No movement. Darin repeated the sequence, beginning with compressions.

"My babies are dead," cried Darlie, who hadn't moved from her place near the kitchen.

Babies, Darin repeated to himself. The word jerked Darin from his daze.

For the first time Darin's attention diverted from his oldest son. His eyes followed a 15-foot bloody trail across the white carpet to the body of five-year-old Damon.

Darin sprang to his feet and dashed to the boy. On his knees again, he quickly examined his middle child. He saw no wounds. But he heard something. Each inhalation Damon took was accompanied by an ominous gurgle.

Darin sagged in shock when he realized what the sound meant—blood in Damon's lungs.

Stunned, horrified, Darin turned toward his wife. Darlie still clung to the black cordless phone, her lifeline to 911. She hadn't come even one step closer to the injured children.

"Check on Drake," Darlie anxiously instructed Darin.

Darin bounded up the stairs. Drake was crying but he was okay. The young father yanked on his jeans and headed back downstairs.

Whatever wounds Damon had were hidden beneath his black T-shirt and denim jeans. Although his breath was labored, Damon was at least breathing. Devon was not.

Darin returned to his oldest son, doggedly resuming CPR. The young father's desperation grew as the air he frantically puffed into Devon's mouth escaped through the deep holes in the boy's chest. The air, mixed with blood, blew across Darin's bare upper torso forming a crimson mantle. Darin then tried forcing air into one of the expanded holes on Devon's chest. Blood seeped from Devon's mouth.

Nothing was working. Nothing.

In the background, Darin heard his wife tell the operator, "I feel really bad . . . I think I'm dying." For the first time Darin noticed the gash on Darlie's neck, the bright red blood flowing onto her white nightshirt. He stared in horror. What had happened to his family?

"When are they going to be here?" Darlie shouted at

the operator as she stood in the bright light of the kitchen, a sharp contrast to the muted glow that barely illuminated the faces of her children a few feet away.

"Who would do this . . . who would do this?" Darlie frantically asked. "Oh my God . . . oh my God . . . oh . . . he's dead."

Darin knelt frozen over the body of his firstborn. His gaze drifted across the room to the small still form of his middle child. *Please don't take my other son,* he silently prayed.

Chapter Two

Gun drawn, Officer David Waddell cautiously walked into the frantic scene. It had taken him less than three minutes to get there after receiving the dispatcher's call.

No amount of training could have prepared the young officer for the gruesome sight: The blood-streaked floor, the still small bodies, a partially clad adult male with blood spatters across his chest, a frantic, blood-drenched woman on the telephone.

The young blonde woman, barefoot and clad only in a nightshirt that had once been white, hovered near the kitchen entry, a bloody towel pressed to her throat.

"Who did this? Where are they?" Waddell demanded.

Between continued hysterical conversations into the phone, Darlie Routier pointed to the back of the kitchen and said, "They're still in the garage."

Waddell glanced in the direction the woman was pointing toward a closed door at the back of the kitchen. The hair on the back of his neck bristled.

"Sit down," Waddell ordered, but the woman didn't move. She clutched the blood-soaked towel to her throat.

"I've been cut. Look what he did to me," Darlie yelled at Waddell.

Turning to Darin Routier, Waddell instructed him to help the largest of the two boys by applying pressure to his wounds.

"It's no use," Darin cried. "I'm just blowing air through his chest." But the young father couldn't give up. He couldn't let his child die. He continued CPR.

"Get towels and put them on that child's back to stop the bleeding," Waddell yelled at Darlie, hoping to be heard over her emotional rantings. He pointed to the smallest boy, spread-eagled on his stomach. The child's eyes were open. To the policeman they seemed filled with horror and pain.

The woman didn't respond, didn't move from her position.

It was obvious to Waddell that nothing he said was going to convince her to budge. Meanwhile, time was flying by. There were other things he had to do.

Police procedures flooded his mind. *Secure the area. Protect those still alive. Preserve the crime scene.*

Gripping his gun a little tighter, Waddell headed for the utility room that separated the kitchen from the garage. This was the intruder's exit route, according to the woman who was still shouting into the phone clutched tightly in her hand.

Waddell's breathing became increasingly rapid. Ever conscious of his surroundings as he moved across the room, he cataloged everything he saw. Blood on the counter. Broken glass. A bloody knife on the center island bar. Jewelry piled on the counter.

He quickly reached the utility room. There were blood droplets on the floor, but no blood trail leading in or out of the small room. A black ball cap . . . perhaps dropped in haste, lay to the left of the blood stains. Blood was smeared on the door leading to the garage.

The officer hesitated just short of the interior exit door.

Sweat beaded on his forehead. Had the assailant escaped or was he still inside, waiting to attack again? The intruder had left one knife behind, but did he have another weapon? Perhaps a gun. Waddell had been taught to wait for backup. If he violated his training and went into the garage alone, the intruder could possibly take his own service revolver. His first responsibility was to protect the family.

Waddell bent toward the door, which was cracked open less than an inch, and listened intently for any sounds from the other side. He could hear the muffled sound from the big screen television in the family room, the voice of the overwrought woman as she stumbled through fragments of information for the 911 dispatcher, and sirens approaching the residence. But there were no sounds from the garage.

Waddell quickly assessed his options. In seconds he would have someone to help in the search. There were things he needed to know before he continued the hunt.

Behind him Darlie Routier still screamed into the phone. "If they don't get here they're gonna' be dead ... my God ... they're ... hurry ... please hurry!"

Waddell returned to the hysterical woman, hoping to gain valuable information. "Can you give me a description of the suspect?" he asked.

Taking a deep breath before speaking, Darlie Routier said, "He had a black ball cap and a dark shirt. I don't know if he was white or black. I fought with him at the bar. He ran across the kitchen to the garage."

Worried about her blood loss and the possibility of shock, the officer again urged the woman to sit down. She obeyed momentarily, then excitedly jumped to her feet as she continued her pleas to the 911 operator.

Waddell walked over to the smaller of the two young victims. Lying facedown on his stomach, the boy struggled to breathe. Each breath was desperate. Damon looked up at Waddell with huge brown eyes, a look Waddell would never forget. The boy's suffering eyes seemed to ask, "Why?"

Anguish filled the young policeman. There had to be something he could do, something that might save this child.

"Get towels to stop the bleeding," Waddell again yelled at the woman, who was still standing near the kitchen counter, still holding the bloodstained rag close to her own throat. For a second time, Darlie Routier did not move.

"He dropped the knife and I picked it up," Darlie said pointing toward the utility room. "God, I bet we could have gotten the prints, maybe."

Waddell stared in shock at the child's mother. *My God! Why won't she help him?* he wondered.

The arrival of backup jerked Waddell out of his stunned revery.

"What happened here?" Sergeant Matt Walling asked as soon as he arrived on the scene.

"An intruder left through the garage. He may still be out there," Waddell responded, as Walling entered the room.

"Let's go."

Waddell led his sergeant on the route he'd taken just minutes before. They passed the wine rack and carefully stepped over a broken wine glass. They slowed their pace as they guardedly approached the door from the utility room to the attached garage.

Walling gripped his service revolver in his right hand and his standard issue, heavy-duty flashlight in the left.

The thinnest sliver of dark showed through the slight crack between door and frame. Whoever had gone through had shoved it closed but hadn't taken the time to make sure the latch bolt clicked into place. Faint smears of blood stained the door, the facing, and the area around the handle. There was no sign of forced entry.

The officers' hearts raced as Walling pushed the door

open and stepped into the garage. Waddell positioned himself in the doorway for backup.

The yellow beam of Walling's flashlight illuminated a few feet of the cluttered garage. Hands damp with perspiration, he gripped both the gun and the fashlight a bit tighter. Gradually he moved about two feet into the massive room. Stacks of boxes, animal cages, and toys lay in disarray. To the left was a large refrigerator or freezer. Walling eased around the appliance, still alert to the possibility of a hidden intruder.

Waddell, stationed at the doorway of the utility room, caught flashes of Walling's badge against the black of his Rowlett Police Department uniform. Then there was complete darkness. Silence. Finally the glare of Walling's flashlight reappeared as he rounded the corner of the large appliance and continued to survey the garage.

At the back of the double-car garage there were several low windows. One was open. The screen sagged from a large cut a few inches from the top, and another down the center. All other windows were closed, their screens intact.

The overhead garage door was securely locked.

"All clear," Walling finally told Waddell.

The policemen returned to the interior of the house.

Retracing their steps, the officers passed back through the kitchen. The glitter of scattered jewelry caught their attention—a woman's gold watch, several gold and diamond rings, bracelets, and a necklace in plain view on the white Formica counter. Nearby lay a red wallet with cash, credit cards, and a large check made out to Darlie Routier. Had the intruder been scared off before he could grab the loot?

These kinds of crimes were usually associated with robbery or rape. If the intruder had come for loot, he had passed it by. Perhaps the motive was rape. The woman with the tear-stained face in the kitchen was obviously a "looker." But the question remained: why had the intruder passed up the jewelry, taken his rage out on two innocent children, and then attacked their mother? A rapist would more than likely use the threat of harming the children if she didn't cooperate. If he killed them first, where was the leverage?

Waddell was annoyed to see that Darlie Routier still hadn't moved from the passageway between the sofa table and the kitchen bar. Nor had she put towels on her youngest son as he had instructed. She simply stood there, whimpering softly as she clung to the rag held to her neck.

Moving back into the chaotic scene, Walling passed between two green leather sofas, only a few feet from the body of Devon Routier.

"God!" He yelled in fright, jumping backward as a wild yowl sounded.

Tucked between the sofa where Darlie had rested earlier and the big screen television was a medium-sized cat cage. As soon as Walling trespassed within three feet of the pen, the extra large, fluffy feline inside had come to life. Frantic, the cat bounced from one side of the cage to the other, screeching in high-pitched tones, and clawing at the slender wires that framed the cage.

Walling took a moment to catch his breath and let the pounding of his heart return to something near normal.

"Secure the front door," Walling instructed Waddell sharply. "Don't let anybody in."

The first ambulance to arrive on the scene had screeched to a halt at the curb while Waddell and Walling had been searching the garage. As he waited, paramedic Jack Kolbye nervously clicked his fingernails on the door handle. "Hurry up. Hurry up," he repeated impatiently, as he waited for the all clear sign that would allow them to enter the house.

Within minutes they saw Sergeant Walling walking toward them.

"You have two children inside. You're going to need some help," Walling told Kolbye and his partner Bryan Kolshak. Walling's face showed telltale signs of stress. His strong voice was marred by a slight quiver.

While paramedics rushed to the house to assist the victims, Walling made his way to the rear of the residence. There he met up with Patrolman Moore. Together they approched the six-foot, white stockade fence that surrounded the backyard. The gate was closed and latched.

Walling flipped up the metal clamp that secured the swinging gate and pushed on the door. It didn't budge. The sergeant put his foot against the bottom of the wooden panel, giving it a hard shove as he lifted the gate. Reluctantly the door opened, scraping against an aggregate walkway.

Inside the yard, the officers quickly scanned the perimeter for any movement, any signs of the assailant. They saw nothing.

They made a mental note of where the window with the cut screen was located. Two upright green plastic chairs stood near the opening, another was overturned nearby. A soccer goal, firmly in place and undisturbed, was located just to the left of the window, and to the right was a light blue dog dish. Beside it lay a child's black shoe.

Further to the right of the porch, light flowed from the sliding glass doors of the family room. The reflection of the television bounced off the glass like a flickering light show. Across the lawn, past the sunken fish pond and wild flower garden, stood a redwood gazebo housing a hot tub.

Walling and Moore crossed the quadrant to search the spa. A beam of light flashed to life from a motion sensor attached to the top of the wooden structure. Both men flinched slightly.

Peering inside, Walling made note of a wet bar, hanging flower baskets, liquor bottles, television, stereo, and a large fiberglass molded hot tub. Wet towels were piled on the floor.

No intruder. No signs of disturbance.

"Search the neighborhood for suspects," Walling orderd Moore, as he headed back toward the front of the house.

As Walling left to search the backyard with Moore, Kolbye grabbed his medical kit from the storage bin on the outside of the ambulance and ran for the house. Kolshak called for additional help and then hurried after his partner, entering the house only steps behind.

Kolbye rushed through the entry hall, glancing quickly to his left into a beautifully decorated formal living room. Across the hall, on his right, was an equally gorgeous formal dining area. The large rosewood table was set with china and crystal as though waiting for dinner guests to arrive. Hearing loud screams from the back of the house, Kolbye hastened into the family room.

Officer Waddell stood near the kitchen, in front of an extended bar. Waddell nodded toward a small child. Arms outstretched, the boy lay facedown on the floor just to the left of the entrance to the family room, near the downstairs bathroom.

A slight hesitation in his step was the only sign of Kolbye's response to the alarming situation. He raced over to the inanimate figure sprawled on the floor and fell to his knees beside the small, motionless body of Damon Routier.

Kolbye lifted the boy's blood-soaked black T-shirt, and sucked in a breath. The damage was horrifying. The youngster's narrow back had been viciously ripped open. Four large gashes and two smaller incisor wounds had penetrated the tanned skin and youthful flesh.

The paramedic tore open numerous four-by-four packages of sterile gauze and pressed them to the fragile back of the young child. Kolbye had to stop the bleeding. He had to save this boy.

Darin and Darlie Routier stood by the sliding glass doors, their heads close together talking. Suddenly, Darin's head jerked backward and he quickly moved away from his wife.

"Help him! Help him!" Darin screamed at the paramedic.

In a surprisingly controlled tone, his wife told him, "Get Karen!"

"Who's Karen?" Waddell asked.

"A neighbor. She's a nurse," Darin answered.

"Get her. We could use some help."

Darin raced from the room. Outside he sprinted across the street toward Karen and Terry Neal's two-story house.

Damon gasped for air as Kolbye gently rolled him over to begin emergency treatment. The boy's eyes, dark as chocolate kisses, looking up at Kolbye possessed a glimmer of light. A flicker of life. But the light was beginning to fade.

This kid's a fighter, he wants to live, Kolbye thought, as he desperately began mouth-to-mouth resuscitation.

Seconds clicked by. For two desperation-filled minutes, the seasoned CPR instructor performed the lifesaving maneuver in a futile attempt to save the boy's life. He felt as though he were moving in slow motion. The minutes seemed like hours.

Then, shaken and repelled at the senselessness of the crime and realizing how hopeless the situation was, the paramedic scooped up the boy and rushed past Bryan Kolshak. Kolbye was shocked to realize his partner was attending a second small boy on the far side of the room. Devoting all his attention to Damon, Kolbye hadn't noticed the second victim.

Doubly stunned, Kolbye continued toward the ambulance. The child in his arms urgently needed advanced life support.

Kolbye stared into Damon's fearful eyes all the way to his unit. "Hold on," he told the boy. "Hold on."

Despite his efforts, Damon had no pulse and he wasn't breathing.

The Rowlett Fire Department engine company wailed to a stop just as Kolbye ran from the house with Damon.

He hurriedly summoned paramedic Rick Coleman for assistance. Inside the ambulance Kolbye fervently resumed chest compressions while Coleman took over respiratory efforts. They worked in tandem in an effort to save the life of the five-year-old.

Coleman inserted a trac tube in the boy's throat, and an IV was put directly into his jugular vein. A cardiac drug was administered in an all-out effort to save Damon's life.

Mike Youngblood came from the engine company unit and climbed behind the wheel of the ambulance. Within minutes, Damon Routier was enroute to Baylor Hospital.

Bryan Kolshak remained in the house, kneeling beside the body of Devon Routier. Two large puncture wounds penetrated his tiny chest. Deep, gaping wounds. One thrust had been driven so violently into his body that it exited his back and penetrated the carpet and concrete slab beneath.

Devon had no pulse, no respiration . . . no life. His large blue-green eyes were open wide in an expression of surprise.

Kolshak's eyes filled with tears. A feeling of defeat consumed him. *There's nothing I can do for this child,* he thought.

Kolshak turned his attention to the woman standing near the kitchen bar beside Officer Waddell. Dressed in a blood-soaked T-shirt and clinging to a bloody towel, at least she appeared to be a viable patient.

Carefully, Kolshak removed the rag from Darlie Routier's clenched fist. A large laceration extended from just below her right ear, nearly four inches diagonally downward toward her chest. A second laceration was present about two inches lower and to the left of the extended wound. He gave the towel back to Darlie.

"Who could have done this to my babies?" she sobbed, the words precise and clear, despite the mayhem surrounding her. Her face contorted in pain but no tears dampened her eyes. She didn't ask how the children were.

Kolshak wanted to get Darlie Routier away from the scene. He needed to keep her calm.

"Come with me to the front porch," the paramedic instructed. The woman followed obediently.

Sergeant Walling was still on the front porch when Darlie Routier, Bryan Kolshak, and Officer Waddell left the house.

"Let's go upstairs and do a search," Walling said.

Waddell followed his sergeant back into the house.

The officers climbed the staircase, pausing momentarily beside a cherry-wood table and oval mirror on the landing. A large 16-by-20 portrait of two smiling boys hung on the wall. Walling stared at the picture. Flashes of the bloody children downstairs darted through his mind.

Walling nodded toward the right and the two officers proceeded down the hall. The first room they checked belonged to one of the boys. Red metal bunk beds with green striped bedspreads stood in the center of the room, a white chest with brightly painted red handles on the far wall. A small bookcase with a number of children's books stood beside a desk. Except for a toy rifle resting on the top bunk, the only other toys visible in the neat and orderly space were two plastic trucks.

The next room must have belonged to the other Routier child. Mickey Mouse wallpaper, bedspread, and rug colorfully accented the area.

Walling and Waddell moved toward the opposite end of the hall. Collectibles, autographs, sports cards, a second big screen television, stereo, and computer system apeared undisturbed in an adult game room. Dozens of Nintendo games were neatly stacked beside the television. A picture of John F. Kennedy hung on one wall, a picture of a black panther on another. The green leather furniture appeared undisturbed.

The upstairs bath was clear.

They found no intruder, no other victims.

There was only one more room to inspect.

Walling was the first to enter the spacious master bedroom.

Without warning he was surprised by one of its occupants. An excited ball of white fluff barked at Walling with the virile attitude of a Doberman. The high-pitched, ear-piercing bark resounded throughout the room. Walling snapped sharply at the dog, who scurried back to his bed on the far side of the master suite.

Walling breathed deeply. Waddell suppressed a smile. Their attention was quickly diverted from the pint-sized attack dog to another, more surprising discovery.

At the far end of the four-poster bed seven-month-old Drake Routier stood in his crib, peering over the top rail with huge brown eyes. Shielded by a ruffled canopy that matched the floral comforter on his tiny bed, the baby appeared unharmed.

Bewildered, Walling and Waddell looked at one another. The parents hadn't mentioned another child in the house. The lawmen left the infant in his crib and went back downstairs.

Waddell returned to his post at the front door.

Walling exited the house and used his portable telephone to check the location of all officers on his watch. He called for the crime scene unit and attempted to secure a Department of Public Safety (DPS) helicopter to aid in the manhunt.

"Sorry, but helicopters just aren't very successful in night searches," the DPS officer told Walling. The sergeant then called the neighboring city of Garland, requesting their K-9 unit. No excuses there. Dogs work day or night. They would be on the scene as soon as possible.

Just as Walling hung up with the Garland officer, an unidentified car sped around the corner, barreling down Eagle Drive. Quickly, Walling moved to the middle of the street and pointed his gun directly at the driver of the black sports coupe.

"Stop!" Walling ordered.

The car halted immediately.

Rowlett police converged on the occupants, slinging open all four doors and pulling out the passengers.

Four teenagers, one female, one black male, and two white males, were shoved forward against the car, their legs spread-eagled behind them as officers patted them down for weapons. The car was searched.

The scene, familiar to viewers of television shows like *Top Cops,* was out of place on the serene Rowlett street.

None of the teens matched the sketchy description of the intruder given by Darlie Routier. No black ball caps. No dark T-shirts. No blood on their clothes.

The juveniles were allowed to leave after a few minutes delay.

Walling had had enough heart stopping events for one night, but there was still work to do. Taking a roll of brightly colored yellow and black crime scene tape from his squad car, he began stringing the tape around the perimeter of the property. He knew the integrity of the scene had to be insured.

When Darin Routier and Terry and Karen Neal ran to the Routier house, the trio were stopped at the front steps by Officer Waddell and told they couldn't go any further.

"But I'm a nurse," Karen said anxiously.

"Okay, you can go ahead."

Karen went directly to Darlie who sat on the porch flanked by paramedics. Karen smothered a gasp, trying not to show her friend how shocked she was at the sight of her blood-soaked nightshirt, or her obvious wounds. Stepping a few feet inside the front door, she could see Devon lying on his back, partially covered by a blanket. Only his right eye peeked from beneath the cover. She recoiled in distress.

Masking her nausea and fear, Karen returned to the porch to see if she could help Darlie.

With bright porch lights illuminating Darlie's wounds, paramedic Bryan Kolshak made a mental note of her condition. Skin color good; temperature, normal; blood return under her nail, typical; able to follow commands normally. No cardiogenic shock. No neurogenic shock.

Crouched on the front porch, Darlie looked up at Kolshak and asked again, "Who could have done this to my babies?"

Kolshak dropped the bloody rag Darlie had been holding to her throat on the porch. She grimaced as he mashed gauze pads against her injured neck, then securely wrapped the entire circumference with bandages just as the ambulance from the Main Street station screeched to a halt in front of the residence.

Partners Eric Zimmerman and Larry Byford jumped from the unit and hurried to the front porch. Byford applied a bandage to Darlie's right forearm, covering a two-inch laceration, just inches below her elbow.

Captain Dennis Vrava of the Rowlett Fire Department entered the residence while his men attended to the female victim. Vrava confirmed there was no life in Devon Routier. He briefly spoke with Darin, then checked the upstairs for more victims.

As Zimmerman and Byford worked on Darlie Routier, Todd Higgins from the second ambulance on the scene wheeled another stretcher up the walk.

"He broke out a window and had a baseball cap," Darlie told them. "Who could have done this?" There was desperation in her voice. She then described an assailant with brown hair, a brown mustache, and added that he was tall.

"Step over here and sit on the stretcher," Kolshak instructed Darlie.

Once Darlie Routier was lying on the gurney, paramedics lifted it and popped down the wheels. Kolshak, Higgins and Byford rushed the patient to the waiting ambulance and hoisted the stretcher into the bed of the mobile unit.

Walling stopped stringing crime scene tape long enough

to speak momentarily with Karen Neal. He requested she take Drake to her home until further notice.

Minutes later, tiny Drake Routier was taken from the nightmare scene in his family home and given to the Neals for safekeeping.

Inside the ambulance, Kolshak quickly snapped an IV bag of saline solution to the chrome hook on his right and began looking for a vein in Darlie Routier's arm. Byford extracted scissors from the lower pocket of his paramedic pants and, in three swift movements—one up the center, the second across the right shoulder, the third across the left shoulder—cut off her Victoria's Secret sleepshirt. The cotton garment fell away from Darlie's nude body. There were no other apparent injuries.

Kolshak swiftly inserted the needle and adjusted for a minimum IV drip while Higgins took her blood pressure. "One forty over eighty," he announced. "She's doing great." Higgins then attached a heart monitor to Darlie's blood-covered chest.

Darin Routier stepped up on the rear bumper of the ambulance, ready to ride to the hospital with his wife.

"You can't ride back here," Higgins said, as he climbed out of the ambulance, pushing Darin back. Paramedic Larry Byford remained inside with Darlie Routier.

"But I want to go with my wife," Darin insisted.

"Sorry, you can ride in the cab, but not back here."

"No," he said. "I have to ride with Darlie."

"Sorry, there's no room," Kolshak said, pushing past him and slamming shut the back doors of the ambulance. Kolshak gave the door a hard couple of taps to signal Eric Zimmerman it was time to leave.

Darin Routier stared in disbelief at the swiftly vanishing ambulance.

Darin shouted at officers, "I want everybody here. Helicopters, police, ambulances. Get the whole police force out here!"

My God! This nightmare couldn't be happening. Devon

was dead. Damon was hanging on by a thread. Drake had been taken from their home and given into the care of the Neals. And Darlie was on her way to the hospital in serious condition. It was like a bad dream.

Darin Routier sank down on the curb in front of his home, lowered his head into his hands, and wept.

For the Routiers, the nightmare had just begun.

Chapter Three

With Eric Zimmerman at the wheel, ambulance number 901 rambled down Eagle Drive to Highway 66, and onto Interstate 30 West toward downtown Dallas. In the back, Larry Byford stripped the bloody latex gloves from his hands. He slipped them in the red bio-hazard bag, and pulled on clean sterile gloves to eliminate the possibility of contamination.

Byford sat across from Darlie Routier as he began charting the patient.

"What's your name?" He asked.

"Darlie Routier."

"How old are you?"

"Twenty-six."

The patient appeared well oriented. Byford continued completing his run report.

"What's your date of birth?"

"January 1, 1970. How much further to the hospital?" Darlie asked anxiously.

"Do you have any drug allergies?" Byford continued with the charting.

"No. Are we there yet?" Darlie's anxiety level was rising.

"Are you taking any medications?"

"Diet pills. Fastin and Pondimin."

Byford noted the drugs on the chart. Leaning forward, he examined the bandage around Darlie's neck. A gleam of gold caught his eye. A thin necklace was embedded in the wound. Darlie grimaced as Byford attempted to pull the chain from the laceration. He decided to leave it in place.

"Are we there yet?" Darlie asked again. Her distress seemed to be increasing, but her blood pressure remained stable.

She's anxious, but she still hasn't asked about the boys, Byford thought.

Zimmerman turned past the bright orange sign marking the entrance to Baylor Hospital's emergency unit from North Hall Street, near downtown Dallas. The vehicle sped past the live oak trees defining the drive and came to an abrupt halt at the entrance to the emergency room. Darlie Routier's vital signs had remained stable during the 25-minute trip from the bloody crime scene in Rowlett to Baylor Hospital in Dallas.

Zimmerman swung open the rear door, pulled the green-sheeted gurney from the vehicle, and, along with Byford, rushed Darlie through the automatic double doors, the same doors her critically injured son, Damon, had gone through only minutes earlier.

As the ambulance carrying Darlie sped toward Dallas, Kolshak slowly walked past Darin Routier, who was still sitting on the curb. He made his way across the two-lane street to the home of Karen and Terry Neal to check on Drake, quite possibly the only remaining Routier son.

Drake was in good shape. He had no injuries. He slept

soundly, unaware of the horrific events that had taken place earlier that morning.

Kolshak walked back to the Routier house at a sluggish pace, visually disturbed by the carnage he had witnessed earlier. He couldn't get the vision of Devon Routier out of his mind. He thought of his own small children. Kolshak wanted to go home, he wanted to hold his kids, and most of all he wanted to get away from the slaughter site. But Kolshak couldn't go home. He still had a job to do.

While Kolshak made his way back to the crime scene, Darin Routier at last rose from his place on the curb and walked sadly to the Neal house. Paramedics and policemen had been urging him for over 30 minutes to leave for the hospital where Darlie and Damon had been taken. But Darin had remained at the scene.

Once inside the Neal house, Darin washed, borrowed a T-shirt from Terry Neal, and asked Terry to drive him to the hospital. The lights of his house faded from view as Neal guided Darin's green Pathfinder out of the once peaceful neighborhood, toward Dallas. Darin would soon be with Darlie.

Back inside the house, Kolshak again kneeled beside Devon Routier, his slender body smeared with blood, his Power Ranger shorts drenched in the red fluid. Devon's arms casually lay at his sides, near his bloodstained Power Ranger pillowcase. His right knee was crooked slightly. But the most disturbing sight was his eyes. Still open. Still with that same questioning look. *If only his eyes could tell me what happened here,* Kolshak thought.

Silently, Kolshak pulled the black-and-white comforter, used earlier as a sleep pallet, over the body of the dead boy. Soon someone from the medical examiner's office would come and pronounce Devon Routier's death official. His small still body would be taken in for autopsy.

Emotionally distraught, the paramedic called the fire department chaplain and left the house for the last time.

* * *

Dr. Alex Santos was preparing to leave the Baylor Hospital emergency room at 3:25 A.M. on the morning of June 6, 1996. It had been a long night, and he was weary. A call from the Rowlett Fire Department paramedics immediately changed his plans.

One child and one adult, each with multiple stab wounds, were enroute to the hospital. Dr. Santos knew he'd need help. He quickly notified Dr. Patrick Dillaw, the trauma resident on duty, and ordered two trauma rooms be readied at once.

Nurse Jody Fitts usually left after her shift was over at 2:00 A.M. But it had been an extremely busy night in Baylor's emergency room. When the call came in that two stabbing victims were on their way, she put on her hospital scrubs, and set up the equipment in trauma room number one.

Santos's head jerked around as he heard the double doors of the emergency room open. The clamor of paramedics roaring into the wide, gray ER hall reverberated throughout the unit. The doctor pointed to trauma room number one, already prepared for the incoming victims. Kolbye and Youngblood carried Damon Routier into the large room on a backboard, a trac tube prominently visible in his throat. They lifted the still body of the small boy onto the ER table, and quickly moved aside so the Baylor staff could take over.

The overcrowed room was packed with X-ray machines, monitors, and overhead IV stands. A drawn curtain was pulled shut for privacy.

Doctors Santos and Dillaw instantly began evaluating the condition of the first of the two Routiers they would see that night.

"White male, five to six years old," Dr. Santos said.

Dr. Dillaw carefully rolled the boy over, exposing the wounds on his back.

"Multiple stab wounds to his back. No signs of life," Santos said.

Santos grabbed Damon's tiny hand, pressing his fingers against the limp wrist. No pulse. He reached for the stethoscope hung loosely around his neck, feeling certain that no heartbeat would be heard. He was right. With his thumb and index finger, Santos opened one of the boy's eyes. Gone was the flicker of life seen by Jack Kolbye just minutes earlier. Santos only saw death. In less than a minute after Damon Routier was brought into Baylor's emergency room, Dr. Santos officially pronounced him dead.

Dr. Dillaw quietly left the room and headed down the hall where Darlie Routier had just been admitted.

With care, Dr. Santos probed Damon's wounds with a gloved finger, exploring the depths of the penetrating injuries. Four gaping stab wounds marred the boy's narrow upper back. The largest of the foursome was two inches in length and a depth of more than four inches. Both the child's liver and lung had been perforated. Two additional lacerations pierced his back, each higher and to the left of the more invasive wounds.

Santos shook his head. Gunshot wounds, stabbings, auto accident victims with broken bones and bloody faces were all part of a day's work. But in his five years of medical practice he'd never become accustomed to the loss of a child or to such senseless carnage.

A nurse carefully placed paper bags over the boy's hands to protect any possible evidence.

"Doctor Santos, we need to send the female stabbing victim to surgery," Dr. Dillaw reported from the opening of the trauma room.

Santos immediately turned his attention from the dead to the living.

Darlie Routier had been wheeled into the emergency room while Santos and Dillaw were in the midst of their examination of her son, Damon.

From outside Darlie's room, some 50 feet from where

her son had just been pronounced dead, nurse Fitts could hear the woman screaming.

"I need pain medication," she bellowed. "Why did they kill my boys?" Her cry then changed to, "Why did he kill my boys?"

As Jody Fitts peered around the corner into trauma room number five, she noticed the angle of Darlie's head. She was looking toward the room where Damon was being examined. Nurse Fitts helped transfer Darlie from the stretcher to the bed and began assessing her wounds. The paramedics took off the dressing they had applied, and began giving Fitts the information obtained on the trip to the hospital.

When Dr. Dillaw arrived in Darlie's room, resuscitation procedures were in progress.

Dillaw quickly made note of the stab wound on her neck. Blood seeped from the wound as he touched the area lightly.

"Did you lose consciousness?" the resident asked.

"No."

"How did your wounds occur?" Dillaw asked, expecting a response of 'stabbed'. But the female patient went into an alert, talkative explanation.

"A white male in a baseball cap. I only saw him from the back," Darlie said.

For the next 13 minutes Dr. Dillaw examined the wound on Darlie's neck, the laceration to her arm, and the gash on her left shoulder. The doctor noted that there were no other cuts on her arms, and none on her hands. There were no signs of head injury.

Darlie was asked again about allergies to medications, drugs she was currently taking, and any surgeries that she may have had in the past.

The long incision on Darlie's neck was clearly through the skin, the fat, and the platysma. Dillaw had a choice, either suture the laceration in ER or take the patient to surgery. Because of the depth of the wound and the possibility of interruption of blood flow to the brain and heart, he decided on surgery. He notified Dr. Santos.

While waiting for Dr. Santos, nurse Fitts carefully removed the gold chain embedded in Darlie's neck. She handed the chain to Zimmerman. He also gathered the bloody nightshirt, and disposable stretcher sheet, and from the other room, Damon's clothing.

Dr. Santos arrived and took little time in evaluating Darlie Routier. From the blood on her chest and body, he could tell the neck wound had bled excessively. He concurred with Dr. Dillaw that surgery was their best option. The doctors scrubbed for surgery as Darlie was prepped and put under general anesthesia.

An anxious Darin Routier arrived at the hospital and was taken to a waiting room where he remained, along with Terry Neal, while Darlie was in surgery. Darin knew that both Devon and Damon were dead. And now his soul mate, his reason for living, was behind the metal doors leading to the Baylor operation room. He couldn't lose Darlie.

She was his world.

Chapter Four

The Garland search dog and Officer B.P. Griffith arrived at the Routier house about 3:00 A.M. Officer Steve Ward relieved Waddell at the front door of the residence, freeing him to work with the K-9 unit. For about 50 minutes Waddell, Griffith, and the specially trained dog walked around the neighborhood, up and down the alleys, searching for the suspect described by Darlie Routier.

No suspect. Nothing unusual discovered. No indication anyone had been there.

Waddell was ordered to stay in the alley behind the Routier house and watch for anyone who might come into the lane. During the four-hour watch on the hot, humid morning, he stopped only one vehicle, occupied by a white female who was on her way to work. She was not detained and no other vehicles or suspects were seen.

Detective Jim Patterson arrived at the Routier house at 3:30 A.M. The lead detective immediately went over to Sergeant Walling to be briefed on the sequence of events that had begun only an hour earlier.

Once briefed, Patterson peered into the house from the

front door. Then he walked to the back where he made a mental note of the cut screen. Within minutes he returned to the front yard.

"Would you go to the hospital and see the female survivor?" Walling asked Patterson.

The detective nodded. He knew the crime scene unit would be there for hours collecting evidence. He'd be back later to talk with them about their findings.

Patterson's attention was diverted to an elderly female who was hollering from across the street. "I want to talk to an officer."

"Can I help you?" Patterson asked in his slow easy manner as he walked toward the excited, elderly woman.

"I saw a car leaving the scene as the police and fire departments arrived," she told him anxiously.

"Who are you?" Patterson asked.

"My name is Nelda Watts. I live across from the Routiers. I saw a car leave right as the police were arriving," she said again.

"What did the car look like?" Patterson asked.

"It was a dark color, maybe black. Small."

Patterson thanked Mrs. Watts for her help and made a mental note of their brief conversation. He would add Mrs. Watts's information to his written report later.

For about 10 minutes, Patterson spoke with firemen and paramedics at the scene in an attempt to grasp what had taken place in the bloodstained house. Their mood was somber.

Speaking rapidly and shaking slightly, a brown-haired woman with glasses quickly made her way to the taped-off boundary line. Patterson joined her at the yellow taped border.

"My name is Barbara Jovell. A neighbor called me and told me something bad has happened. I work with Darin Routier and Darlie is my best friend," she said with a thick Polish accent. "My mother was at the Routiers yesterday.

She saw a black car about three forty-five or four o'clock. The car was in the alleyway behind the house."

Patterson thanked her for the information, took her mother's name and phone number, and headed for his car. Two reports of a black auto in the neighborhood. Later he would canvass the neighbors for any other sightings, any further description of the car. But for now he needed to question the only witness to the frightful crime as soon as possible.

A little after 4:00 A.M. Patterson climbed into his green Ford Taurus and drove westward to Baylor Hospital to interview Darlie Routier.

Just as Patterson was pulling away from the crime scene, Officer Thomas Ward parked his marked patrol car at the curb. Rousted out of bed at 3:00 A.M. with the news of the stabbings, he'd quickly dressed and gone directly to the Rowlett Police Department to pick up needed equipment, and the marked car before heading to Eagle Drive.

"I want you to supervise the outside perimeter," Sergeant Walling told Ward. "Stop anyone leaving for work and ask if they saw anything. Also sweep the area for possible evidence."

Ward positioned an officer at each end of the dark alley to stop any and all traffic. Meanwhile, he met with Officer Steve Ferrie and began an exhaustive search of the back alley dividing Eagle Drive and Willowbend. Ward took the Eagle Drive side of the lane, Ferrie Willowbend.

Flashlights glowed like minisearchlights as Ward and Ferrie scanned backyards, driveways, and fence lines. Ferrie carefully approached a covered boat at the residence directly behind the Routier home. Slowly he lifted an edge of the canvas boat cover. Poking the flashlight through the slight opening, he scanned the interior. All clear.

The six-foot wooden stockade fences surrounding the majority of houses along the row presented a challege to the officers. They had to look inside each of the backyards.

The suspect could be crouched behind the fence or huddled next to a house.

Tentively, Ward hoisted his overweight frame onto one of the two silver water meters stationed between the first two houses on the Eagle Drive side of the alley. From his vantage point atop the foot-high meter, he grasped the top of the fence and peered over the wooden enclosure. Once again, all was clear.

Ward repeated the process at the next house. Ferrie worked the Willowbend side of the alley in much the same manner. Occasionally the men would use the two-foot-tall green utility boxes, sporatically located up and down the paved inlet, as step stools.

Slowly, thoroughly, the officers searched each brown two-wheeled trash can, and each red recycling bin that lined the alley.

"Search the trash cans like you're looking for your lost paycheck and you gotta' find it," Ward told Ferrie.

Each man threw the attached lids back and rifled among the rank contents. No blood. No weapons. No suspect.

Behind the third house on Ward's side of the alley, he stopped abruptly. The ray of his patrol flashlight picked up a bright white spot beside the trash container. He moved in for a closer look.

On the bare ground, beside the receptacle and only inches away from an open concrete drainage ditch, was a single white sock. Wade leaned forward. His light illuminated a single spot of blood. The stain, the size of an elongated nickel, was the only visible blemish.

Without touching the tube-type sock, Wade studied the fabric. The sock appeared to be in good condition. Leaving it where it was, Wade thoroughly scanned the surrounding area.

He cautiously lifted the lid on the trash container beside his discovery. The sour stench of wet cut grass assaulted his nostrils. He shook his head, as if to clear the smell. He emptied the bin, about two-thirds full of the grass clippings, on the ground. No blood inside the container. No blood on the outside. No blood in the grass. No other sock. No shoes.

"Come here," Wade called to Ferrie. "Think I've found something."

Ferrie moved to the opposite side of the alley, behind the house three doors down from the Routiers. He looked at the white object on the ground.

"Go get a crime scene investigator," Wade instructed. He remained with the evidence while Ferrie returned to the Routier home.

Officer David Mayne had arrived at the residence at 4:15 A.M. He was preparing to take photos of the crime scene and secure any discovered evidence when Ferrie requested him to follow him down the alley to where Wade had secured the sock.

Mayne took seven photos of the sock from various angles, as well as shots of the surrounding area. He then gently picked up the sock with latex-gloved hands and dropped it into a clean brown grocery bag, tagged it for evidence, and secured the top folded edge.

While Wade and Ferrie resumed their search of the alley, Mayne field-tested the sock. The instant results revealed that the red-colored spot was indeed blood.

Fifty-five minutes later the extensive alley search had uncovered no additional evidence, no blood in the alley, or any blood on the fences that lined the narrow lane. The thorough search had even included looking inside a manhole cover, but with negative results.

Satisfied that their inspection was complete, Ferrie was assigned to relieve the officer stationed at the front door while Wade began canvassing the neighborhood.

After waking up those residents who managed to sleep through the sirens and commotion, Wade broke the unbelievable news of the assault on the Routier family.

"Did you hear anything?" Wade asked. "See any unusual activity? Any strangers in the area?"

The officer also questioned anxious neighbors who stood in their yards, and sat on the curbs. Fearfully they clutched their children to them wondering who could be next.

Wade received negative responses to each question from the stunned neighbors. No one had seen anyone matching the description of the intruder.

Daylight chased away the darkness and shed new light on the horrors of the tragedy. Thomas Ward made a second sweep through the alley. Visibility was better, and he wanted to make sure he and Ferrie hadn't missed something on their initial hunt.

Sure enough, as Wade went back down the alley, he made a disturbing discovery he had missed in the darkness.

In the backyard of a home on Willowbend, through the six-foot, locked white iron gate adorned with black scrolls and a four-foot green hedge surrounding the yard, he saw a knife thrust into the ground, another metallic silver knife lay flat on the grass. Two-thirds of a butcher knife protruded from the ground. Beside that, a screwdriver had been deeply embedded. Wade studied the objects intensely and then began to scan the entire backyard.

Rubber edging, partially embedded into the ground, led up to the knives and the yellow-handled screwdriver. At the end of the tool was tied a string. Fresh mud coated the handle of the metal knife and muddy finger imprints were visible on the wooden-handled butcher knife.

No visible signs of blood.

Someone must be landscaping, Ward thought. *Looks like they are inserting edging.*

But Ward knew every lead had to be investigated. He made his way to the front of the house.

Eighteen-year-old Gustavo Guzman, Jr. was awakened by the ringing of his front door bell and a loud pounding. He had gone to bed late and was groggy from lack of sleep as he stumbled to the door.

Ward identified himself as a Rowlett police officer and told the teen that he needed to ask him some questions.

"Have you seen or heard anything unusual in the last few hours?" Ward asked.

"I played roller hockey until about midnight at the high school with some friends. I came home with a friend that lives down the street. I didn't get here until about one o'clock. Then I watched some TV in the kitchen. I saw some cops with flashlights looking at the grass and around the fence . . . behind the house in the alley. I ignored them and went upstairs to bed."

"Have you been doing some gardening?" Ward asked.

"I've been putting edging around the bushes along the back fence, along the alley. The white metal fence has five or six-inch gaps between the bars. I was laying down edging where the bushes are messy . . . to separate the bushes from the grass."

"How are you doing that?"

"I'm using knives, spoons, and a shovel."

"Where did you get the knives?" Ward asked.

"They're old kitchen knives. I cut deep into the ground, then use a shovel. I tie a rope to the end of one knife, then to the end of the other. It makes a straight line."

"Did you finish the job?"

"No. I left it until next week. The knives were muddy so I left them outside to go play street hockey."

"Mind if I take a look?" Ward asked.

Guzman led Ward through the house to the backyard. As Ward had earlier determined, the tools were covered in mud and appeared to have been lodged in the ground for some time. *These aren't our murder weapon,* Ward thought. He left them there and returned to the Routier house.

About 5:45 A.M., as Ward was busy searching the alley a second time and questioning Guzman, James Cron arrived. Called earlier by the Rowlett dispatcher, Cron was familiar with the Rowlett Police Department (RPD) and many of the officers. He had conducted crime scene schools at the RPD and was pleased that Sergeants Matt Walling and David Nabors had called him into this investigation early. Older and more experienced, the 39-year veteran was reported to know crime scenes better than anyone.

Some 15 minutes after arriving, Cron met with Sergeants Walling, Nabors, and Mayne. They all ducked under the crime scene tape, and halted in the front yard of the Routier home to talk.

They waited several minutes to enter while Karen Neal retrieved Domain, the Routier family dog. Only minutes earlier when Walling attempted to reenter the house, the white Pomeranian pup had met him on red alert. Barking and growling at the uniformed officer, the dog inched him back out the door. Having retreated, Walling summoned Karen Neal to remove the small animal from the premises. The last thing they needed was an animal with an attitude traipsing through the crime scene and disturbing evidence.

Once Neal and the dog were gone, Mayne was cleared to enter the house to capture the crime scene on film.

The click of the shutter and the flash of the light were repeated more than 100 times as David Mayne photographed the bloody interior of the Routier family room—the overturned table, the flower arrangement resting on the floor, the blood-streaked carpet, the cockeyed lamp shade, and the covered body of Devon Routier. Last of all, he photographed the exposed, lifeless form of the dead child.

The medical examiner arrived, pronounced Devon dead, and arranged for the body of the eldest Routier son to be taken to the Southwest Institute of Forensic Science in Dallas.

Mayne's photos depicted the savagery that had occurred in the still, quiet hours of the morning, but the camera's eye could not answer the "why" of the vicious crime, or name the person responsible.

Those were questions the police hoped James Cron would be able to help answer.

While Mayne worked inside the house, the officers talked with Cron outside.

"What situation do you have here?" Cron asked Walling.

"A stabbing," Walling answered. "Possible intruder."

"How many bodies?"

"Two children dead. One female victim alive. She's at the hospital," Walling said.

Cron looked at him questioningly. It was unusual for children to die at the scene and an adult victim to be left alive.

"We'll do an initial walk-through of the house to get a game plan. We'll do a visual inspection, decide what action to take, and determine what equipment we'll need," Cron told the sergeants.

At 6:10 A.M., with Domain still safely across the street in the Neal home, Cron, Walling, and Nabors entered the house.

The crusty, retired crime scene specialist began evaluating the crime scene the moment he stepped up on the front porch. He made note of blood, medical tape and gauze, and a bloody rag. Clearing the threshold of the house he immediately began to notice the floor, walls, and ceilings of the dwelling. Quietly, he looked for blood movement. He discovered the blood from the entry and hall continued into the family room and kitchen. Several areas of the carpet contained excessive amounts of bright red blood.

A dead child lay in the back of the room.

Cron slowly rubbed his chin without speaking, then continued his mental inventory: No blood on the paper flower arrangement. No broken flowers. No blood on the vase. The vase not broken or damaged. No cracks or breaks on the glass-topped table. The lamp was standing, with the lamp shade only partially pulled down. No tears, creasing or damage to the shade. No blood on the lamp or bulb. No blood on the stand.

No real physical damage present.

Cron carefully looked for carpet indentations before moving on to the kitchen. He studied the blood spots on the linoleum, the broken glass, the overturned vacuum. He noted the wine rack standing upright. Kitchen drawers had been left open and bloody cloths had been dropped nearby. A blood-coated knife lay on the white counter top. Cron followed blood drops to the utility room.

A black ball cap lay on the floor next to more blood drops. Bright red blood ran down the side of the washing machine. Blood stained the door facing.

In the garage Walling pointed out the open window and cut screen, and the closed and locked garage door. Cron found no blood on the floor, and no bloody prints on the garage door or window. A thick layer of dust—undisturbed—coated the windowsill. He looked for a blood trail, but it appeared to have stopped at the utility room door.

"Let's go around to the back," Cron said.

The officers backtracked through the house and made their way to the backyard. Cron was making a mental plan of what needed to be done once the initial walk-through was complete.

The veteran investigator was looking for signs of an intrusion. He needed to find footprints, blood, impressions in the damp vegetation, any signs of another point of entry or exit—cigarette butts, weapons, anything that indicated who would have entered the Routier house.

There were no skid marks in the driveway, no blood, no discarded objects. The fence was clear of blood or scuff marks. The patio door and garage door showed no pry marks.

The flowers and bushes appeared intact. Cron tested the mulch to see if it could have been disturbed. He first walked fast, then ran through the thick bark mulch. Both disturbances caused a natural unsettling. A dark stain from the dampness beneath the mulch seeped to the surface.

The officers and Cron made their way back to the front yard where they inspected the four lower windows that spanned the front of the house. Again, no signs of attempted intrusion, no indication that foliage or grass had been disturbed.

About 30 minutes after James Cron began his initial walk-through of the crime scene, he was feeling uneasy. Something wasn't right.

"You need to record everything. You'll need the usual photographs, blood samples, fingerprints. And I think we might need some help. Get Charles Linch from SWIFS (Southwest Institute of Forensic Science) over here," he said.

Cron looked at Walling and Nabors perplexed. With wrinkled brow, he sighed, and gave a slight shake of his head.

"Looks to me like there was no intruder here."

Chapter Five

Detective Chris Frosch talked with Darin Routier in a private family room at Baylor Hospital while he waited for Detective Jim Patterson to arrive.

"I want dogs, a helicopter, and the Dallas P.D.," Darin said excitedly to Detective Frosch. "This is the biggest thing to hit Rowlett. Make sure you get your shit done right."

"We aren't a bunch of idiots, Darin. We can figure it out. Give us the benefit of the doubt," Frosh said.

Within minutes Frosch had calmed Darin down. The grief-stricken father looked remarkably good under the circumstances.

"My wife is so beautiful," Darin said. "She has thirty-eight double D breasts."

Frosch looked at Darin with interest. He had been talking about his wife since Frosch had arrived. Darin obviously held Darlie up on a pedestal. *He wouldn't have hurt her,* Frosch thought. *He wouldn't have let anybody else hurt her.*

Detective Patterson stared at the closed brown wooden door of the private family room at Baylor University Hospital. It was his job to talk to Darin Routier, but what could he say to a man who had just lost two of his children? Reluctantly, he opened the door.

Darin was sitting on a green and mauve side chair. His fingers tapped nervously against the wooden armrest. Terry Neal was on his left. Detective Chris Frosch sat in a solid green-upholstered chair at a 90-degree angle to Darin's right.

Darin stood as Patterson entered the room.

"Hello, Darin, I'm Detective Jim Patterson."

"Hello," Darin replied.

"I know this is a hard time for you, but I need to talk to you about what happened tonight."

Patterson asked Terry Neal to leave the room while he and Frosch talked to Darin for a few minutes. After Neal closed the door behind him, Darin asked a surprising question.

"Have you seen Darlie? Have you seen how pretty she is? Did you notice her big breasts?" Darin asked with pride.

Unable to conceal his shock, Patterson shot Frosch a wide-eyed look of surprise. How could this man be talking about his wife's breasts at a time like this? Two of his sons were dead and his wife was in surgery.

Patterson shook his head in dismay. *How strange,* he thought.

In the operating room, Darlie Routier slept soundly under general anesthesia. Her blonde hair was neatly tucked beneath a surgical cap, her delicate nose and mouth covered by an oxygen mask. The laceration to her neck seeped only small quantities of blood. The penetrating wounds to her shoulder and forearm had stopped bleeding altogether.

Minutes earlier Darlie had been prepped for surgery. A routine drug screen was performed. Darlie tested positive for amphetamines. She had told the nurse she was taking diet pills. The drug screen indicated the use of a stimulant but was not conclusive as to the type of drug. Her vital signs remained good. The surgeons, scrubbed and masked, entered the operating room ready to work.

Doctor Alex Santos carefully explored each of Darlie's wounds before determining treatment.

The neck wound, which ran nine centimeters long, a little over four inches, from right to left past the midline of her throat, was determined not to be life threatening, as first feared. The zone two cut, appearing above the collar and below the chin, had penetrated the skin, fat, platysma, and barely nicked the neck muscle. The knife that had caused Darlie Routier's wound stopped at the sheath of the carotid artery, only two centimeters away from the main blood vessel itself. Had the carotid artery been severed, Darlie Routier would have bled to death within two to three minutes. Two centimeters had determined the difference in a superficial wound and the death of Darlie Routier.

With Dr. Dillaw assisting, Dr. Santos retracted the skin surrounding the neck wound and looked for damage to Darlie's windpipe. Finding no injury, Santos immediately began tying off the oozing blood vessels. Electric current seared those veins too small to surgically close. Finally, the diagonal cut was closed with sutures neatly tucked under the skin to avoid excessive scarring. The wound was taped with steri strips to hold the edges of the skin together.

Once the major laceration was closed, the surgeons directed their attention to the one-and-one-half-inch cut on the victim's left shoulder and the penetrating stab wound, about the same size, on her right forearm. No foreign objects were found in any of the injuries. All three of these superficial wounds could have been stitched in the emergency room, but Santos and Dillaw were playing this one safe.

The patient was checked for any further injuries, particularly her forearms, palms, and fingers. No other wounds were found. No noticeable head trauma had been experienced.

Forty-five minutes after surgery began, Darlie Routier was ready to be taken to recovery. Anesthesia was stopped at 5:00 A.M. and she was allowed to emerge from the sleep naturally.

"Take her to ICU," Dr. Santos ordered. Normally, Santos would not have sent a non-critical patient to the intensive care unit but, from what little he knew of the events surrounding the woman's injuries, he thought it best to keep her isolated.

"I don't want the media to get to her," Santos commented. "I'm afraid all this may be to much for her to handle right now. I'm not sure of her psychological state. We can keep a close eye on her up there."

Nurse Christopher Wielgosz received Darlie Routier into the second floor ICU unit of Baylor Hospital just after 5:00 A.M. Wielgosz, normally responsible for two patients in the four-bed pod of ICU, had both beds empty on his shift.

"What's your name?" Wielgosz asked, testing Darlie's coherence.

"Darlie Routier."

"Do you know what time it is?"

"Just after five o'clock."

"Do you know where you came here from?" the nurse continued his questioning.

"Surgery."

Satisfied that the patient was alert and responsive, Wielgosz began his medical assessment. He worked around the monitoring systems connected to Darlie by long, thin tubes. An arterial monitor established her vital signs. An IV pumped fluids into her left arm. A catheter in the radial artery monitored her heart rate. Although not a critical care patient, Darlie Routier looked like a woman clinging to life by thin wires.

"How could anyone do this to my children?" Darlie asked her attentive male nurse.

Wielgosz stiffened slightly. He knew that both her children were dead. Unsure of Darlie's emotional condition or how much she knew about her boys, Wielgosz said nothing.

"I picked up the knife after the attacker dropped it and my prints might be on it," Darlie babbled. Wielgosz noted her concern.

Wielgosz continued to examine his patient. He noted some dry blood on her hands and slight cuts on her left fingers. Cuts so minor, similar to paper cuts, that Wielgosz did not chart them. The laceration on her right arm had been closed with five sutures. A small nick above the bottom stitch, toward her wrist, had not been closed. Darlie made no comment during the exam. She asked no questions.

Darlie dozed on and off for the next 30 minutes as Wielgosz charted her progress at his station some six-to-eight feet away. Occasionally Darlie would make a statement, then fade back into sleep.

"I wonder if I obscured the fingerprints," she said.

Her concern finally prompted Wielgosz to respond. "I'm sure the police will do everything they can."

"My neck hurts," Darlie groaned. "My arm hurts. Can I have something for the pain?"

The young nurse had been informed earlier that the Rowlett police wanted to talk to Darlie as soon as possible. He called his supervisor.

"How long till the police get here to see Darlie Routier?" he asked. "She's alert, but she says she's in pain. I don't want to give her anything that would make her drowsy."

"They're ten minutes away," the supervisor answered.

Darlie continued to ask for medication.

On a scale of zero to ten, Wielgosz estimated her pain to be about a three. He decided to give her a the low dosage of Demerol prescribed by the doctor. Twenty-five milligrams would take the edge off her pain but would not subdue her. The medication was administered at 6:05 A.M.

Ten minutes later, Detectives Jim Patterson and Chris Frosch arrived.

Wielgosz sat at the desk a few feet from Darlie's bed, completing some of the paperwork required for his patient. He caught bits and pieces of the conversation between Darlie and the detectives standing at her bedside.

"We want you to tell us what happened at the house," one of the detectives said. "Just start at the beginning."

"I woke up with the intruder leaning over me with a knife in his hands. I was on the couch. We struggled, then he walked off, through the kitchen into the utility room. I saw him drop the knife. I picked it up. Shouldn't have. I probably covered up the fingerprints. I shouldn't have picked it up. Then I realized I was bleeding. I put the knife on the kitchen counter. I went into the den. I saw Damon standing in the hallway; he was bleeding. I saw Devon lying on the floor with blood all over him. Then I called 911," Darlie stated.

The officers switched their questioning to focus on the attacker. "Can you describe him?" Detective Patterson asked.

"I think he might be white. He was wearing a black ball cap, black T-shirt, and blue jeans." Darlie said.

"Was there writing on his shirt? Did he wear a belt?"

"No, no writing. I think he had on a belt."

"Was the bill of the cap turned forward or backward?" Patterson asked.

"I think it was forward."

"Any writing on the cap?"

"No."

"Did you see his face?" Patterson asked.

"No."

"What about his hair?"

"It was brown, straight, shoulder length," Darlie said, looking at Frosch.

"Did he have on shoes and socks?"

"I did not see if he had on shoes or socks."

The description seemed vague. Patterson asked about the intruder's build. "Was he built similar to me, or to Detective Frosch?"

"Like him," Darlie said, pointing to Chris Frosch who was much taller at 6″ 3′ than Patterson.

Patterson asked her to elaborate on the description, trying to get more precise facial features. Darlie was unable to give him anything specific. She claimed she had slept through the attack.

"Were you sexually assaulted?" the detective inquired.

"No, I would have felt that," Darlie said.

How can someone know they weren't sexually assaulted yet claim to have slept through a physical attack? Patterson asked himself. Something didn't add up.

"Did you notice anything stolen or missing?" Frosch asked.

"No. I had left a lot of my jewelry on the kitchen counter and I had my jewelry box out. My rings have precious stones and diamond baguettes," Darlie said proudly, describing in greater detail each of the pieces of jewelry she owned.

Still at his nearby desk, Wielgosz watched attentively as the policemen questioned his patient. His notes indicated she appeared alert. There was no shock, no telltale signs of anesthetic hangover, and no obvious effects of the pain medication. She answered the questions calmly and completely. The detail to her jewelry struck him as odd under the circumstances.

BEEP . . . BEEP. . . . BEEP, the alarm on the blood pressure monitor sounded loudly. Darlie jerked and snapped her head around to look at the light flashing on the machine. Her hazel eyes followed the tube leading from the machine to her left arm and wrist. The detectives quickly looked over at the male nurse writing at the table.

Wielgosz immediately stood up and checked the readings on the monitor.

"It's okay, just a false alarm," he said to the detectives.

"If you'll keep your left arm still the alarm won't sound," he told Darlie. Her eyes filled with tears but her facial expression stayed flat, almost indifferent.

Odd, Wielgosz thought again. Her demeanor was not at all what he would have expected. Pale and rather distracted, she'd shown little emotion since being brought into ICU. Mascara-stained tears now slowly ran down her cheeks. No sobs. No sniffles. Only silent tears.

Sometime around 8:30 A.M. Nurse Jodi Cotner arrived at Baylor. As trauma team coordinator, Cotner made her usual rounds of all trauma patients brought into the hospital during the night. She connected with Darlie Routier on Four West of the ICU.

"Hi, I'm Jodi Cotner, trauma coordinator," the nurse told Darlie.

"Hi," Darlie responded.

Jodi noted on her chart: patient awake; alert; no trouble communicating; does not appear to be groggy from anesthesia.

"Do you know what happened?" Cotner asked.

"Me and my sons have been stabbed. I chased him through the house to the garage. I picked up the knife."

Cotner took Darlie's hands in hers and studied them for injuries.

No puncture-type wounds to the back of the arms or the hands. No slices or nicks. Doesn't appear to have any characteristic defensive-type wounds, Cotner thought.

"Am I going to have a scar?" Darlie asked, gently touching her throat.

Cotner studied Darlie Routier closely. She had dealt many times with moms who had lost their kids. There had always been a wide range of emotions displayed. Some cried, others screamed. Some were so overcome with emotion that they fell to the floor. But Cotner had never seen the reactions she observed in Darlie Routier.

Darlie seemed withdrawn. She shed few tears. She appeared almost detached from the events that had shattered her life. Cotner stared inquisitively at the woman who lay in the elevated bed. *Why doesn't she ask about her children?* the nurse wondered.

While Darlie was being observed in ICU, Darin again talked with Detectives Frosch and Patterson. He answered their questions, recalling the nightmarish events that haunted his mind.

"I heard a glass break and then heard my wife scream. I put on my glasses and ran down the stairs. I saw Devon laying by the table. It was on its side. I started giving him CPR," Darin said. His story had not changed from earlier that morning.

A nurse knocked softly on the door of family room number one. Swinging the door partway open, she announced, "You can see your wife now."

Darin took the short walk down the hall to his wife's room. He was stunned to see multiple tubes running from monitors and plastic bags attached to his cherished wife. Jodi Cotner was checking the IV in Darlie's right arm for blood in the tubing when Darin Routier walked in. Perhaps intimidated by the medical paraphernalia, he made no move to embrace her.

Although sedated, Darlie was able to ask her husband, "Why did someone kill my babies?"

Darin had no answer.

"Darlie, we need to do a rape exam. Do you understand?" Cotner asked.

"Yes."

"Do you think you were raped?"

Darin listened with concern.

"When I woke up I felt a pressure down there," Darlie said. "Damon was shaking me saying, 'Mama.' He woke me up. There was blood on him. He was hurt. He followed me into the kitchen. I told him to lay down. I believe Darin was in the room at the time."

"I heard you screaming and it woke me up," Darin said.

Through the fog of sedatives, Darlie shot Darin a serious look. "No, you didn't."

While Darlie rested, the police took Darin, who still wore the bloody jeans he'd had on while giving his son CPR, down the hall. Darin was fully cooperative, willing to help the police in anyway he could. The officers photographed Darin, took his bloody clothes, and photographed him again, nude. The hospital provided a set of surgical scrubs for him to wear.

Darlie's family and friends began arriving. Darlie Kee, Darlie's mother, and Dana, her 16-year-old sister, cried hysterically as Darlie lay stoic in the bed.

"Will you bring me pictures of the boys?" Darlie asked Darin.

By the time nurse Diane Hollon came on duty at 8:05 A.M., Darlie was clinging to the photos of Devon and Damon.

"I can't believe my babies are gone," Darlie said. "My babies are gone," Darlie said again, her hands resting on the pictures of her two dead sons. Tears welled in her eyes.

"My older boy would go to the neighbors' house and pick flowers from their yard. Then he'd bring them to me. I'd get upset with him," the young mother said as she clung to memories of the good times she'd had with her son, Devon. All she had now were memories.

Nurse Hollon cried softly. She pulled a tissue from the bed table beside Darlie and dabbed her eyes. She started to offer a tissue to Darlie, but then she noticed the tears that had dampened Darlie's eyes were not rolling down her cheeks.

Nurse Cotner came back into the room carrying an adorable boy with large brown eyes and an engaging smile, Darlie Routier's only surviving son. Darlie looked at Drake with sadness in her eyes. Cotner held Drake out to Darlie for a kiss or a hug. His outstretched arms reached for his mother. She turned away.

Stunned at the young mother's cold reaction, Cotner held the baby closer and kissed him on his smooth, soft face and held him close. Finally, after Darlie made no move to respond to the child, she handed the baby to his father.

During the day, Darlie told nurse Hollon the story of the intruder three times. She had been sleeping downstairs. She felt pressure from him. She chased the man out.

Hollon noticed that Darlie had not suggested pressure on her from the assailant until asked if she had been raped.

"I saw a car out front that didn't belong there," Darlie said once. "I'd seen it before. It was suspicious." That was the first time she mentioned a car in any of her narratives.

Darlie and Darin repeated fragments of the story over and over to friends and family members who moved in and out of the room throughout the day.

"I'm positive I locked the window," Darin said. "The boys must have unlocked it."

Diane Hollon finally asked Darlie to stop talking about the incident, and encouraged her to get some rest. Darlie clung to the photo of her dead sons and wept softly.

Eight-month-old Drake was brought back into his mother's room a second time by the Routiers' neighbor, Karen Neal. Again the child was extended to Darlie, and again she turned away. Karen sat Drake on his mother's lap, far enough away from the IV tubes and monitor cords so that the rambunctious infant could not pull them out. The only attention Darlie paid to him was to play with the baby's tiny toes as she talked with family and friends.

During Hollon's shift the members of the Rowlett Police Department arrived to collect evidence. The medical examiner took scrapings from Darlie's fingernails. The dried blood on her palms and around her cuticles had not been washed off in anticipation of evidence collection. Her wounds were photographed. Both the Routiers were fingerprinted.

* * *

Pastor David Rogers of the Shepherd Heart Fellowship Church arrived at Baylor University Hospital about 10:00 A.M. He had met Darin Routier through Darin's cousin, Randy Reagan, a parishioner at his church. Rogers had received a call at 4:00 A.M. that morning telling him about the murders of Devon and Damon. Since the Routiers had no church home, Reagan requested Rogers to pray for the family.

The cool air conditioning of the hospital was a sharp contrast to the hot, humid air outside. Rogers welcomed the chilly change. He was directed to the family room where Darin waited with Rowlett detectives while other family members visited with Darlie. Pastor Rogers laid hands on Darin and prayed.

"Darin, we need to get a written statement from you later," Detective Frosch said.

"Okay," Darin agreed.

"We'll need the keys to your house, the boat, the shed, and your business now. The more information you can give us, the closer we'll get to the killer," Frosch said.

Darin handed over the requested keys, and gave permission for officers to search everywhere.

While Frosch stayed with Darin a little longer, Detective Jim Patterson headed back to the house on Eagle Drive.

Something wasn't right. In his 18 years of police work, he had never seen parents lose their kids and not go a little crazy. Darin Routier didn't ask about his boys. He didn't seem to care where their bodies had been taken. He focused only on his wife's beauty, her physical attributes, not his loss. His behavior was inconsistent with the norm.

Patterson couldn't help but wonder if Darin Routier had killed his own flesh and blood.

Chapter Six

James Cron waited in the front yard of the Routier house for Rowlett crime scene investigators. Officer Steve Ferrie, posted at the front door, had kept a complete log of who had entered and left the residence on his watch. So determined to maintain the integrity of the scene, Ferrie had refused to allow even Rowlett Police Chief Randall Posey inside.

At 6:59 A.M. Cron, Sergeant David Nabors, Sergeant Lamar Evans, and Robin Price of the Dallas Medical Examiner's office slowly walked down the Routier's front sidewalk. The concrete path, flanked by large urns near the street, led to the front door with leaded glass insets on both sides and above the door. To the left of the door was the first sign of the Routier boys—two pairs of small, scuffed athletic shoes, evidently tossed aside before the boys entered the house. It was a chilling reminder of why the investigators were there.

Again, Cron noticed the bloody rags and soiled medical waste strewn across the front porch. A large blood smear contaminated the area directly in front of the threshold.

They opened the door, adorned by a grapevine wreath of entwined white flowers, and stepped into the entry.

A glass chandelier illuminated a massive cherrywood table and an ornately scrolled mirror. Photos of the boys, taken during happy times, greeted them from their places on the table. Blood spotted the floral throw rug just inside the doorway.

To the left of the entry was a large formal living room. A floral chaise lounge occupied one corner. The room was accented by cherrywood antique tables, a small, dainty desk, and an oil painting on an easel prominently featured near a heavily draped window. A white wedding gown, carefully draped across a red brocade sofa, was the only item seemingly out of place in the attractive room. The out of place garment, in the otherwise orderly room, seemed strange to Cron.

Across the hall an immense rosewood table, with a six-inch dropped carved border, dominated the center of the room. The pink-clothed table, set for eight with china, crystal, and silver, looked like a picture out of Martha Stewart's magazine. Pink linen napkins had been swirled and tucked neatly into wine glasses. Everything was neat and orderly, each piece precisely placed and obviously picked by someone on a mission to create a picture perfect room. A large, teardrop chandelier hung like a glimmering crystal ball over the table. The pretentious room, like the formal living area across the hall, showed no signs of burglary, property damage, or even use.

The investigators crossed the hardwood floor of the entry to a staircase on their left. They looked questioningly at one another. Nabors leaned forward for a closer look.

"It's Formica," Nabors said.

Darin Routier had painted the top of each step leading to the upstairs with a deep wood-toned stain. But it was what he had done to the face of each step that intrigued Nabors and the others. Darin had cut strips of green marble-like Formica the size of each stair front, and glued them in place.

"I guess he was going for a marbled staircase effect," Nabors said, rolling his eyes.

The crime scene analysts followed a bloody trail beginning near the staircase into the family room at the back of the house. The dark red bloodstains were a somber contrast to the pure white carpet.

Just as they entered the room, Cron pointed out a large red stain to his left, the results of the blood that had oozed from the body of Damon Routier. A 15-foot trail of red smudges led from the blood-soaked spot, across a plastic carpet runner, between the two green leather-look sofas, to a second bloody stain across the room.

"Looks like he was first stabbed in front of the sofa and crawled toward the stairs, then he was stabbed again," Nabors said.

The plastic runner was an enigma in a house decorated with such elegance. Was Darlie Routier so obsessed with keeping her carpet clean? The boys's, dirty little shoes lying on the front porch indicated she didn't allow shoes in the house to mar the pristine purity of the carpet.

Why have white carpet in the first place? Nabors thought.

At the end of the runner, near where Damon's body had been found by paramedics, lay a black portable phone. It was the phone Darlie had used to summon help for her boys. At the other end of the runner was Drake Routier's white plastic walker, smeared with blood.

To the left of the clear plastic strip was a sofa table, adorned with a green-colored Roman bust. To the right was a counter that separated the kitchen from the family room—the room the Routiers referred to as the Roman room. Nothing appeared to be disturbed on the table. No dust spoiled the surface. No blood.

Cron, Nabors, Evans, and Price walked single-file onto the carpet, careful to avoid stepping in the blood of the victims. Cron pushed against the heavy coffee table base with his knee. *Not easily moved,* he thought. He then lifted the glass tabletop, still on its edge, to judge its weight. He noted that there were no chips on the edge, no scrapes on the top, no sign of the violent shove it would have taken to push the glass top off the base during a struggle. *Had the carpet cushioned the glass top to keep it from cracking?* Cron wondered.

As Cron tested the table, Nabors scanned the room. A molded border encircled the perimeter. Nabors studied the treatment with interest. It was a standard-embossed wallpaper, approximately one-foot in depth with a raised urn design. Nabors, a self-proclaimed handyman, recognized the treatment but had never seen it finished in quite the same manner. Darin Routier had spray painted the border with gold paint. The uneven streaks gave the paper an unusual look, one Nabors wasn't sure Routier had meant to achieve.

The tawdry molding was a contrast to the expensive, tasteful, framed urn lithograph hanging on the wall and the bronze cast clock on the mantel.

"Check this," Cron said to Nabors and Mayne. Near where the body of Devon Routier had been found was a bloody knife imprint. The serrated blade was about six inches long and two inches wide at the base.

"Be sure to get a shot of that," Con told Mayne.

Mayne photographed the knife impression, then moved to the end of sofa in front of the sliding glass doors. He opened the lid of a green file box which sat between a caged cat on one side, and less than a foot from the sofa where Darlie Routier had slept the night before.

"Looks like important papers in here," Mayne said as he slipped off the rubber band that secured the folders and leafed through a number of labeled files. "Birth certificates, marriage license, insurance policies, the boys' social security cards. This one's interesting, a six-hundred-thirty-dollar receipt from Alliance Funeral Home, for a cat," Mayne said somewhat surprised.

Mayne flipped through a spiral notebook. He read a handwritten hodge-podge of personal information.

> A.L. Williams
> Darin - $350,000
> Darlie - 50,000
> Massachusetts General Life
> agent John B. Tanner
> Darin - $350,000
> Darlie - 100,000
> If death occurs by plane, American
> Express will also pay for us.
> Guardianship - Sarilda & Lenny Routier
> joint custody - Darlie Kee (Mauk)
> Executor of Will - Darlie Kee
>
> House to be sold by Mary K. Molloy,
> and any profit to be put in
> trust fund for Devon, Damon, and Drake
> until age twenty-one.
>
> All items in safety box are to remain
> in place until Devon, Damon, and Drake
> reach age twenty-one. Darlie Kee will
> have access to this box until the boys
> reach twenty-one.
>
> Money from Insurance:
> Money remaining after funeral
> arrangement is to be divided into
> three trust funds for Devon, Damon,
> Drake.
>
> Funeral Arrangements:
> Funeral to be paid for from
> insurance money. Arrangements to be
> made by Darlie Kee and Sarilda Routier.

Then Mayne read notations on another smaller pad.

> *Mink Coat, diamond heart necklace,*
> *leather furniture, formal dining table*
> *and chairs, leather furniture - Darlie*
> *Kee*
> *All autograph pictures and remaining*
> *jewelry and guns go in safety box for*
> *Devon and Damon until age 25. Also any*
> *remaining items in house are to be sold*
> *by Darlie Kee and put in a trust for D&D*
> *until age twenty-one. 1986 XJ6 Jaguar*
> *- Deon Routier and stereo w/big screen*
> *t.v. Armanti statue, two diamond and*
> *gold watches - Arenda Routier 1987*
> *thirty-foot boat - Lenny and Sarilda*
> *Routier, also green marble three-piece*
> *clock set and large vase in entrance.*
> *Three-piece bedroom suite to Barbara*
> *Jovell*

Though none of the unsigned, personal notations were dated or notorized, the document resembled a will. The handprinted pages appeared to be written in a woman's hand.

As Mayne photographed the documents contained in the green file box, Nabors walked to the end of the sofa nearest the kitchen. He bent forward, picking up a bed pillow tucked inside a maroon and green pillowcase. His heart stopped as he drew in a quick breath. The carpet under the pillow was marked by a tiny bloody handprint. From the location, it had to be Damon Routier's.

"Come take a look at what I found," Nabors said.

Cron, Evans, and Mayne walked to where Nabors was staring at the carpet. Nabors's face was pale.

Mayne quickly photographed the print.

Cron pointed out another heavily blooded spot, this one

near the tabletop, where Devon Routier had been laying only minutes before.

Cron gave the lamp, lamp shade, and flower arrangement another look. He agreed with Nabors that they should be dusted for prints.

No nicks or cuts were observed on the sofa or chair. No nicks or cuts on the maroon-and-green pillow that had concealed the bloody handprint, or the gold pillow where Darlie Routier had rested her head. *Such little property damage for so much human devastation,* Cron thought.

Cron, Nabors, and Evans scanned the family room. "What did the mother say about a struggle?" Cron asked.

"She said she struggled with the intruder and she ran after him," Nabors said.

"Well, there's no evidence of a violent struggle here," Cron said. "The children wouldn't have put up much of a fight, but this was not a peaceful killing."

As the investigators crossed the family room toward the kitchen, they passed a green imitation leather side chair, a match to the twin sofas at right angles across the room. In the seat was a large cherrywood jewelry box. The lid was open, revealing a number of better jewelry items. *Strange,* Cron thought. *Why would an intruder leave something like that behind?*

The idea plagued Cron again when he passed the bar that divided the family room and kitchen. As he had noted on his initial walk-though, two gold watches, 13 rings, a bracelet, and a wallet with cash remained on the counter in plain sight. A large soup tureen sat next to the jewelry. "We aren't dealing with a burglar, we're dealing with a murderer," Cron said.

Charles Linch and Kathryn Long of SWIFS arrived. After speaking with Cron, Nabors, and Evans, Linch began to collect trace evidence items such as hair, fibers, and paint chips. He also cut a swatch from the carpet—the square that held the tiny, bloodied handprint—evidence that a small hand had reached out for help. Long took blood samples and performed presumptive testing.

"You might want to cut out that section of carpet," Cron suggested, pointing to a place where several bloody smudges made by footwear appeared. The lab would compare them later with the shoe prints of all emergency personnel who had been in the house.

"We'll wait. The crime scene people may just want to take the whole carpet," Linch said.

Charles Hamilton of the Rowlett Police Department got there a short time later. His assignment was to dust the house for latent fingerprints. He would do so meticulously, dusting every surface a suspect may have touched coming or going.

With the SWIFS team working in the family room, Cron, Nabors, and Evans moved into the kitchen. The room was in disarray. Drawers were opened. Towels hung over the edges. Heavy blood smears stained the front of the cabinet where the stainless steel kitchen sink was located. The green floral rug in front of the sink was also bloodstained.

One of the officers opened the cabinets under the sink. Blood had dripped down the interior of the doors. *These doors had to be opened when the blood was dripped, then closed,* he thought.

Inside the cabinets were the normal household cleaners: Ajax, Sun Lite, a blue cleaner in an Amway spray bottle, brushes, and bar soap.

The countertop itself was cluttered with a floral arrangement, a decorative bottle, portable phone recharger, and a butcher block. One knife was missing from the block.

Cron noticed bloody wheel-roll marks leading to a vacuum cleaner lying facedown between the kitchen island and the family room divider. *This vacuum was placed here,* Cron thought. *I wonder why?* "We need to move that vacuum," Cron said.

Before Mayne lifted the upright, green-and-black Hoover, he first photographed the vacuum. He set it beside the wine rack.

Visible through the remains of a shattered wine glass, was a clear, distinguishable bloody footprint.

Cron bent down and picked up a piece of the broken glass to see how sharp it was. It drew blood.

"Need to see if your complainant has cuts on her feet," Cron told Evans as he put his bloody finger in his mouth and walked to the vacuum.

Cron stepped closer to the wine rack, comparing the broken glass to the undisturbed ones on the glass shelves. It was identical.

Traces of blood could be seen on the handle, body, wheels, and some on the top of the vacuum bag. From the smears on the handle, and the direction and shape of the drops, it looked as though the blood droplets fell when the vacuum was in an upright position.

"Killers will often use ordinary things to try to cover up evidence," Cron explained. "It's like, if we don't see it, we won't find it."

They found other, lighter footprints leading away from the sink toward the family room. None led to the utility room. Only one heel print from a shoe or boot was found. Officer Mayne photographed all the footprints.

The investigators looked around to see where the broken wine glass could have come from. The most logical place was the iron wine rack across from the kitchen island. Cron studied the rack with care. No blood on the rack, bottles, or glasses. Nothing broken. One glass was missing.

Cron shook the wine rack, bumped into it, and jarred it to see if any of the remaining glasses would fall off. Nothing moved ... not even the ice tongs balanced on top of the ice bucket. Although Darlie Routier claimed the intruder ran into the wine rack while fleeing the scene, there was no evidence to support her story.

The most disturbing sight in the kitchen was a bloody butcher knife, lying on the white island counter top. The handle matched those found in the butcher block near the sink. Nabors and Evans leaned forward to get a better look. They could see different density lines on the blood caked blade—lines they felt probably denoted the differences in penetrations to the boys' bodies. Nabors turned away, sickened by the sight.

The men moved into the breakfast room, just off the kitchen. A glass-topped table, surrounded by white-upholstered chairs, stood in the middle of the room. To the side of the attractive informal setting was a baby's high chair and a miniature yellow-topped plastic table with blue legs. Three red chairs were neatly tucked under the little table.

The kids had a separate eating place? Nabors questioned to himself. He shook his head slightly, trying to understand the family who resided there.

Like the formal living and dining rooms, this room, with its beautiful floral arrangements and perfectly placed paintings, showed no signs of burglary or property damage.

As Nabors walked from the breakfast room toward the laundry area, he stopped in his tracks. Taped to the front of the refrigerator was a brown construction paper sign: *I Love You Mommy and Daddy*. It was signed *Devon*. A chill crept up Nabors's spine. There would be no more refrigerator art, no more "I Love You's" from the slain child.

As Cron and Nabors headed for the utility room and garage, Mayne began picking up evidence and placed the items in brown grocery bags from the local Albertson's.

Cron entered the utility room, again noting, as he had earlier in the day, the smeared blood on the door facing and the door handle leading to the garage. A child's black ball cap, embossed with Planet Hollywood on the crown, lay just inside the room, just inches from another spatter of blood drops.

Cron stepped into the garage, piled high with junk. Something he hadn't seen on his first trip through the garage caught his eye. There was a blood smear on the floor going out of the utility room, several feet into the garage.

"Looks like a transfer stain," Cron said to the Rowlett officers. "Someone has tracked blood into the garage from the house."

The men began searching boxes and open containers for anything that might prove useful to their case. Nabors dug through the contents of a green box stacked among the garage rubble. Notes and letters filled the container. Some of the notes appeared to be from Darlie to Darin, some from Darin to Darlie, and some were from a person named Dana. *Who's Dana?* he wondered. There were also some unsigned notes. He would have to read them more closely later.

Cron made his way to the back of the garage, where the cut window screen still lay inward. He noticed two tabs at the base of the screen. *The screen could have been snapped out easily, why cut it? And, if the intruder exited by the window, the thin, flexible metal screen would have been lying outside,* he reasoned.

Most importantly, Cron noticed that the thick layer of dust covering the windowsill was undisturbed. There was not the slightest sign that anyone had gone through that window.

Cron and the Rowlett officers walked back into the house. Linch and Long were busy collecting blood samples. Hamilton was still dusting for prints. Patterson had arrived after interviewing Darlie Routier at Baylor Hospital. Patterson joined Cron and the others who made their way upstairs to check the rest of the house.

Closing off the upstairs rooms from the staircase landing were double French doors, ornately decorated with brass lion head pulls. On the wall to the right of the double doors, next to the 16 × 20 portrait of the boys, hung a Glamour Shots photo of their mother.

Down the hall, the "Mickey Mouse Room," as the Routiers called it, was a vision of the cartoon character. The black mouse was everywhere you looked—the wallpaper, rug, bedspread, curtains, clock. There was even a large framed picture of the Disney character on one wall and an expensive, original cartoon cel hung on another. The room looked like a photo out of the Disney Store catalog. It seemed too perfect, as if only for show.

It appeared that the next room down the hall was were the boys actually slept. Red metal bunkbeds, like those advertised at Wal-Mart for $149.95, were in the center of the room. Other furnishings consisted of two laminated cardboard dressers, a small metal desk and a single chair, and a two-shelf bookcase that held books and two toy trucks. A play rifle lay on top of the upper bunk. A gumball machine was near the door. Two trucks were the only other toys in sight.

One of the detectives carefully inspected the green-striped bedding. A small amount of blood stained one of the comforters. "The lab people will need this," he said, holding up the corner of the cover.

Entering the Routiers' bedroom, investigators noticed an immense contrast. The boys' room had been sparsely decorated; the master bedroom was opulent—expensive wooden furniture, an entertainment center, custom-made bedding and drapes, a fancy fireplace. The parents had spared no expense on themselves.

Matching nightstands stood on each side of the king-sized four-poster bed. Officers Sarah Jones and Duane Beddingfield searched the contents of the tables. A small amount of marijuana was found in one and three vibrators in the other.

Jones picked up a black book, trimed in gold and began leafing through the pages.

1995

This book belongs to Darlie Routier
Born-January 4, 1970

I was born in Altoona, Pa. Later in life we moved to Texas. I have gone on to marry a wonderful man and have brought three gorgeous boys into this world. My only prayer is for God to watch over us all and keep us all strong throughout the trials of life.

Jones flipped to the final entry, dated May 3, 1996.

I hope that one day you will forgive me for what I am about to do.

Jones called Nabors to the bedroom. The book could be a significant piece of the murder puzzle.

"Looks like a diary," Jones said. "We better take it with us." She tagged it for evidence and passed it to Nabors.

Patterson made his way across the room to the walk-in closet. Three-fourths of the massive closet obviously belonged to Darlie. Dozens and dozens of women's garments hung neatly in a row. There were too many shoes to count.

At the top of the closet the men found two videos, marked XXX. Nabors slipped one of the tapes into the video player, fast forwarding through the film. Then he played the second tape. Both were commercial-type porno flicks, obviously dubbed, possibly from a station picked up by the satellite dish perched on top of the garage roof.

In a plastic bag next to where the videos had been stored were two dildos and a number of motion lotions. One tin canister of Spanish Fly was on the shelf and in a Victoria's Secret box were two *Playgirl* magazines.

On the second shelf of the closet, hidden inside a Clinique makeup box, investigators found a small gray plastic tray with a white residue, scratch marks, and a razor blade. The officers suspected it was cocaine.

Among other photos of Darlie Routier, there was a roll of film, presumably taken by Darin, of Darlie leaving the grocery store. The entire roll of film was shots of Darlie in varying poses in front of the local market. *How odd*, Nabors thought.

The detectives took the items into evidence and proceeded to the game room down the hall.

Once again they found quality furnishings, all neat and precise. More than 70 Nintendo cartridges were stacked orderly into a tower. The expensive electronics equipment was undisturbed. Just as in the other upstairs rooms . . . no damage, and apparently no burglary.

"Let's take a look out back," Cron said.

Nabors, Evans, and Patterson followed Cron to the alley at the back of the Routiers' house.

The wooden gate separating the Routier backyard from the alley had been strangely rigged. Metal posts had been cemented into the ground beside the rotted wooden posts. Shoestrings held the wooden and metal poles together at the top.

Flipping the latch, Cron attempted to swing open the gate. It was hung on the aggregate walkway on the other side and wouldn't budge. Cron lifted the door and pushed hard against it. The bottom of the gate dragged against the ground, the top flopped around like a kite in the breeze.

Once again, Cron and Rowlett detectives meticulously went over every inch of the backyard. Noticing the motion detector light come on outside the spa, Cron asked, "Did anyone time that light to see how long it stays on?"

"I did," Sergeant Walling answered as he entered the backyard. "It stays on for eighteen minutes."

"And how long did it take to respond to the 911 call?" Cron asked.

"We had a unit here within three minutes. I was here in about five."

"Did you notice the light on when you came back here?"

"No, sir. I triggered the light when I was checking out the backyard," Walling said.

Cron nodded.

The investigators had been searching the house for nearly eight hours. They were near completion.

FLESH AND BLOOD

Officers hadn't anticipated the added burden of the press. The first media to arrive was a Channel 4 television truck, a FOX affiliate, just after 4:00 A.M., only an hour-and-a-half after Darlie Routier's call to 911. By the end of the critical evidence search, three other television trucks were parked out front.

"Get that camera out of here!" Nabors yelled at a cameraman. "If I see you back here again, I'll break that camera," he threatened. The man, who had climbed the back fence and was filming investigators as they searched the yard, hurriedly scurried down the alley.

The investigators didn't want their evidence showing up on television, so they took special precautions. Most of the evidence was hurriedly removed during the lunch hour, when reporters were busy giving their live stand-up reports, or it was taken out of the house at night. When officers arrived at the Rowlett Police Department they were forced to drive into the sally-port, under the station, to unload evidence from the scene. The procedure was a hassle, but the integrity of the case had to be protected.

As Cron and the detectives continued to scour the backyard for any evidence, they entered a landscaped area of the yard that displayed rock formations, tall grasses, and Tiki torches. In the center of the park-like setting was a headstone.

"Come look at this," Nabors yelled.

The granite and bronze headstone standing beside a stagnate pond was the final resting place of Fluffy. A photo of the deceased feline adorned the front of the headstone near the top, and a heart-shaped plaque had been prominently placed in the center. *This must be the six-hundred-and-something dollar purchase from the Alliance Funeral Home for the cat,* Nabors thought, shaking his head.

"What kind of people would spend money on something like that?" Nabors asked aloud.

Chapter Seven

Darin and Darlie Routier grew up nearly 1,700 miles apart, geographically, and worlds apart in family values.

The South Plains city of Lubbock, Texas, population 170,000-plus, known for its miles of flat, dry cotton fields, sprinkled intermittently with an oil rig or two, was the boyhood home of Darin Routier. The son of a hardworking machinist, Leonard Routier, and his assertive wife, Sarilda, Darin was raised in a Christian home, along with his brother, Deon, and his sister, Arenda. Darin was known as the All-American boy. He played football, ran track, was a member of Future Farmers of America, the cotton and cattle judging team, and worked in the Distributive Education Clubs of America (DECA) work-study program at Cooper-Lubbock High School. Voted "Most Likely to Succeed" by his high school peers, Darin was destined to make a name for himself.

Darlie Lynn Routier was born Darlie Lynn Peck in Altoona, Pennsylvania, a city of 55,000 surrounded by the Allegheny Mountains. An industrial and transportation center, Altoona was a world away from the agricultural plains of Lubbock.

Darlie's father, Larry Peck, a railroad worker, and her mother, Darlie Mauk Peck, divorced when Darlie Lynn was seven-years-old. Her mother remarried the following year to truck driver, Dennis Stahl.

The Stahls, along with Darlie and the couple's two daughters, Dana and Danelle, lived in a squat, three-bedroom home high on Brush Mountain in Altoona. That's where Darlie spent an uneventful adolescence.

Darlie Peck did not participate in any sports or belong to any clubs at Roosevelt Junior High School. Most of her time was spent with her childhood sweetheart, Eddie Nyiri.

The reportedly "boy-crazy" teen was meticulous in her appearance. Friends and neighbors thought Darlie was destined to be a model.

In 1984, Dennis Stahl decided he no longer wanted to pay child support for the three sons he'd fathered with a previous wife. He moved his new family to Lubbock, Texas. Darlie was a high school sophomore.

Darlie Maul Peck Stahl began working for Western Sizzler Restaurant as a waitress. There she met a hardworking, energetic young man named Darin Routier.

At 15 Darin had begun washing dishes at the Lubbock restaurant, becoming assistant manager by the time he was 18. Whatever Darin Routier did, he gave it his best.

"You have to meet my daughter," Darlie Stahl would often say to Darin. "She is a beautiful girl." And likewise she would say to Darlie, "There's a great guy at work you need to meet."

Finally, Darlie Stahl introduced her daughter to Darin Routier on Mother's Day 1985. It was love at first sight.

Darlie, with her good looks and beautiful smile, captivated the 17-year-old Darin. From that moment on, the two were inseparable. Darin provided the love and attention she lacked at home.

Darin took his new love home to meet his mother. Sariilda Routier noticed how beautiful the young girl was, but distracted by the illness, and ultimate death of her own father, she didn't realize how serious the relationship was becoming.

The following winter, Darlie joined the Routiers on a family vacation in Purgatory, a ski resort tucked high in the mountains of Durango, Colorado.

"Mama, I think I'm serious about Darlie," Darin told his mother.

"What?" Sarilda said, a bit shocked at the declaration. Sarilda Routier liked Darlie Peck just fine, but didn't feel she really knew the girl her son seemed to love.

Snuggling on the cold, slow-moving ski lift surrounded by tall, leafless Aspen trees, Darin proposed to Darlie. There was no hesitation in her response. "Yes," she blurted out with a huge grin. They hugged and kissed.

Darin, two years Darlie's senior, graduated from Cooper-Lubbock High School in 1986. He was looking forward to attending technical school in Dallas.

Darin's mother threw him a big graduation party to celebrate the happy occasion. Her firstborn had graduated and was making plans for the future.

At the party Darlie became discontent. According to party-goers, Darin, rather than Darlie, was the center of attention. To add to her displeasure, Darin was not giving Darlie the attention she was used to getting from him.

"I want to go," Darlie said to Darin.

But Darin wasn't ready to leave. It was his party and he intended to enjoy every minute of it.

"If you don't go now, I'm leaving alone," she declared.

Darin watched his fiancée walk out the door.

In about 30 minutes Darlie returned. She claimed to have been attacked by a man. "He tried to rape me," she told Darin breathlessly.

Darlie refused to let Darin call the police or to let him and his friends look for the perpetrator.

"I just want to go the hotel," she whimpered. Darin dutifully obliged.

Had this episode been an eerie precursor to the attack Darlie Routier would later suffer—or the first clear evidence of her penchant for high drama when she felt abandoned or thwarted?

Darin left Darlie behind while he attend Video Technology Institute in north Dallas for a 16-month course of study. In the meantime, Darlie completed her education at Dunbar High School, participating in the work-study program in cooperation with Western Sizzler.

Darin often returned to Lubbock to see Darlie, and, in turn, Darlie frequently visited Darin in Dallas. Barbara Jovell, a coworker of Darin's at Q-Plex, a computer testing company in Plano, north of Dallas, became fast friends with the young, future Mrs. Routier.

On August 27, 1988, a little more than three years since they met, Jovell, 15 years Darlie's senior, stood up with the young bride as matron-of-honor at her marriage to Darin Routier. The bride looked radiant in her long white gown. Darin was handsome in a black tuxedo. Darin's best man, Shannon Petty, stood on his right.

A colorful arch of balloons framed the blissful bridal couple. Coordinating balloons dotted the wooden fence enclosing the backyard of Leonard and Sarilda Routier on Woodrow Street in Lubbock. With very little money at her disposal, Darlie had worked hard to create a romantic, fantasy setting for their vows at the rear of the modest Spanish-style house. The hot West Texas sun beat down on them, but that didn't matter. Darlie and Darin were happier than they had ever been. They knew that one day they would be able to afford the wedding of their dreams.

Romping in the Jamaican surf, Darin and Darlie hadn't a care in the world. Convinced that they had each found their one true soul mate, they laughed and loved the honeymoon away in the balmy paradise.

Just as they had been in high school, the couple were

nearly inseparable. They lived in a small apartment in Garland, northeast of Dallas, and both worked at Q-Plex.

But Darin had bigger dreams. He wanted to own his own company. At night he and Darlie would sit and watch television while snapping together parts for testing circuit boards. They were partners in business, partners in life.

Darlie clung to that love, love she craved, love she had never received as a child.

But Darlie's dream life was reportedly shaken during the young couple's first year of marriage. According to relatives, the young wife was devastated to learn that Darin had been unfaithful. The news nearly destroyed her.

The young couple worked through their problems and reaffirmed their commitment and devotion.

Devon Routier, a sign of the couple's pledge, was born on June 14, 1989, just 10 months after their marriage. The new mother was only 19 years old. In spite of her young age, Darlie had experience raising children. Darlie's mother would later brag that as a preteen Darlie had been responsible for much of the rearing of her two younger sisters. Mama Darlie, as her mother became known, claimed to have been building a career. Some say she was busy enjoying a social life. Nonetheless, even Mama Darlie herself admitted that during her youth, Darlie Lynn was responsible for most of the child rearing of her two sisters.

The Routiers' part-time business grew and in 1992 they moved their new company, Testnec, to a building in Rowlett. Darin would build fixtures to test the continuity of circuit boards to determine if they were good or bad. Darlie kept the books and helped Darin test if the workload was too great. The couple worked together to build a future.

On February 19, 1991, just two days before moving into their first house, Darlie was at the new house on Bond Street making preparations for the move. With the pizza deliveryman at the front door and the realtor in the house, Darlie's water broke. Moving had to be put on hold. Their second son, Damon, was ready to arrive.

Testnec Electronics prospered. The Routiers moved from their first small house on Bond Street to an impressive 3,400-square-foot house on Eagle Drive. They began to acquire the trappings of the newly affluent: a thirty-foot boat, big screen televisions, a satellite dish, a $9,000 redwood spa, and rooms full of antiques. Life was good.

The young couple spent a lot of time with their children. "One of the things the boys loved to do was eat out," grandmother Sarilda said. "They didn't just take them to McDonald's. Those boys loved prime rib. They took them to good restaurants." They also took them to a variety of restaurants, Chinese, Vietnamese, Italian, telling others that this taught their children cultural diversities.

Movies became a favorite family outing. The parents made certain that their children saw the latest kids' movie the first weekend it was released. They always took a few of the boys' friends with them and, of course, Six Flags Over Texas became a yearly excursion.

Darlie wanted her children to be liked and accepted, just as she craved friendship and acceptance herself.

"Darlie always had to make certain that the boys always took the biggest and best birthday present to any party. If they couldn't go, she'd always send a gift," Sarilda, Darlie's mother-in-law, said.

Darlie's inclination for the excessive carried over into Devon's classroom.

"Darlie always made big bags for Halloween. She would go to post-holiday sales and put things back for the next year, so the bags could be even bigger bags. She loved doing it for the kids," Sarilda Routier said.

All seemed happy in the Routier household.

Dana Brown had moved to Lubbock from Colorado about the same time Darlie Peck arrived from Pennsylvania. They met as classmates at Monterey High School. Both girls were pretty, with the typical Texas "big hair," and became fast friends. They lost touch with one another when Darlie transferred to Coronado High School, then to Dunbar. It was years later that the two renewed their friendship after learning that they were both marrying brothers.

Deon Routier and Dana Brown were married in a doubling-ring ceremony on October 9, 1993. Her good friend and sister-in-law, Darlie Routier, attended the outdoor affair with her husband Darin, and oldest son, Devon.

Relatives noticed a pronounced difference in Darlie. The petite young mother now had sizably larger breasts. "Thirty-eight double Ds," she announced with pride. Darin grinned from ear to ear at the attention being paid to his beautiful wife. She was his most prized possession.

"Why did you do it?" a close friend reportedly asked.

"Well, I was pregnant again. I didn't want to have another child. Devon and Damon are so much to handle. Darin wouldn't agree to an abortion unless I agreed to breast implants. They look great, don't they?" Darlie asked with a little giggle.

Darlie did look great. All the males at the wedding certainly seemed to agree. But what kind of tradeoff was a child for larger breasts?

Family members would later brush off questions about Darlie's new, enlarged dimensions with a variety of responses. "Her breasts sagged so badly after the two boys were born, that the doctor said she either had to 'fold them up,' forfeiting sensitivity, or have them augmented."

Another explanation was that Darlie had been born with a heart murmur and pigeon chest. The breast augmentation would make her look more normal, although she had been well-endowed even before the cosmetic surgery.

In January 1995, Darlie again became pregnant. A number of family members observed that Darlie seemed greatly depressed. The young mother exiled herself to her room for three days upon learning of the unexpected pregnancy. Few knew this was Darlie's fourth pregnancy. Eventually, Darlie adopted a positive attitude and began preparing for the birth of her first daughter. She bought clothes, including a red velvet dress. She began picking out names.

But Darlie's joy was short-lived. She was devastated in her fifth month of pregnancy to learn from a sonogram that she would be bearing a third son. She again retreated to her room, this time not for three days, but for three weeks.

Drake Routier was born on October 18, 1995. He was the third Routier son to bear a name beginning with the initial "D."

Many psychologists believe giving all the children in a family names beginning with the same initial letter is a symptom of the fear of rejection and the fear of separation. Some psychologists also believe that the person naming their children with the same first initial had little or no emotional attachment to their own mother. Using only one letter of the alphabet restricts just how far a parent will go emotionally, fearing that if they get closer they will be hurt. It is a way to see the family all together even though they lack emotional bonding.

If both parents are from families that indulge in the naming practice, their restrictions on emotional bonding are narrowed even further. Both Darin and Darlie Routier came from families who named their children with the letter "D."

Same initial names are also used as a symbol or a sign. A way to get attention. Darlie Routier loved attention. The naming of Drake increased Darlie's immediate "D" name family to five. Even the dog's name started with "D."

Devon and Damon were happy about their new baby brother. They visited him in the hospital, and did their best to entertain the infant. The older boys would take the latex gloves from the night table beside their mother's bed, and put them on their heads. Darlie laughed at the silliness. She cherished the photo taken of the two older boys holding the new baby.

But again, Darlie's joy was short-lived. After taking Drake

home, the pressures of raising three small boys was overpowering. She felt as though Darin did little to help her with the children. Darlie began to slip back into deep depression. She attempted to talk to Darin, but her concerns fell on deaf ears. She turned to her friend and sister-in-law, Dana Routier.

"I don't know what to do, Dana, I'm so depressed. I don't know what's wrong with me," Darlie said.

Dana was concerned. She saw the pain in Darlie's eyes. She heard the anguish in her voice.

Dana attempted to talk to Darin about the problems his wife was having, but Darin only said, "Darlie's okay. She'll be fine. She just has the baby blues."

But Darlie continued to feel the pressures of raising three sons. Upset that she was unable to lose the last 15 pounds from her pregnancy, she began taking diet pills. Darlie, usually dressed nicely and with her makeup applied to perfection, no longer had time to attend to her looks. When business slowed, the couple felt financial stress. Darlie's car was broken more often than not. Feeling almost overwhelming despair, she cried almost continually. Darin wouldn't listen and the young mother felt like she had no where to turn.

Chapter Eight

Darlie Routier was recovering as expected from her knife wounds. She was alert, articulate, and appeared to enjoy the attention of family and friends who crowded her small Baylor hospital room.

Paige Campbell, an intensive care nurse, began attending Darlie at 7:00 P.M. on the evening of June 6, 1996. Campbell noted on the chart: patient lying calmly in bed, no complaints, stable condition, friends visiting.

When visiting hours ended at 9:30 P.M., Darlie's friends and family left for the evening. Campbell and her patient were alone. "If you don't want people around, I'll kick them out," Campbell told Darlie. "I'll be the bad guy."

"I just need a lot of friends and family here at this difficult time," Darlie said.

"What happened?" Campbell asked with genuine concern.

"A man was over me. He tried to stab me," Darlie answered.

Campbell took Darlie's left hand, noticing the cuts across her fingers. "What are the cuts from?" she asked.

"That's where I tried to grab the knife," Darlie said.

Strange, Campbell thought. *They look like paper cuts and they're already scabbed over.*

Campbell had bathed Darlie's small feet about 8:00 P.M. The soles of both feet were coated with dry, dark brown blood. Campbell inspected the bottoms of Darlie's feet carefully. There were no cuts.

"Did you get any cuts on your feet?" Campbell asked.

"No," Darlie answered.

A number of times during the night Darlie Routier had moaned, "My babies, my babies."

Campbell never saw a tear run down the woman's face. She never asked for a tissue, and Campbell never felt it necessary to offer one.

At 1:00 A.M. Friday morning, June 7th, Campbell and another nurse, Denise Faulk carefully bathed the rest of the patient's body. With care they lifted Darlie's right arm to wash away dried blood and antiseptic stains, mindful of the five sutures that closed the wound on her forearm.

"Can I see the picture of my boys?" Darlie asked in what Campbell would later describe as a whining voice.

At 4:00 A.M. Faulk sat at Darlie's bedside and talked with her while Darlie lay on her right side, propped up by pillows.

"Do you remember anything that happened?" Faulk asked.

"I was downstairs in my house, asleep on the couch. The two boys were watching the big screen TV I woke up when I heard my little boy crying. My husband was upstairs with the baby. I felt a struggle, like in my neck, and I started struggling with him. I was on the couch. I started yelling and he ran off. He dropped the knife. I picked it up. He ran into a wine rack holder and it made a big crack. I remember the knife came from my butcher block because it had a white handle. I turned the light on. I saw the boys. I screamed. Blood was everywhere. My husband came downstairs and I realized I was cut. Darin did CPR on

Devon while I called 911. While Darin was doing CPR he kept saying, 'Hang in there baby, just hang in there'."

Faulk glanced at the heart monitor. Darlie's heart rate was elevated just a little, but appeared calm. Her eyes watered, but no tears ran down her face. She had a flat affect, almost a numbness.

Faulk thought this was unusual. The normal reaction is for the mother to go ballistic, be beside herself, in disbelief, denial, or show signs of anger. Darlie didn't display any of those characteristics.

Later in the day, around 10:00 A.M., Darlie had a number of friends in the room visiting. Darlie whispered to her friend, Barbara Jovell. "Basha," she said using her nickname, "I need to talk to you." Then she announced to her visitors, "I need to talk to Basha. Would you all step out for a few minutes?"

The two friends looked into each other's eyes for a long time. Jovell was scared. She thought something horrible was happening to her best friend. Finally, Jovell spoke, "Darlie talk to me."

Darlie looked at her friend with deep concern in her eyes. "Basha, I'm afraid the police will find the sex toys when they search the house."

Basha looked at her friend with astonishment. "My God, you shouldn't worry about those things. The babies were killed, you were almost killed. Don't worry about those things at a time like this. Lots of people have those things. Don't worry," Basha said, trying to ease her friend's anxiety.

Darlie Routier didn't know that as she was expressing her concern for the hidden sex toys at her house on Eagle Drive, investigators had already begun their slow and precise collection of evidence. And they had already found the dildos and pornographic material.

The tedious crime scene investigation continued on

throughout June 7th and 8th. Neighbors, friends, and family were interviewed and statements taken. Police scrutinized every possible lead in an attempt to solve Rowlett's worse homicide in the city's history.

While police investigators carried on with their search for clues, Darlie and Darin began to discuss funeral arrangements for their murdered sons. The young couple were not churchgoers and had no church affiliation to call on. They agreed to ask David Rogers, the round-faced pastor of Darin's cousin, to officiate. The funeral would be held at the Rest Haven Funeral Home chapel in Rowlett on June 9th.

Darin began thinking of music to be played at the service. "We'll have to play the boys' favorite song," Darin said. *"Gangster's Paradise."*

Chapter Nine

Robbery Ruled Out in Rowlett Slayings

The headline topped the front page story of the *Dallas Morning News,* June 8, 1996.

Rowlett officials had to make some statement to the public. Nervous neighbors of the Routiers had been calling the police station day and night for any information on the assailant. "Do we need to worry?" "Is there a crazed killer on the loose?" "Are our children in danger?" Police had to calm the community's fears and at the same time make no indication that the Routiers themselves were under extensive scrutiny. Dean Poos, Rowlett Public Information Officer, released limited information.

"Something doesn't make sense about someone randomly popping into this house and doing this," said Sergeant Poos. "It was not some crazed lunatic walking down the alley and making some left turn and attacking them."

Poos had canceled an afternoon news conference, to be held June 7th, less than two hours after he'd invited the news media to listen to the 911 phone call from Darlie Routier.

"We do not want to publicly release information that may be crucial evidence only known by the suspect," Poos told Michael Saul of the *Dallas Morning News*. He declined to elaborate.

"Everybody is a suspect," Poos added. "Nobody is ruled out."

Saul's story ended with information about a memorial fund established for the family, and a $10,000 reward offered for an arrest and indictment in the boys' slayings.

Also on the morning of June 8th, Darin Routier spoke with Detective Frosch by phone.

"It's time for Darlie to go home," Darin said. "We'd like to have police protection, someone to pick us up."

"Okay, Darin, I'll arrange it, but we need you to come to the PD and give us your statements," Frosch replied.

Within an hour Sergeant Latham Evans and Detective Keith Needham were at the entrance to Baylor Hospital in Dallas to pick up the Routiers.

Evans and Needham sat in the front of the unmarked police car while Darin, Darlie, Sarilda Routier, and baby Drake rode in the back. The Routiers engaged in conversation among themselves, but did not talk to the officers on the ride to Mama Darlie's house in Plano.

Needham and Evans leaned against the car in the driveway and waited for the Routiers to change clothes before heading to the Rowlett Police Department to make their formal statements. They thought it was best to wait outside, rather than go into the small Plano house filled with lots of family who had come in from out of town for the funeral. After giving their statements, the Routiers would attend the viewing of their boys' bodies at the Rest Haven Funeral Home.

At last, Darlie emerged from the house dressed in a simple black dress. Darin was in a jacket and slacks.

"Can you take us by the florist?" Darlie asked Needham once they were on their way to the police station.

"No, we're not going to do that," Needham said. "We need to get to the station."

After the 20-minute ride to Rowlett, the couple was met in the station lobby by Detectives Patterson and Frosch.

"This is what we're going to do," Patterson said. "Darlie, you will go with me and I'll take your statement. Darin, you'll go with Chris and he'll take yours."

There was no objection by either of the Routiers.

Darin sat with Frosch, pen in hand, and began writing his voluntary statement.

06/06/96 We were watching TV in the Roman Room (Living Room SW corner of house) Watched MASH movie on HSO (satalite) [sic]. Baby Drake had fallen asleep about 10–10:30. I took him up to bed in parents room. Put blanket on him and turned out lights. I went down stairs to talk to Darlie. We talked about the boys not being able to start baseball yet because we were so busy with the baby right now. We talked about the business, bills and how Darlie was having a hard time with taking care of the baby's (all) today. Darlie said she wanted to sleep on the couch because she would sleep better because the baby would keep her awake. The boys were asleep with pillows + blankets on the floor. Devon was asleep face up in front of T.V. and Damon was asleep between couch + coffee table, by the couch mom was. So I went upstairs to get her a blanket & pillow and came back downstairs to cover her up. We talked a little more about her going to Cancun with some friends across the street and I gave her a kiss goodnight. Told her to dream about me and went upstairs around 1:00 A.M. I went and turned on T.V. in our room and watched for 10 to 15 min. and couldn't sleep with it on so I turned over, took my eyeglasses off and turned T.V. off. I couldn't go to sleep for a while but finally I fell asleep. Unconsciously I heard a noise and then Darlie screaming *Loud*. She was yelling Devon! Devon!!! oh my God Devon! I woke up quickly grabbed my glasses on the night stand and ran down stairs as fast as I could. Going into the Living Room (Roman) I ran over to Devon laying on the floor where he was when I saw him last and I nealed [sic] down over him to see if he was hurt and then looked at the coffee table to see it tipped over on him. When I looked again at his chest there were two holes in his chest with blood and muscle piercing [sic] out. I slapped his face to get him to say or look at me. No response. I started CPR and when I blew into his mouth air came out of his chest. I blew 5 or 6 times and held my hand over the holes on his chest. Then when that didn't work, I blew into one of the holes in his chest. I looked over at Darlie and she was on the phone calling 911. I ran over to Damon, laying on floor in hallway between wall & side of couch. Near the bathroom he had no pulse but I could not see any injury [sic]. 2 police came in and I told them that my babys were stabbed and she told them that he went out the garage. I ran upstairs to put my pants on. I looked over and Drake was crying and I felt relieved he was ok. I noticed my wallet hitting the floor but all I could think to do was to go to Karen's house for help. I needed someone to help some and held [sic] the paramedics when they arrived. I went downstairs, ran out the house and ran across the street to Karen and Terry door. I banged 5 - 6 times as hard as I could until Terry came to the door 1st and when I told them that Devon + Damon were stabbed they were in shock and ran over with me to the house and that was when they were putting Devon on a stretcher. I knew that Devon was dead before I ran across street and Damon had no pulse but the paramedics carried him out in a blanket out the front door. I ran out yelling that we have to find who did this and Karen told me that Darlie was cut too! I never knew that she was hurt yet she had blood all over her from the neck down to the bottom of her nightshirt. She was standing in the doorway and the paramedics said she needed to go to the hospital so we helped her onto the stretcher and she said, "Darin, you have to promise me we will FIND THIS MAN! HE KILLED OUR BABYS." [sic] I walked back to the house, pushed my way through the police and saw the knife on the floor in kitchen w/blood all over it. and went to garage + door to look at the window that the police had said he entered and I went out of the house and walked across the street and neighbors were there to comfort me and ask me what had happened. I sat for a minute on a curb and walked over to the ambulance where Damon was and asked paramedic was he alive and they said no. I was in shock. Karen told me to go with Darlie in the ambulance so I got in and they threw me out and said they needed to work. So then they asked the questions (fire dept) (ss# + address + name) and I asked what hospital and no one knew. So Terry found out where Darlie went (Baylor Dallas) and drove me to the hospital. At hospital I was questioned by Det. Frosch for hours.

The document was signed by Darin Routier and notarized by Steven Stanley.

Down the hall Detective Patterson gave Darlie Routier instructions on completing her voluntary statement. She wrote for nearly an hour.

Darin and my sister Dana came home from working at the shop. The boys were playing with the neighborhood kids outside. I was finishing up dinner. Damon came home and Devon called and I told him to be home soon because we were going to eat. Darin played with the baby (Drake) with Dana while I pulled everything together to eat. Devon came home and we all ate dinner together. After we ate we cleaned all the plates. I was changing Drake while Darin put everything in some containers for leftovers. We all talked a little about how happy we were that the shop had been so busy for the past three weeks and that we hoped it would continue since worked [sic] had been slow for a couple of months. Devon and Damon asked if they could play with one of their friends a little longer so we said okay. Darin, Dana, and I just sat around and watched a little t.v. Later, I'm not sure of the exact time I asked Darin to drive Dana (my sister) home because I wasn't feeling to [sic] well. While Darin was gone the boys brought down their blankets and pillows and asked if they could watch t.v. I said yes. They came downstairs and played on the floor in front of the t.v. with Drake while I made some popcorn. About 20 or 25 minutes later Darin came in and sat down with us while we watched t.v. Drake started to get fussy so I made him a bottle and I believe Darin fed him the bottle. Soon after the boys both feel [sic] asleep. Darin took the baby upstairs and put him in his crib and came back downstairs. We talked about a few problems we were having with the car and the boat and had a few words between us. Since I had the baby I have been having some depression. I told Darin I was depressed because I hadn't been able to take the boys anywhere because we only had one car. He told me he loved me and asked me if I wanted him to sleep downstairs with me because I wanted to stay up a little and watch t.v. I told him no because I didn't think he would be able to sleep on the couch and get any sleep. I had been sleeping on the couch the past week or so off and on because the baby slept in our room in the crib and when he moved he woke me up. Darin and I layed [sic] together for a little while and then decided to go to sleep because he had work the next day, this was around 12:30 or 1:00, I'm not sure. He kissed me and said he loved me, and I told him I loved him and would see him in the morning. After awhile I started to get sleepy. The next thing I woke up and felt a pressure on me. I felt Damon press on my right shoulder and heard him cry, this made me really come awake and realized there was a man standing down at my feet walking away from me. I walked after him and heard glass breaking. I got halfway through the kitchen and turned back around to run and turn on the light. I ran back towards the utility room and realized there was a big white handled knife lying on the floor, it was then that I realized I had blood all over me and I grabed [sic] the knife thinking he was in the garage. I looked over and saw the door shut to the garage so I thought he might still be in there and I needed to get Darin. I ran back through the kitchen and realized the entire living area had blood all over everything. I put the knife on the counter and ran into the entrance, turned on a light and started screaming for Darin. I think I screamed twice and he ran out of the bedroom with his jeans on and no glasses and was yelling, what is it, what is it. I remember saying he cut them, he tried to kill me, my neck, he ran down the stairs and into the room where the boys were. I grabed [sic] the phone and called 911. Darin started giving Devon CPR while I put a towel on my neck and a towel over Damon's back. I remember telling Damon to hang on, mommy was there. I looked over at Darin, and saw the glass table had been knocked halfway off and the flower arrangement had been knocked over. I then stood up and turned around and saw glass all over the kitchen floor, I tried to glance over to see if anything was out of place or if anything was missing. I took a few steps and opened the door and screamed for Karen. I was still on the phone with 911 and I don't recall what all was said because everything was happening so fast. I went back to Damon and by then he had stopped moving and the police walked through the door. The perimedics [sic] came and tried to work on the children. Darin was screaming Who Did This Who Did this? I starting [sic] asking if my babies were dead. Darin was crying and said yes. After that I just remember screaming and showing Darin my neck. Darin took me out to the front of the house and by then Darin ran upstairs to make sure the baby was okay, he showed me Drake was okay and then handed him to Karen, our neighbor. I remember then holding a towel on my neck and wrapping my arm and then they put me in the ambulance. Darin got in but the [sic] told him he needed to leave to [sic] they could take care of me. I remember get [sic] to the hospital and then them telling me they were taking me to surgery. They took off my necklace and put me to sleep. I woke up and minutes later the detectives were there asking me all kinds of questions.

The voluntary statement was signed by Darlie Routier. It was notarized by Stanley.

Patterson, who had already read Darin's completed statement, noticed several discrepancies between the two declarations. Most notably were the discriptions of what Darin was wearing when he entered the family room. Darin claimed he was wearing glasses and no pants. Darlie claimed he was wearing pants and no glasses. Since Darin had told Frosch that he couldn't see two feet in front of him without his specs, the detective had to assume that Darin's recollection was correct.

Darlie claimed to have gone to the front door and screamed for Karen Neal, their neighbor. Darin didn't mention Darlie yelling for Karen, but said he had run across the street to get Karen.

Darlie said she put a towel on Damon's back, but Darin never mentioned Darlie going to aid either of the boys. Police later stated no matter how much they urged, she never tried to help her children.

The discrepancies may have seemed minor, but they made Patterson question what really happened in that house.

After reviewing the Routiers' written statements, Patterson asked, "Can you give us a description of the assailant?"

"He was tall, had broad shoulders, and longish hair," she said. "I didn't see his face."

Patterson called Frosch into the interview room. "Did he look more like me, or more like Chris?" Patterson asked.

"More like Chris," Darlie said.

At 6′ 3″ 32-year-old Chris Frosch stood three inches taller than the 45-year-old Patterson. Recently assigned to the criminal investigation division from undercover narcotics, Frosch also had shoulder-length brown hair.

Darin and Darlie Routier were impatient and increasingly irritable. The viewing for the boys's bodies had been scheduled for earlier in the evening, and they were late. They wanted to leave.

Patterson and Frosch sat in the front seat of Patterson's police-assigned green Ford Taurus, while Darin and Darlie Routier rode in the back.

On the way to the Rest Haven Funeral Home on Highway 66, Darin told his wife, "Darlie, they asked for consent to search the boat, the shop, and the storage shed. I said it was okay."

Darlie immediately lashed out at Darin for giving the police permission to search their property.

"They're taking a lot of time with us, and not looking for the guy," she said irritably.

Within minutes they were at the Rest Haven Funeral Home where a number of family and friends waited somberly for the young parents. Darlie and Darin were met at the back door by Pastor David Rogers and Randy Reagan. The men hugged the Routiers and expressed their sorrow. Darin cried. Darlie remained dry-eyed.

Devon and Damon Routier looked content, as though they only were sleeping in the cherrywood casket. The horror of their untimely deaths did not show on their sweet, innocent faces. Because the boys were best friends, as well as brothers, the parents had elected to bury them together. They lay side by side, holding hands. Dressed in matching white tuxedos, the boys looked like heaven-bound angels.

Dana Routier admired her sister-in-law. Dana herself couldn't stop crying. She already missed Devon and Damon. But Darlie was being so brave . . . so strong . . . she had it all together. *What's wrong with me? Why can't I be more like Darlie?* Dana thought.

Tears filled the eyes of friends and family members who filed by the small wooden casket. Darlie greeted each one with a smile, aglow in the attention paid to her by viewers.

At the end of the viewing, when friends had departed, the family was left alone to say their good-byes.

Tears streamed down Darin's face as he stared at his boys. Darlie began to wail, falling to her knees beside the casket. Detective Frosch saw no tears in her eyes. He moved closer to the casket as Darlie Routier leaned forward to tell Devon and Damon good-bye. Frosch maintained his composure as he overheard Darlie speak to her children.

"I'm sorry," Darlie whispered. Then she turned and left the funeral home.

Chapter Ten

Later that same night, after family members took the Routiers back to Mama Darlie's house, Detectives Patterson and Frosch, along with Sergeant Nabors returned to the Eagle Drive house.

The detectives and the crime scene investigator were there to spray Luminol, which gives indications for the presence of blood. The established test, with a strong track record, is unique in that its reaction with blood results in the production of light as blue-white luminescence.

Luminol was chosen because it is relatively non-destructive to blood, it can cover and screen large surfaces quickly and easily, and it reveals trace bloodstains otherwise unnoticeable to the naked eye.

The police had deliberately waited until dark so the luminescence could be easily seen. They began in the family room where the victims had been attacked. Nabors sprayed the chemical carefully across the green leatherette sofa where Darlie Routier claimed to have been sleeping. No blood appeared where her head was reported to have been laying.

Nabors moved to the opposite end of the sofa, spraying its arm and down the front. In moments, Nabors gasped. Patterson stiffened. The hair on the back of Frosch's neck stood up. Their eyes widened in the darkened room as a single, small handprint appeared on the sofa arm.

Frosch played the developing scenario of the killing in his mind. He was sure he knew what had happened in that room. He felt it in his bones, in every gut instinct of his years of police training—Damon had been trying to get away from his killer.

Nabors felt an eerie chill run down his back. He shivered slightly and mumbled, "Oh, my God."

As the remainder of the Luminol developed, blood smears could be detected on the front of the couch.

Nabors, nauseated by the sight, told Patterson, "Looks like the little boy fell against the sofa. You can see his butt print right there. He may have gotten up, or tried to get up, but he slid back down the front of the sofa."

Their eyes followed the now visible bloodstains on the carpet—a trail from the sofa to the area across the room where Damon had been found by paramedics. Had he crawled?

Or had someone moved him?

Because of the slick surface of the sofa and the liquid properties of the Luminol, the small handprint began to dissipate and disappear from view as the officers watched. The tiny handprint faded into nonexistence . . . as had the little boy who had made the print. They were all thinking the same thing. Someone had to have washed off the sofa. Who would have done that? Who would have had the time?

Nabors, Patterson and Frosch moved into the kitchen area, spraying the vinyl floor between the kitchen and the Roman room. Several footprints appeared. The men looked at one another questioningly. Then they sprayed the chemical across the floor to see where the prints led. Two clear prints, a right and a left foot, stopped at the sink in a mass of luminous blood.

"Be sure we get footprints from everyone who was in this house," Patterson said, surprised by the amount of blood found in the kitchen.

Nabors studied the stain. It was obvious that the killer had moved back and forth between the sink and the Roman room. But why?

"Someone wiped up the prints," Nabors said. "But who would do that? And why? We know an intruder wouldn't have taken the time."

"Neither Darlie nor Darin mentioned being at the sink in their statements," Patterson said.

"Let's spray the sink," Nabors suggested.

Under the black light the shiny, silver-toned, stainless sink glowed in a haze of blue-white. Blood. There had been a lot of blood in the sink, but it had been washed away. Blood had also been wiped from the counter top.

"Okay," Nabors said. "Let's take the sink, the P-traps, everything that might have been used to clean up the blood."

For two nights Patterson, Frosch, and Nabors Luminoled the house, checking and re-checking the evidence they found. A number of other officers, including Detective Beddingfield and Officer Sarah Jones, helped methodically collect the trash from trash cans around the house. Believing that perhaps someone had done a quick load of wash after cleaning away the evidence, they took the damp clothes from the washing machine. They collected the pillows from the family room, the phone and cradle, a pair of blue jeans and blue jean shorts, and three hand-written pages detailing costs of a wedding were among items removed from the house. Dirty dishes in the sink and a bowl of popcorn from the counter were gathered up to be tested for traces of drugs.

The drains in the kitchen and all three bathrooms were Luminoled for blood traces. The P-traps from all the sinks were removed. They even took the kitchen sink itself.

The garage was sprayed with the chemical, with negative

blood results. They even sprayed the back fence. Those results were also negative.

As they worked thruough the long, tedious hours of evidence collection, the officers began to desperately hope that the little boys who smiled in the photos displayed around the house had been sedated before the attack. They hated the thought that the boys may have seen their killer. More than anything, they hated that the killer may have been someone they knew ... someone they trusted.

Chapter Eleven

On June 9th, the Rest Haven Funeral Home was filled with more than 400 mourners. Dozens of wreaths, floral baskets, potted plants, and balloons surrounded the small, single, cherrywood casket topped by a cascade of red roses, reportedly paid for by the boys' paternal grandmother, Sarilda Routier. The overflow crowd was forced to stand along the walls, unaware of the plainclothes police officers among them.

Detective Frosch scanned the faces of the mourners. Officers were certain that the killer was someone the boys knew and the evidence was pointing to one person in particular. But they hoped they were wrong. Killers often hang around the scene of a crime, attend funerals, and visit grave sites. The detectives were at the funeral to see if anyone acted unusual, or if someone was there who didn't seem to belong.

Frosch, Patterson, and their supervisor, Lieutenant Grant Jack, studied the crowd closely. Most of the mourners sat silently, clutching the folded programs featuring a color photo of Devon and Damon on the front. The detectives watched the mourners' sad faces turn to questioning stares as the lyrics to *Gangsta's Paradise* filled the sanctuary.

Grief-stricken friends sat silently in disbelief as they heard the rap song's words. Questions of why, on such a tragic occasion, the parents would play such a violence-based song, were whispered throughout the chapel.

However, Frosch, Patterson, and Jack focused on the uncanny lyrics that spoke of aroused anger, reference to what's going on in the kitchen, and power and money, money and power. The irony was almost more than the seasoned detectives could handle.

Frosch scanned the crowd, noticing a man sitting in the rear of the chapel, rapidly writing on a tablet. Frosch didn't recognize him. Casually, he walked to where the man was sitting.

Mike Saul, of the *Dallas Morning News* was quickly taking down the funeral events for the next morning's edition of Dallas's only newspaper. Frosch shook his head slightly. *Reporters, they're everywhere,* he thought.

The second song, *I'll Always Love You*, began to play. Tears welled in the eyes of everyone. The heart-wrenching pain that always accompanies the death of a child engulfed the room.

Pastor David Rogers delivered the address, *Jesus Loves Me* was played, and then it was time for the mourners to say good-bye to Devon and Damon.

As the family began to file past the casket, Rest Haven staff escorted Mike Saul from the chapel. It was a time for private grieving.

Darin Routier sobbed openly. He hugged family members and continually spoke about the boys, their past experiences, their likes and dislikes. The father of the slain boys hugged both Detectives Frosch and Patterson tightly.

"Thank you for your efforts on this case," Darin said with tears in his eyes.

Darlie paused only momentarily beside her sons' coffin. Then she began to pick trinkets from the wreaths and floral arrangements surrounding the two forever-stilled children. Teddy bears, notes, a miniature wooden airplane, and a small picture of the boys filled her hands as mourners continued to say their good-byes.

Inside the casket lay a deck of cards, stuffed animals, silver coins, flowers, poems, and letters. But the most astonishing items were two red Swiss Army knives. Friends wondered how anyone could put knives in a casket beside two slain boys who had been stabbed to death. The gesture struck many as bizarre.

Detectives Frosch and Patterson had worked quickly to set up surveillance equipment at the grave site just prior to the funeral. Before implementing their plan, Sergeant Evans cleared the maneuver with Greg Davis of the Dallas County District Attorney's Office.

A microphone had been hidden in an urn provided by Rest Haven, and placed where the head of the boys' casket would later rest. The dozens of floral arrangements would effectively hide the opening of the urn, yet the police surveillance team would be able to hear clearly. A video camera was positioned nearby to capture anyone who might go near the grave within a 14-hour period. Police hoped that if anyone decided to confess to the grisly murders, they would be both seen and overheard.

But the results were negative. No one confessed, and the person all their evidence pointed to as the guilty party did not go near the casket at the grave site following the funeral.

On June 10th, Darlie and Darin Routier arrived at the Rowlett Police Department, as requested. They continued to fully cooperate with the police.

Officer Jones photographed Darlie, noticing for the first

time a large, ugly bruise that extended from the inside of her right wrist to under her armpit.

Sergeants Evans and Nabors began taking both Darlie's fingerprints and footprints. Darlie seemed to be enjoying the event. She laughed and joked with the officers, flipping her hair to the side and batting her eyes. The scene was more than Officer Jones could stand. Unable to take Darlie's flirting any longer, she left the room.

Detective Patterson took Darlie into an interview room on the first floor of the law enforcement building. He read Darlie her Miranda Rights and asked her to draw a diagram of the family room of her house on Eagle Drive.

As she drew, Patterson asked her to, once again, go over the events of June 6th.

"I woke up with a man standing at the foot of the sofa," Darlie said. "He ran off through the kitchen. I heard glass break. I then saw him run through the utility room into the garage. I chased him. Then I stopped at the utility room and went back to turn on the light at the other end of the kitchen. I looked across the island and saw the knife."

After telling Patterson the story of her attack and the murders of her children, Patterson asked about her diary and the entry that referred to suicide.

"Explain to me about being depressed," he said.

"Last month [May 1996], I was going to commit suicide. I've been writing in a journal that I kept in the top draw of my nightstand. I bought some over-the-counter sleeping pills from the drugstore and started writing a suicide note for Darin. He came home, we talked, worked out our problems, and flushed the pills down the toilet," Darlie explained.

"Why were you depressed?" Patterson asked.

"I was depressed about my weight, we only had one car, and I wasn't getting to do what I use to do."

"What did you use to do?"

"Party," Darlie laughed.

"Dope?" Patterson asked.

"Yes. The last time I bought coke it was for Darin's birthday in January. I got him eight lines. He really pissed me off because he did all eight lines," she said angrily.

Patterson knew by the amount of marijuana and cocaine found in the house that the Routiers were recreational drug users. They didn't have heavy habits.

"How was your relationship with Darin?" Patterson asked.

"Sex was okay; it's been better. The last time we had sex was Sunday before the murders. We've been having heavy arguments over our finances and I'd been sleeping downstairs for about a week and a half."

Wanting to know about the lifestyle of the young Routiers, Patterson began talking about a variety of subjects. At one point the discussion turned to tattoos.

"Do you have a tattoo?" Darlie asked him.

"Yes. I have an eagle on each arm," Patterson said. "Does Darin?"

"Yes, he got a tiger about a year ago. I have one, do you want to see it?"

"Sure," Patterson said, expecting Darlie to show him her ankle or perhaps a shoulder blade.

Darlie stood up, unzipped her shorts, and lowered them to expose her pierced belly button and her underpants. She then pulled her underwear to the side of her crotch, proudly showing off a tattoo of two small flowers surrounded with tribal art. She giggled with pride.

Stunned, all Patterson could do was blush.

While Patterson was questioning Darlie, Detective Frosch was talking with Darin in another interview room.

"Darin, I want you to draw me a diagram of your house," Frosch said after reading him his Miranda Rights.

As Darin drew, he became extremely emotional. His breathing was labored. Frosch was afraid he was going to hyperventilate. Frosch talked calmly with Darin, successfully calming him down within minutes.

Darin talked about the mechanical problems he was having with their 24-foot cabin cruiser and his 1987 Jaguar. Darlie had been hounding him to get them fixed. "Darlie told me, 'It's driving me crazy,'" he said.

His young wife was also dissatisfied with their relationship. "She complained that I didn't pay attention to her," Darin said with a small perplexed shrug.

After Darin completed the drawing of the Roman room, as he proudly called the family area, Frosch asked, "Where was Darlie while you were doing CPR?"

"I'm not paying attention to Darlie!" Darin shouted. "I'm trying to save my son!" Darin had obviously become irritated by the questioning. Again, Frosch needed to help Darin gain his composure.

"We're working on this case day and night," Frosch assured Darin. "We've followed hundreds of leads. We're missing our kids's ballgames, neglecting our families, all because we want to catch this guy."

Frosch talked about Darlie's good looks, a subject Darin was always ready to discuss, and eased into the personal question he needed to ask. Darlie Routier had not been wearing underwear when she arrived at Baylor Hospital. None was found at the scene. If she had been wearing underpants the night of the attack, where were they?

"Does Darlie normally sleep nude?" Frosch asked.

"When she sleeps with me she does," Darin answered with a broad, crooked-tooth grin.

Darin loved to talk about his wife. On every interview he mentioned her large breasts and her good looks to Frosch. Darlie was his trophy.

"We were in Colorado skiing when Drake was conceived," Darin boasted.

With equal pride, Darin portrayed himself as the perfect family man and the consummate business person. "I started from zero, look where I'm at now," he bragged. "I have a beautiful wife, and a beautiful house."

The department had run a thorough background check

on both Darlie and Darin Routier immediately after the murders. During that routine check Frosch learned that Darin was licensed to carry a concealed weapon under Texas's new gun law. Frosch was cautious when questioning Darin, and once, in an effort to insure the safety of everyone, made the comment that it was against the law for a citizen to bring a gun into the police station. No one knew how the grieving father was holding up emotionally.

"Chris, I can't wait till this is over and we can go to the range and shoot our guns sometime," Darin said, as he hugged Frosch good-bye before leaving the Rowlett Police Department.

On June 14th, eight days after the murders, and the day Devon Routier would have turned seven years old, a private service for the boys was held at the cemetery in the neighboring city of Rockwall. At the grave site, in the midday heat, a tearful prayer service was led by Reverend Gordon Thomas.

Randy Reagan, Darin's cousin, spotted a *Dallas Morning News* reporter standing near the dozen or so people invited for the final farewell. Reagan requested that he respect the family and remain a reasonable 100 yards back from the grave site. The reporter moved back, as requested.

Once the scriptures, thoughts, and prayers had been said, both Darlie Routier and her mother, Darlie (Mauk Peck Stahl) Kee, now on her third marriage, walked to the reporter to grant an interview.

Eight-month-old Drake fretted and fussed as he was passed from one person to another. He was hot, tired, and confused by the disruption of his schedule.

The Reverend Thomas noted that Darlie talked with Darin about a gold bracelet that seemed to be of concern to her. To him, the young mother appeared to want to impress people more than to grieve over her lost children.

114   *Patricia Springer*

As soon as the service was concluded, Reverend Thomas left the cemetery.

Then, to the shock of many onlookers, a joyful birthday party followed—a party that would eventually come back to haunt Darlie Routier.

A rainbow of helium-filled balloons were stirred by a light breeze. "Happy Birthday" was written on one. Dana Stahl, Darlie's 16-year-old sister, had brought additional balloons and a sack full of party toys.

"I brought you balloons," Dana said with a giggle. "Devon, the big one's for you. I brought Silly String, and poppers, too."

Dana handed a can of the Silly String to Darlie. The sisters giggled as they shook the cans of confetti-type material and popped the caps.

Darin Routier stood nearby, dressed in cutoff jean shorts, a blue-and-white knit shirt, black socks and black shoes. His hands were shoved down in his pockets. He did not laugh. He did not smile. Darlie was comfortably dressed in a blue denim blouse and short blue denim cutoffs. A small silver cross was pinned to the corner of her right collar. Darlie's one-inch, dark-brown roots were a sharp contrast to her straight, light blonde hair. She had four earrings in her right ear, and three in the left.

Darlie Routier giggled joyfully as she began spraying the Silly String across the grave of her two sons. She smacked her gum and threw her head back in laughter as she pointed the can upward, shooting the string 10 feet into the air. Dana was enjoying the event with an equal amount of enthusiasm. Darlie laughed and shot the string at Drake.

Family and friends waited, but did not join in the merriment. With an unconscious step backward, Darin seemed to distance himself from the revelry, his hands still shoved deep into his pockets. The gaiety lasted only a few minutes but the scene would be forever fixed in the minds of the public.

Joe Munoz, a good-looking news correspondent from

NBC's Channel 5 of Dallas, was off-camera watching the party. He had called Darlie Routier earlier in the day and, out of respect for the grieving parents, asked if he could film the gravesite. Darlie had said, "Sure, we'll be out there in about thirty minutes. We'll meet you there."

Munoz had no idea what he and his camera crew were about to chronicle when he made that call. He had hoped for a simple interview. He got a piece of footage that would change the course of Darlie Routier's life.

After the cans of Silly String were emptied, Munoz made his way toward Darlie and Darin.

In the exclusive interview, and the first public comments since the murder of her sons, Darlie and Darin Routier spoke about the investigation, their sons, and the man who they believed killed their children.

Darlie appeared well rested ... no dark circles under her eyes, no puffiness, no tears. She began by complimenting the hard work and dedication of the Rowlett police.

"The support and hard work these police are putting into this is incredible," Darlie said.

"They're using some high tech stuff on the investigation," Darin added. He grinned broadly, as though he had something to be very proud of. "Stuff I haven't even seen in the movies."

Each time Darin began to speak, Darlie interrupted with an animated comment. Happily, Darlie told Munoz about the number of people praying for their deceased sons. "God's hot line must be swamped," she said with a little laugh. "Darin and I tried to save the babies but they're gone," Darlie added in a high-pitched voice. Her nose was wrinkled, but there were no tears in her eyes.

"What are your sweetest memories of the boys?" Munoz asked.

"They were good kids. We tried to teach them right," Darin said. "They didn't see anything bad. They still believed in everything we're taught as kids—"

Darlie interrupted Darin with her own thoughts. "They

believed in everything as equal. They didn't believe anybody had a different color. They didn't see the world as cruel, as adults have to see it. They saw it like, okay, I'm just like you and you're just like me, and that's just the way they were," Darlie said with another grin and a nod of her head.

"They knew we were more fortunate than other people," Darin added.

Darlie again cut in with, "But they were giving, very giving."

Darin continued. "Like when the Rowlett children's fund started, they wanted to go home and get their old toys, plus we bought new toys. They were a giving-type people. They learned that from us," Darin said. Once again a huge grin lit his face. "But we saw it through them."

Munoz again asked for their sweetest memory of the boys.

"I have a lot of sweet memories," Darlie replied, beaming in motherly pride. "I could talk for days and days and days." A giggle punctuated her words. "You'd have to come and move in," she said, throwing her head back and laughing.

The couple, who showed no outward signs of the grief experienced by most parents, told Munoz the story of how Devon and Damon had nicknamed their house the *Home Alone* house, after one of their favorite movies. Darlie and Darin were happy with their memories.

Darin smiled as he reminisced about watching old videos of the boys. While Darin talked, Darlie looked away, chewed her gum, and waited for Munoz's next question to her.

"Darlie, why the balloons, the confetti, and the happy birthday song?" Munoz asked.

Once again Darlie came to life. She smiled and began to talk. "Even though we're sad because Devon and Damon aren't here, we try to hang on to what we can to get us through these times. And, if you knew Damon and Devon, you'd know they're up in heaven, and they're up there having the biggest birthday party that we could ever imagine. And they wouldn't want us down here being sad. Even though our hearts are breaking, I know Devon and Damon would want us to be happy. They'd want us to celebrate as if we were with them. They'll always be with us," Darlie said. Her voice was joyful.

"Who do you think could have done this?" Munoz asked.

"I think he's a coward because he went after two somethings so innocent that couldn't fight back and then he tried to come to me, but he went to them first. To me, that is such a cowardness," Darlie said. "I don't know why God spared me."

"Like an animal that goes after a weak sheep that is asleep, completely lifeless, and attacks the weakest person in the room first," Darin said. As he spoke, Darlie mumbled something inaudible and walked off-camera. "To get off on whatever he thinks he's going to accomplish. I keep hoping he had stolen something out of my house, that he picked me and my family because I had more than some. That way, in my heart, I could think that living large is why we got targeted. Now we don't know why. Now we know that this is a sick individual, who took absolutely nothing from our house, except the two most important things to us, away from us."

Darlie picked up her youngest, and only surviving son Drake and held him over a framed photo of Devon and Damon. She urged him to give them a kiss. Suspended in air, Drake looked questioningly up at his father with his huge brown eyes. He didn't know the two children in the framed picture.

He never would.

* * *

A couple of days after what came to be known as "the Silly String incident," the Rowlett police received a Xeroxed copy of a handwritten letter. Someone in attendance at the birthday party had seen Darlie lay the letter beside the boys' grave, someone who thought it might be of interest to the Rowlett police.

> *Dear Devon and Damon,*
> *It's mommy again!*
> *I know you probably get tired of hearing me all the time but we miss you so much. We are trying not to be selfish and we just loved you so much. You both touched everyone in ways people only wish for and you will live on in our hearts for ever [sic]. Baby Drake misses you both, he will be the luckiest baby in the world because his two big bubbas will allways [sic] be looking out for him. Someday we will all walk together again, until that day help us to have strength and peace, help guide us in the right path. I know God and Jesus have you both under their light and I thank them for that. You never knew of hate or how cruel the world can be, you never saw color and your life was peaceful, and I am happy that the Lord spared both of you, but I can't help but to miss you both so much. So young to be taken away, but what a full life you both lived. Keep the light on for us! I will talk with you both again later. I love you both more than I can ever say and this paper doesn't go long enough to show you "how big."*
>
> *Hugs and kisses,*
> *Mommy XXOO*

Chapter Twelve

Greg Davis, Assistant District Attorney for Dallas County, sat in his living room, staring at his television set, speechless. He watched as Darlie Routier chewed gum, laughed, and shot Silly String across the grave of her children. Davis was stunned.

What kind of cold individual could stand out there at a gravesite and joke about children who had been killed eight days earlier? Davis asked himself. *No grieving mother could do that.*

Four days earlier Davis had met with Jim Patterson, Chris Frosch, and Lamar Evans concerning the deaths of Devon and Damon Routier. The detectives had laid out the evidence that had been collected to that point, and expressed their gut feeling about the perpetrator.

"The evidence just doesn't support an intruder," Patterson told Davis, after pointing out inconsistencies between Darlie's story and the physical evidence found at the scene. "That leaves only three people who could have killed those boys. Darin, Darlie, or Drake. I think we can safely rule out the baby and Darin's story has remained consistent."

Davis gazed at the bodies of Devon and Damon in the crime scene photos that lay on the table. A father himself, Davis struggled with the concept that parents could murder their own children, especially a mother. The thought of the monstrous betrayal of the unspoken bond between mother and child repelled him. Society expects mothers to be gentle, nurturing, unselfish, even willing to sacrifice their own lives to keep their children from harm. Could Darlie Routier have shattered the sacred bond of creation itself? It was unfathomable.

But Davis knew that parents did indeed murder their children. Even mothers.

To the disbelief of society, 1,400 to 2,000 children are killed in the United States each year. Four or five children die at their parents's hands each day, nearly all before they enter first grade. Half of them are killed by their mothers. Prominent in the statistics was a specific category of mothers: young, often in their twenties, married, the biological mother of a child or children they bore early—and with no history of previous arrest. The children of these mothers were often killed in their homes.

In many ways, Darlie Routier fit the profile.

Most of these women killed to protect a sense of themselves, their own sanity. They often manufactured a story to cover their acts. The story usually came after they initially killed—a way of dealing with their own sense of guilt, shame, or their own shock at what they had done. They relied on society's deep resistance to believing they could be responsible. To deal with the overwhelming guilt, they went into denial. Denial supported by an outpouring of sympathy and support.

But motives for killing could also include revenge. Had Darlie been trying to get back at Darin? Or one of the children?

Often the killing is simply in response to overwhelming levels of stress. The unfinished suicide note written only a month earlier by Darlie Routier could only be perceived as a cry for help. She had tried to communicate how scared, how worried, how overwhelmed she was, but people didn't listen. Her's was a cry unheeded.

Perhaps she couldn't stand the thought of her children growing up without her.

Most women who kill their children are pushed to their mental limits and have diminished ability to deal with raising their children. Some suffer from personality disorders in which they never grew up. Some had never acquired moral values. Frequently, they were reenacting their own childhood traumas, including sexual abuse or the divorce or death of a parent. Was this the case with Darlie Routier?

As Davis sat watching the graveside interview presented on the news, data presented to him by the Rowlett detectives flooded his mind: The mother's failure to aid her dying children. The great human loss with little, if any, property ruin. The lack of evidence of an intruder. The blood wiped from the crime scene. The bread knife with window screen fibers housed in the kitchen butcher block. The dispassionate lack of grief. Her own admission of depression and stress.

The Silly String tape became a turning point for the observant, audacious assistant district attorney.

Investigators were working 16 hours a day, seven days a week to solve the case. Every lead was scrutinized. Every neighbor, friend, or family member of the Routiers's was interviewed.

On the wall of the detectives's division at the Rowlett Police Department hung a photo of Devon and Damon Routier. Under the photo read the caption, "That's why we're doing this." The investigation had begun to take an emotional toll.

David Nabors, crime scene investigator, saw his own son laying on the bloody carpet every time he closed his eyes. He clung to his seven-year-old son whenever he had a chance to get home. Nabors threw out all the Power Ranger clothing his boy owned.

"I'll buy you whatever you want," Nabors told his son, "but you can't have the Power Ranger stuff." The haunting image of Devon Routier in bloody Power Ranger shorts kept replaying in his mind. His son seemed to understand.

Like Nabors, Detective Chris Frosch embraced his five-year-old son whenever he was home. He squeezed the boy, hoping to separate the cold image of Damon Routier from the warmth of his own child.

Frosch's eight-year-old daughter clung to him and asked when the murderer would be caught. The young child was constantly asked by her peers and their parents for the latest news in the case. Frosch wanted the ordeal to be over, not only for him, but for her.

The night of June 14th, just after the Silly String tape played on the local news, Jim Patterson walked into the garage of his Rowlett house and began to tinker with his Harley Davidson motorcycle. It was his wife's birthday.

"What's wrong, Jim?" Monica asked as she stepped into the garage.

"I know it's your birthday. I know I should be taking you out to celebrate, but I just can't," Patterson said in a quivering voice. "Today would have been Devon Routier's seventh birthday."

Monica went to her husband, they embraced, and cried together.

The morning of June 17th, Darlie and Darin Routier arrived at Southwest Institute of Forensic Science (SWIFS) to comply with blood tests requested by the Rowlett Police Department. Their youngest and only remaining son Drake, accompanied them.

Detective Patterson scrutinized Drake carefully. The eight-month-old child appeared to have a black eye.

"He fell backward out of Darlie's arms while she was feeding him," Darin explained. "He hit his head against the table."

FLESH AND BLOOD

Patterson was concerned about Drake's welfare. If he continued to live with his parents at his maternal grandmother's house, could he be in imminent danger? The detective believed he had no choice. He had to report the incident to Child Protective Services.

Later that day, the yellow-and-black crime scene tape was removed from the perimeter of the Eagle Drive property. The house was returned to the Routiers.

Frosch and Patterson were back at the Rowlett police station completing their reports of the events that occurred at SWIFS. Frosch's phone rang.

"Chris, this is Darin. Look, we have a psychic coming out to the house. Me and Darlie are going out there, do you want to go?" Darin asked.

Frosch hung up with Darin and immediately dialed Patterson's extension. "We're going to the house," Frosch told him, then explained the phone call he had received from Darin.

Except for her Spandex pants, the hefty "Psychic Fran"—a woman with long flowing dark hair—reminded Frosch of a witch he'd seen in a story book as a child. The psychic's accompanying son, maybe 20-years-old, was barefoot and wore cutoff blue jeans held up with a rope at the waist. Frosch repressed a laugh. The detectives were a distinct contrast dressed in their dark suits, dress shirts, and conservative neckties—not only to the psychic and her son, but also to Darin, Darlie, and Dana Stahl who had come to the house casually attired in shorts and T-shirts.

A strong, musty odor forced Frosch to take a step backward, instantly covering his mouth and nose with his hand. The smell, somewhat akin to marijuana, was sickening. Stale blood, mixed with the Luminol chemicals, had created a nauseous stench.

As Patterson followed Psychic Fran and Darin Routier around the house, Frosch stayed close to Darlie. She moved through the foyer showing no emotion. She barely glanced into the family room where her two children had been slaughtered.

Darlie walked into the kitchen with her younger sister, Dana as Frosch watched her carefully. Darlie stopped in front of the kitchen sink, flinching slightly. The sink was gone.

"I remember when I went to the sink and got towels and threw them to you," Darlie said to Darin, who was standing by the sliding glass doors of the Roman room.

Darin stared at Darlie with a blank, unresponsive look.

Frosch made a mental note. This was the first time Darlie Routier had ever mentioned going near the sink the night of the murders.

"Where's the walker?" Darlie asked Frosch, referring to baby Drake's white, circular chair on wheels.

"It had blood on it. We took it to the lab," Frosch said.

As Darlie walked through the utility room to the back door, she talked to Dana in a whiney voice, loud enough for Frosch to hear. "I know I didn't touch that," she said, pointing to a bloodstain on the utility door frame. Then she added, "It might be my blood, but I didn't put it there."

Psychic Fran roamed around the family room, occasionally stopping to pick up an object and hold it for a moment. Finally, she made her declaration to the detectives and the Routiers.

"Whoever did it drove a van," Psychic Fran said. "A white van. Something was written on the side. It's a construction business."

With that said, the psychic and her son left the house on Eagle Drive.

Frosch and Patterson returned to the Rowlett police station where Patterson, more convinced than ever, began preparing an arrest warrant.

Chapter Thirteen

ARREST WARRANT
DALLAS COUNTY, TEXAS
___X__ FELONY _____ MISDEMEANOR
COURT NO. F96-39972-R
Rowlett OFFENSE NO: 96-18574
State of Texas v. Darlie Lynn Routier
Arrest Status: at large   Race: W   Sex: F   DOB: 1/4/70
Residence address: . . . Eagle Dr., Rowlett, Dallas County, TX

THE STATE OF TEXAS
COUNTY OF DALLAS

THE STATE OF TEXAS, to the Sheriff or any Peace Officer of Dallas County, Texas or any Peace Officer of the State of Texas, GREETINGS:

WHEREAS, the Affiant whose name appears on the attached affidavit (which said affidavit was attached hereto at the time this warrant was issued) is a Peace Officer under the laws of Texas and did heretofore this day subscribe and swear to said Affidavit before me (which said Affidavit is here now made part hereof and incorporated herein for all purposes), and whereas I find that the verified facts stated by Affiant in said Affidavit show that Affiant has probable cause for the belief expressed therein and established existence of proper grounds for issuance of this Warrant;

Now, therefore, you are commanded to arrest instanter Darlie Lynn Routier, a white female, born on 1/4/70, 5 feet 4 inches tall, about 130 pounds, blond hair, hazel eyes, and safely keep her so that she may be dealt with according to law, and to hold her to answer to the State of Texas for an offense against the laws of the State, namely: Capital Murder, a capital felony under Tex. Penal Code S19.03, of which offense she had been accused by written complaint, made before me under oath.

ISSUE THIS THE 18 of June A.D., 1996, at 3:30 o'clock P.M., to certify which witness my hand this day.

Janice Warder
District Judge, Dallas County, TX

AFFIDAVIT FOR ARREST WARRANT
STATE OF TEXAS   COUNTY OF DALLAS

My name is Jimmy Patterson, and I am a peace officer with the State of Texas. I have been a peace officer for seventeen years. I am presently a Detective assigned to the Criminal Investigations Division, Crimes Against Persons, of the Rowlett Police Department, and I have been a detective for more than seven years.

On June 6, 1996, at approximately 2:31 A.M. a call was made by Darlie Routier to 911 at the Rowlett Police Department that "they" had just broken in and "stabbed me and my children" at her home at . . . Eagle Drive, Rowlett, Texas, Dallas County. Rowlett Police Officer D. Waddell arrived at the location first. Darlie remained on the phone with the 911 operator dispatcher until after officers arrived, for over 5 minutes. I have reviewed the 911 tape and talked to Waddell and the other officers and paramedics at the scene about what they saw and learned. I arrived at the scene about 1 hour after the 911 call came in.

From my review of the 911 tape, and my discussions with Darlie, her husband Darin Routier, and other officers, I know the following:

Officers and paramedics arriving at the scene found Darlie Routier, Darin Routier, and their sons, Devon Routier (6 years old) and Damon Routier (5 years old), in the downstairs portion of the house in the rear living area on the southwest corner of the house. Devon had been stabbed multiple times, including major penetrating wounds to his chest. Damon had multiple wounds, including approximately five major penetrating wounds to his back. Darlie had a slashing wound to her neck, a minor stab wound to her left shoulder, minor cuts to the creases of the last knuckles on the palm side of her left fingers, a minor cut or scrape on the left side of her chin, and a laceration to the top of her right forearm.

When the 911 call began, Darlie referred to the assailant as "they" although she told Sgt. Walling, the second officer at the scene, that the assailant was a single white male, possibly wearing a dark colored ball cap, blue jeans, and a black shirt. Darlie told me later, shortly after 6 A.M. that morning, that the assailant was one male, probably white, with shoulder length hair, a black baseball cap with bill facing front, a pullover, black, short-sleeved tee shirt, blue jeans. Darlie told the 911 dispatcher that "my little boy's dying" and later "my babies are dying." Despite the fact that she knew that one or both boys were still alive, Waddell has told me that Darlie never made attempts to stop their bleeding, touch them, or render other first aid. Before going to the garage, Waddell told her twice to take the rag that she was holding and apply pressure to the wounds of the younger child, who had been stabbed in the back, but she never went to the child or attempted to help him (although she said in a later written statement that she put a towel on his back before police arrived). Waddell remarked that Darlie was instead pre-occupied with the minor wound on her neck, and she kept the rag pressed to it.

Darlie told Waddell upon his arrival that the assailant had gone out the utility room and into the garage and out of the house through the garage. Waddell went to the utility room and garage to look for the assailant. He saw no one in the garage. While Waddell and Walling were in the garage, they saw that one of the garage windows leading into the backyard of the house was open and that the screen was split.

Darlie initially told officers at the scene, and me at the hospital that same morning, that she was asleep in the family room on the couch, which sits parallel to the west wall of the house, and awoke to find the assailant standing over her with the knife in his hand, she had then struggled with him, and that he then walked away through the kitchen, into the utility room, and out of the house through the garage (which adjoined the utility room); in this story Darlie told us that she saw the assailant drop the knife in the utility room. Darlie told officers at the scene that she realized that she had been stabbed only after she found the knife. When she gave me a written statement on June 8, 2 days later, she changed her story to say that she woke with Damon, the younger child, pressing on her shoulder and that the assailant was "standing" down by her feet at the end of the couch "walking away" from her. In the written statement, Darlie said that she "walked after him and heard glass breaking." In the written statement Darlie did not mention the knife until she says she "realized there was a big white handled knife laying on the floor of the utility room" when she followed the assailant there from the kitchen. In the written statement Darlie said she picked up the knife "thinking he was in the garage." When Darlie later drew a diagram of the house for me, which is attached to this affidavit as exhibit A, she told me that the assailant "ran away" and that she "ran" behind him into the kitchen. At that time, Darlie told me that she didn't see the knife on the utility room floor until she went back to the kitchen doorway near the family room to turn on the light, and that she then saw the knife by looking over the kitchen island toward the utility room floor. When I examined the scene after she told me her story, I was unable to see the utility room floor from the vicinity of the light switch by looking across and over the kitchen island because the island is too large, and I am taller than Darlie.

During the 911 call, after about 4 minutes had passed and the first officer had apparently arrived, Darlie said, "Look out in the garage. They left a knife lying on the . . ." The dispatcher told her, "don't touch anything" to which Darlie replied, "I already touched it and picked it up." Darlie later told the dispatcher again that she had touched the knife, 5 minutes into the call and while her dying children were still on the floor in front of her, and she said, "I wonder if we could have gotten the prints maybe."

During the 911 call, there is no mention of, or sound from, Darin (Darlie's husband) until 43 seconds into the call, after which a male voice is first heard. Darlie told the 911 dispatcher that "my husband . . . just ran downstairs," but she never asks him [about], or mentions during the call, her 8-month-old baby, who Darlie and Darin later told us was sleeping upstairs with Darin at the time of this offense.

I know from talking to the officers involved and reviewing their reports that Rowlett patrol officers secured the crime scene and maintained it until crime scene physical evidence officers arrived at the scene within 2 to 3 hours of the 911 call. Sgt. Nabors, Rowlett Police physical evidence supervisor, personally surveyed the scene and made a preliminary report which I have read. Nabors also sought the assistance of Retired Dallas County Sheriff's Lieutenant James Cron to help examine the crime scene because

Cron has extensive experience in examination of murder crime scenes. Cron has also sent some preliminary reports which I have reviewed. We also have received assistance from Richardson Police physical evidence supervisor Jeff Craig, who helped obtain blood evidence from the kitchen and other areas. From my own investigation of the scene as well as my discussions with Sgt. Nabors, Lt. Cron, Mr. Craig, and my review of their reports, I have learned the following facts inconsistent with Darlie Routier's stories to us:

Although Darlie has consistently said that the assailant fled the house through the garage, there was no blood found in the garage, on the window in the garage, or on the white wood fence or gate surrounding the backyard, even though the assailant would have had to leave the backyard over the fence or through the gate. The overhead garage door, the only way out of the garage besides the windows, was closed and latched from inside when police arrived, and Darlie has never told us that she heard that door open or close. The windowsills had a layer of dust on them which was undisturbed. Mulch on flower beds between the garage and backyard gate was undisturbed in the early morning hours after the offense when Cron examined it.

Although Darlie told us that she followed the assailant through the kitchen and heard him breaking glass ahead of her, the only broken glass found in or around the house was a wine glass which was broken on the kitchen floor. Bloody footprints were found on the kitchen floor and photographed by physical evidence investigators at the scene. These footprints were all made by a single-size set of bare feet. Darlie was barefoot when officers arrived at the scene. The broken wine glass in the kitchen floor was found lying on top of one of the bloody footprints—the footprint appeared to have been left on the floor before the glass was broken on top of it. We examined Darlie's feet and took footprints with her consent on June 10th. I have seen the footprints on the kitchen floor and the footprints taken from Darlie and her husband Darin, and the footprints on the floor appear to me to be the same size as Darlie's prints. Although the broken glass was near and on top of the prints on the floor, Darlie had no injuries to the bottom of her feet four days after the offense. Darin also had no injuries to his feet, and his feet are much larger than Darlie's. All of the bloody footprints on the kitchen floor lead from the kitchen sink area back toward the family room where the offense occurred. There are no bloody footprints leading into the utility room where Darlie says she followed the assailant. There was also an upright vacuum cleaner overturned in the kitchen with blood on its handle—the vacuum would have appeared to have been overturned in a struggle or by accident, except that it was overturned on top of blood drops and bloody bare footprints leading back into the family room.

Although Darlie at some times has told us that she found the knife on the utility room floor, Cron has examined that floor and told me that he has found no blood splatters or other marks consistent with the bloody murder weapon being dropped on that floor.

Although Darlie has never mentioned to us being near the kitchen sink, which is on the west wall of the kitchen, during or after the offense, the physical evidence investigators examined that area and determined that there had been significant quantities of blood shed or dripped immediately in front of the kitchen sink. Although attempts had been made to clean the counter top and sink, tests with Luminol revealed blood on the top of the counter in front of the sink. Nabors, Cron, other officers, and I have all examined the couch where Darlie says she was sleeping when she was attacked; although there are quantities of blood throughout the room and around the boys, there was no appreciable blood on the couch where Darlie's head, neck, and shoulders were located at the time she says she was stabbed by the assailant. Cron's opinion from his blood evidence is that Darlie self-inflicted her wounds while standing at the kitchen sink.

The murder weapon, a wooden block knife-holder from the kitchen, and the cut screen and uncut screen from the garage windows, among other things, were seized at the scene by Rowlett officers and turned over to Charlie Linch, a forensic analyst employed by the Southwest Institute of Forensic Sciences in Dallas. Mr. Linch performed tests on the undamaged screen taken from the garage and compared residue from that screen and residue found on one of [the] knives taken from the kitchen, and his expert opinion is that the garage screen found cut by Rowlett police, and through which the assailant supposedly exited and/or entered the house, was cut from the outside of the house using a knife from Darlie's kitchen, which knife was recovered from the wood block container after the offense. Linch has also told me that the murder weapon matches the set contained in the wood block container taken from the kitchen, and the murder weapon is consistent with the slot in that wooden block container from which one knife was missing when the block was seized by police.

Although Darlie initially told us that she "struggled" with the assailant, Cron's expert opinion is that the blood splatters in the family room are inconsistent with a violent struggle.

Although Darlie at some points has told us that she chased her assailant through the kitchen, the blood splatters left in the kitchen lack the "high velocity" spread pattern which would be consistent with splatters left behind by someone running through the area.

I spoke today to Mike Bosillo, an investigator with the Dallas D.A.'s Office, who spoke today to Dr. [Joanie] McClain of the Dallas County Medical Examiner's Office. Dr. McClain told Bosillo, and he told me, that Dr. McClain performed the autopsy on the old [est] child, Devon, who McClain says sustained two incised wounds to [the] chest. The larger of the wounds, the top of which began above the child's right nipple and which extended 2" in length in a downward direction, had a maximum depth of penetration of 5", exiting in the right chest wall on the child's back. The wound penetrated the child's rib cage, breaking the child's ribs.

At my request, Dr. [Janice] Townsend-Parchman of the Dallas County Medical Examiner's Office examined Darlie's injuries on June 6, and she has told me that the wounds could possibly have been self-inflicted.

Based upon the above information which I have received from investigating officers, my own investigation, and Dr. McClain and Dr. Townsend-Parchman, I believe that the wounds inflicted upon Darlie were of a completely different character and severity than those inflicted upon her sons. None of her wounds were deep, penetrating wounds to vital areas of her body such as those received by her sons.

Based upon these facts, I believe that someone from inside the house took a knife from the kitchen, cut the garage window screen from outside of the house prior to the offense, and then replaced the knife in the kitchen block container. I further believe that Darlie Routier's stories to Rowlett police are internally inconsistent and inconsistent with all the physical evidence at the scene. I further believe that her repeated statements to the 911 dispatcher about her fingerprints on the knife, her lack of concern and attempts to help her dying son, and her lack of concern for her remaining infant child who was upstairs during the offense and whose condition was apparently unknown to Darlie during the call, are indicative of her guilt and inconsistent with her story that she had awakened after the violent assault on her two older sons and after she had been wounded. I further believe that her story, that she slept through the violent stabbings of her sons only a few feet from her and through multiple cuts inflicted upon herself, is incredible.

Based upon the above facts, I believe that Darlie Routier

committed the capital murder of Damon Routier and Devon Routier in Dallas County, Texas on or about June 6, 1996.

Jimmy Patterson
Affiant

WHEREFORE, AFFIANT REQUESTS THAT AN ARREST WARRANT BE ISSUED FOR THE ABOVE ACCUSED INDIVIDUAL IN ACCORDANCE WITH THE LAW.

SUBSCRIBED AND SWORN TO BEFORE ME ON THE 18th DAY OF June, 1996.

>Janice Warder
>MAGISTRATE, IN AND FOR
>DALLAS COUNTY

***

MAGISTRATE'S DETERMINATION OF PROBABLE CAUSE

ON THIS THE 18 DAY OF JUNE, 1996, I HEREBY ACKNOWLEDGE THAT I HAVE EXAMINED THE FOREGOING AFFIDAVIT AND HAVE DETERMINED THAT PROBABLE CAUSE EXISTS FOR ISSUANCE OF AN ARREST WARRANT FOR THE INDIVIDUAL ACCUSED THEREIN.

>Janice Warder
>MAGISTRATE, IN AND FOR
>DALLAS COUNTY, TEXAS

While Detective Patterson procured the arrest warrant on June 18th, Darlie and Darin Routier cleared away the memorials for their sons placed lovingly on their lawn by friends and family.

About 11:00 A.M., Nelda Watts, in the one-story house across the street, heard a noise outside her front bedroom window. It sounded like children playing.

Mrs. Watts went to the bedroom window to see what was going on. The retired schoolteacher had lived across from the Routiers for about two years, and although she did not know them well, she had seen them outside their house on many occasions. That day, she saw Darlie and Darin in the front yard of their house, playing catch.

Watts watched with curiosity as Darin would pluck a stuffed animal from one of the memorial wreaths, then toss it to Darlie, about 10 feet away. Darlie, dressed in short-shorts and wearing no bra under her T-shirt, would jump up to catch the toy in midair. Then, with a giggle, she would toss it back to Darin, who in turn, pitched the stuffed animal into the back of his green Pathfinder. Some of the toys fell short, landing in the yard. But if Darin was successful in making the shot, Darlie would cheer, jumping up and down with glee.

Watts was aware of the murders that had occurred in the house only 11 days earlier. She watched the antics of the parents of the dead children in shocked disbelief for several minutes, then returned to the chore of packing her suitcase for a planned trip. When she finished packing, Mrs. Watts again looked out her window. She saw Darin pull an 8x10 inch American flag from one of the wreaths. With Darlie cheering him on, he climbed the two-tiered fountain prominently stationed in the Routiers's front yard, and placed the flag on top of the cement figure. Both parents laughed.

Watts later walked across the street to her mailbox as Darin was dragging wilted wreaths to the back of his house. The couple left the neighborhood a short time later.

Chapter Fourteen

Jim Patterson picked up the phone on his desk at the Criminal Investigation Division of the Rowlett Police Department. He had to get Darlie Routier to the station.

Patterson had been working on the murders of Devon and Damon Routier for 11 days and nights. He had gone over the evidence again and again. Some of the evidence was indisputable, like blood splatters and footprints. Other less tangible pieces of the puzzle were Darlie's mental attitude and her demeanor. He was consistently surprised at the evidence they were finding that pointed to Darlie Routier as the killer. It was like a funnel. All the evidence ran right down on Darlie's head.

"Hello, Darlie? Jim Patterson," the detective said. "I need you and Darin to come by the station after six o'clock this evening. I have a few more questions."

After Darlie agreed to meet with Patterson, he hung up the phone, leaned back in his chair, and exhaled deeply. The media had been hounding him for two weeks. Rowlett citizens had phoned, afraid to go to sleep at night. The extended Routier family was anxious. Now finally, all his hard work, and the work of scores of other men and women, was about to pay off in the first step toward retribution for Devon and Damon.

Making his way past the mobile media units parked in front of the Rowlett Police Department, Bill Parker, a 20-year veteran of police interrogations, arrived just after 6:00 P.M. The retired investigator had been asked by Patterson to question Darlie Routier. Although Parker, now a private investigator, had never worked with the Rowlett Police, he was known to be one of the best at getting confessions. Rowlett detectives hoped Parker could crack their prime suspect.

Parker reviewed the evidence while waiting for the Routiers to arrive at the station. He had met with the detectives and Chief Randall Posey a few days earlier, reviewing both the crime scene photos and video, as well as investigative reports. On the 17th, Parker met detectives at the Routier house, piecing together what had taken place on the tragic morning of June 6th. The quick review of the facts on the evening of the 18th was just to refresh his memory before talking with the suspect.

Darlie and Darin Routier arrived at the Rowlett police station just before 7:00 P.M. It was still light outside and was a warm, balmy evening. Darlie was dressed in her familiar short-shorts with rolled cuffs, a blue peasant-style blouse with string tie at the front, and white sandals. Darin, also in shorts, wore a Bud Light T-shirt.

The couple exhibited their familiar smiles and cooperative attitudes. Darin hugged Detective Frosch, which had become his habit, but didn't seem to notice the extra pats on the back from the cautious detective. Frosch had to make certain that Darin wasn't packing his pistol. No one knew how Darin would react when Darlie was taken into custody.

Darlie was led to a room on the second floor of the station by Patterson.

"Let's take a ride," Frosch said to Darin.

Frosch drove the unmarked police car while Detective Keith Needham sat in the front beside him. Darin sat in the back. In retrospect, probably not a good idea, Frosch would later comment.

As Patterson sat across from Darlie Routier, he thought of the caustic evidence that pointed to the young blonde mother of the two victims. The one question he wanted to know most had not been answered. Why did she kill her own children?

"Darlie, I have to read you your rights," Patterson said.

Darlie showed no expression, no concern. She was at ease. After all, Patterson had read her her Miranda Rights more than once over the course of the last 12 days. The eight-year criminal investigator was certain Darlie Routier had no idea she was about to be arrested for the murder of her two children.

She waived her right to speak to an attorney.

"You know, I've always wanted to be an actress," she said. "One day I'll be famous."

Patterson blinked. Darlie Routier may have just predicted her own future. But this wasn't fantasy. The dropped sock was straight out of the O.J. Simpson case or the cut screen was something you'd see on TV. Patterson believed that beyond a doubt Darlie Routier killed her children. He knew they wouldn't find any one-armed man.

"We have an investigator here we'd like you to talk to," Patterson said. "His name is Bill Parker. He's a private investigator. Will you talk to him?"

"I'll be happy to," Darlie said with a coy grin.

She thinks she's so smart. This is nothing but a game with her, and she seems to be having a good time, Patterson thought. He left to get Parker.

Darlie Routier sat alone in the interview room in the upstairs criminal investigation section of the Rowlett Police

Station. She twisted the string tie on her peasant blouse, chewed her gum, and idly looked around the barren room.

Parker had requested a chamber with a two-way mirror, and/or a recording device, but none was available. He could have interviewed Darlie at another location, but decided it was easier to do it at the Rowlett police station. No one knew how things were going to go down once Darlie was informed she was under arrest.

Parker spoke pleasantly to Darlie as he entered the interview room. He immediately informed her that he was acting as a police department agent and would be asking her some questions.

Darlie smiled and appeared to understand what Parker meant. She did not seem to be impaired, but anxious to talk.

"I have your voluntary statement with me," Parker said, tossing the 10-page document on the table in front of her. "I would like for you to read it."

Darlie took the written statement in her hands and began reading. It took her less than five minutes to read all 10 pages.

"Has anything occurred to you that you need to add?" Parker asked.

"No. That's exactly what happened," Darlie replied.

For three hours Parker questioned Darlie Routier concerning the events that led to the murder of her two children. Six times he confronted her directly that she had killed Devon and Damon. Darlie never denied killing the boys. Once she simply shrugged. Five times she responded to Parker's accusation by saying, "If I did it, I don't remember."

Parker finally decided that there was no confession near at hand.

About 9:00 P.M., Sergeant Lamar Evans informed Darlie that there was a warrant out for her arrest. She whispered over and over, "I did not hurt my babies."

About 10:00 P.M., Evans informed Darlie she was under

arrest and that she was not free to go. She nodded her head, saying nothing. Patterson led her from the Criminal Investigation Division interview room, and took her to the Rowlett City Jail for booking.

As Officer Sarah Jones completed the arrest sheet, Patterson fingerprinted Darlie.

"I didn't hurt my babies," Darlie said clearly. There were no tears in her eyes. She seemed in control.

"I know you did it, and you know you did it. At this point you're trying to convince yourself. You need help, Darlie. You need to tell someone before it's too late. You need to talk with God," Patterson said.

"If I did it, I don't remember."

As his wife was being questioned and booked for the murder of his two sons, Darin Routier cruised the streets of Rowlett with Frosch and Needham. They talked about the murders, about his life with Darlie, and his business.

Finally, Frosch was given the signal to return to the station. Darlie had formally been taken into custody, booked, and was secured at the jail.

Moments after the detective altered his course to return to the station, Darin's mobile phone rang.

"Hello," Darin said. "What? No!"

Darin was speaking to Mama Darlie. She had been watching television in her Plano home when a news break announced that an arrest was imminent in the murder case of Devon and Damon Routier. She had put two and two together and had come up with the impending arrest of her daughter.

Darin closed the phone.

"Mama Darlie says you're going to arrest Darlie. Is that true?" he asked Frosch.

"That's a bunch of shit," Frosch said as he stomped on the gas and sped back toward the station. As Frosch turned the car onto Rowlett Road he could see the station, lit up like Las Vegas: TV cameras, communication trucks with huge satellite dishes, and additional lights perched on standards engulfed the police building.

Frosch pulled into the sally-port, and he and Needham whisked Darin past the television cameras, into the police station.

Frosch guided Darin into a room where he and Needham planned to inform him of Darlie's arrest. They asked Darin to sit behind a desk on the opposite side of the room, while the detectives stood near the door. Frosch wanted to make certain that there was some distance, and a barrier between him and Darin when they gave him the news. He had no idea how Darin would respond. Frosch was a bit more at ease, feeling certain that Darin was not carrying his gun.

"Darin, Darlie has been arrested for the murders of Devon and Damon," Frosch said.

"No! No! No! You're wrong! You're kidding. Prove it to me," Darin shouted.

Frosch slowly read Darin the arrest warrant. He wanted him to understand the evidence. He wanted to help him believe his wife had ripped his children from his life.

Darin began to question the evidence. "The man went out the window," Darin said, objecting to the warrant indicating there was no intruder.

"Explain how anyone could go in or out of that window without dumping stuff over or bumping into that huge cat cage," Frosch said.

Darin's anxiety level was high. He was pacing, shouting, nervously running his fingers through his short-trimmed beard.

"Maybe there were two people. One took off the screen and he murdered them. The other guy put the screen back on and left," Darin said. He was desperately trying to find rational answers to an unrational act.

* * *

FLESH AND BLOOD

The Dallas press could smell a story. It hadn't taken them long to discover that an arrest warrant had been issued. Reporters began to call with questions, and more crew trucks began arriving. Sergeant Dean Poos, Information Officer, knew he would have to make a statement as soon as the arrest was made. At 10:20, he made the calls. "She's busted. News conference at eleven thirty."

News crews already in Rowlett caught on tape Darlie Routier being escorted from the Rowlett jail. Her wrists handcuffed behind her, she walked briskly to a waiting squad car for transport to the Dallas County Jail. Head down, she avoided looking at the cameras, a sharp contrast to the laughing, playful mother captured on the Silly String tape only four days earlier.

Within an hour, while Frosch and Needham talked with Darin, a visibly shaken Poos read a statement to the press:

> On the morning of Thursday, June 6, 1996, an investigation began into the murders of Damon and Devon Routier. A significant event has now occurred in this very intensive investigation.
>
> At approximately 10:20 P.M. this evening, investigators from the Rowlett Police Department arrested Darlie Routier, a white female, age 26. Mrs. Routier was charged with two counts of Capital Murder stemming from the stabbing deaths of her sons Damon, age 5, and Devon, age 6. This arrest is the result of the most intensive and exhaustive investigation ever conducted by the Rowlett Police Department.
>
> Darlie Routier was arrested at the Rowlett Police Department. She was booked at the Rowlett City Jail and arraigned by Municipal Court Judge Owen Lokken. Judge Lokken ordered Mrs. Routier held without bond. Mrs. Routier was then transferred to the Lew Sterrett Justice Center. [Dallas]
>
> I can not comment on the details of this investigation other than to say we believe that the white male

suspect described by Darlie Routier as the man that attacked her and murdered her children never existed. We also believe that the wounds present on Darlie Routier were self-inflicted. As for the father, Darin Routier, at this point we do not believe that he was involved in, or participated in, the murders.

The proper time and place for the details of this investigation to be released is at the time of trial, and in a court of law. The full story will be revealed at that time. Any further questions should be directed to the Dallas County District Attorney's Office.

For nearly five hours, Darin Routier questioned the evidence, defended Darlie, and concocted scenario after scenario. He was in denial. He couldn't, or wouldn't, let himself believe Darlie had killed their children.

Frosch and Needham were exhausted. It was nearly 2:00 A.M. There was no reason for Darin to stay at the police station, but they couldn't convince him to go home. Over and over they asked him not to say anything further without an attorney. But Darin couldn't stop. It was as though, if he gave into the fatigue and went to sleep, he would never wake from his nightmare.

Finally, Frosch was told that attorney Peter Lesser was downstairs to see Darin.

"Darin, we can't talk to you anymore. We're exhausted, and your lawyer is downstairs," Frosch said.

But for 15 minutes longer, Darin continued to talk.

"Darin, you have to keep quiet," Frosch said.

Frosch escorted him to the door, and surprisingly, in Darin's usual manner, he hugged Frosch good-bye.

"Thanks for the work you've done on the investigation," Darin said.

Flabbergasted, Frosch stared at Darin as he dejectedly walked toward his attorney.

Family and friends of the Routiers, along with dozens

of Rowlett residents and a horde of press, waited outside the station.

"I'm thinking this is pretty sick when a woman goes and kills her kids," Ryan Bertz, a resident of Rowlett, told reporters. "It is pretty weird, especially in Rowlett—you think people are pretty peaceful."

Darin walked from the back door of the police station, through the sally-port, to his car. In one hand he held a red Coca-Cola can, the other arm was wrapped around the shoulders of Darlie's youngest sister, Danelle, her head nestled into his body.

Darin declined to comment on his wife's arrest.

Randy Reagan, Darin's cousin, was among those who waited for Darin outside the station. He approached Chris Frosch.

"Did she do it, Chris?" Reagan asked.

"Yes, she did," Frosch answered.

"I kinda thought she might have."

Chapter Fifteen

Darlie Routier huddled on the floor in the corner of her cold, bare jail cell at the Lew Sterrett Criminal Justice Center in downtown Dallas. The small cubicle was void of any furnishings except for a stainless steel sink/toilet combination that hung on the wall. Darlie was given a paper sheet and a paper blanket to cover her naked body. She had no shampoo. No toothbrush. It was the suicide watch cell.

Darlie's family was angry. They didn't understand that it was jailhouse procedure to lock anyone accused of capital murder in the suicide watch cell. Often despondent and depressed, prisoners charged with capital murder were known to attempt to take their lives in a variety of ingenious ways, from tearing their clothing in strips and trying to hang themselves, to setting fire to their bedding. The suicide watch was for Darlie's own protection.

Five hours after arriving at the Lew Sterrett jail, Darlie was taken to a regular, single cell within the unit.

* * *

While Darlie acclimated herself to her new surroundings, the shocking statements of disbelief and astonishment that Darlie Routier had been accused of killing her kids rumbled across Rowlett.

"What? Are moms going ballistic these days?" Dawn Daniel of Rowlett asked.

"She needs to be electrocuted," Leslie Madden said to the *Dallas Morning News*. "They were little helpless kids—they didn't do anything wrong."

"I'm in total shock," former neighbor Dan Morgan said. "They loved their kids more than anything, and were both great parents. Still, something's making me believe it."

After the initial shock of Darlie's arrest, the people of Rowlett began to breathe a little easier. The fears of a mad psychotic killer roaming their streets were eased, but replaced with disbelief.

"The arrest brings a conclusion, an answer, to a horrible nightmare," Brigitte Baxter, who lived across the alley from the Routiers, said.

But not everyone agreed with the accusation made against the young, sexy blonde accused of taking the lives of her children.

Friends continued to call the Routier house to offer their support. But Darlie was in jail and Darin was staying with Mama Darlie. Callers heard a cryptic message from Darin Routier on the answering machine. "Yes, the boys were killed by an intruder. Darlie has been falsely arrested. She didn't do it. Don't believe what you read or what you hear. Believe in us."

Karen Neal, who had been in the Routier house soon after police arrived on the morning of the murders, doubled over when she heard the news, placing her hands on her knees. She believed in Darlie. "I feel in my heart she didn't do it," Neal exclaimed.

Neal and Darlie had been friends for some time. Neal knew Darlie not as a killer, but as a loving mother and giving friend.

"She bought school clothes for my children because I went through chemotherapy and could not afford clothes," Neal said. It was also rumored that Darlie paid the Neals's house payments, totaling nearly $8,000, while her friend was off work recuperating from cancer.

That was one thing neighbors remembered most about Darlie, the extravagant gifts, the lavish parties, the materialistic approach to life. Had Darlie been trying to buy friendship?

Darlie Routier was a puzzle. Even her neighbors couldn't agree whether she was the June Cleaver-type mother, or more of the *Knots Landing*-style neighbor.

Whatever the answer, the residents of Rowlett slept a bit better at night and their children were once again allowed outside to play after the arrest of Darlie Routier.

The Routier family remained frightened. They believed the murderer was still free. Free to kill again.

Darlie Kee, Darlie Routier's mother, loudly accused the Rowlett police of succumbing to public pressure.

"They don't have anybody else, and everyone's pushing them to make an arrest on this because it's two little kids," Kee said. "I don't know if they're trying to make this into a Susan Smith thing or what," she continued, referring to the 1994 case in which a mother drowned her two small children by letting her car, with them inside, roll into a South Carolina lake.

"We're going to fight this," Kee said. "This is an unbelievable nightmare." The fire in her eyes and the hostility in her voice gave further credence to her words.

On June 19th, the day following the arrest of Darlie Routier for the murder of her two eldest sons, eight-month-old Drake was taken from his father by Child Protective Services (CPS) and placed in a foster home.

"Darin has said he intends to stay with and support his wife. It is believed he [Darin] would be unable to protect his last surviving son," a CPS worker told the press. CPS officials added that they were concerned about Drake's safety in the event that his mother bonded out of jail.

"The bottom line is the mother is charged with this," Margie Wright of CPS said. "The father is standing firm that she didn't do it. They're talking about bonding her out. If they bond her out, who's to say she wouldn't be right back there with the baby?"

Darin Routier had lost everything.

"We went from a family of five to one," Darin said in his first public statement since Darlie's arrest. "With her [Darlie] being in jail and my boys now gone, my life is gone."

But Darin wasn't giving up. He planned to do whatever it took to prove his wife didn't kill their children. Those plans included selling Darlie's story to the highest bidder. Darin and Mama Darlie signed an agreement on June 20th with Larry Garrison of Silvercreek Entertainment for *"The True Life Story of Darlie Kee and Darlie and Darin Routier."* That agreement was solely for a movie deal. Darin and Darlie planned to acquire their own book deal, with Darlie penning her own memoirs. "That way we can cut out the middle man [an author] and get all the big bucks ourselves," Darin said.

Larry Garrison set to work contacting potential movie producers. Meanwhile, everyone waited for the trial of Darlie Routier to begin.

On June 26th, Darlie Routier entered a courtroom at the Lew Sterrett Criminal Justice Center in downtown Dallas in white prison overalls. Gone were her glamorous looks. Her freshly scrubbed face was void of the heavy black eyeliner and thick black mascaraed lashes. Her straight blonde hair was pulled back and secured at the nape of the neck. Wisps of blond strands loosely framed her face.

Darlie was there to face her accusers.

Sitting beside her court-appointed attorneys, Doug Parks

and Wayne Huff, Darlie turned to Darin, sitting in the second row, and mouthed, "I love you."

Lieutenant Grant Jack told the court that he believed Darlie was responsible for the deaths of her sons. As he reiterated that the physical evidence collected at the scene contradicted Routier's version of the events, Darlie shook her head from side to side and rolled her eyes.

Detective Jim Patterson testified that, "She made it sound like she was crying on the tape." The remark infuriated the Routier family.

At the end of the long court session, with hours of testimony by Jack and Patterson on the evidence gathered at the crime scene, Judge Phil Barker found probable cause to hold Darlie Routier for trial. He maintained her bail at one million dollars.

"You guys did a good job on this, looks like," Judge Barker commented to the Rowlett investigators outside the courtroom.

But the investigation was not complete. There was more work to be done. More evidence to gather. With no apparent motive and no confession, investigators wanted to insure the circumstantial case was as strong as it could be.

Darin Routier, Darlie Kee, and the rest of the Routier family were ready to fight. As Darlie was being taken back to her isolated cell at the Dallas County jail, Darin remarked, "I'll sell everything I have to prove her innocence."

Two days after Judge Barker found probable cause to hold Darlie Routier for trial, a grand jury indicted her on two counts of capital murder.

Citing extensive pretrial publicity, Judge Mark Tolle imposed a gag order in an attempt to ensure an impartial jury. The gag order included Darlie, any attorney associated with the case, law enforcement personnel, witnesses, and perspective witnesses. Tolle sternly warned that violators would be subject to punishment of up to six months in jail and a fine of $500.

Routier family members, however, continued to be very outspoken in both the local and national press. Darin gave numerous statements and appeared on the nationally broadcast NBC program *Dateline*. In every way they could, Darlie's family attempted to gain public support for her. Nothing slowed them down. Not even the court's gag order.

The next court appearance for Darlie Routier was a bail reduction hearing. Her attorney, Doug Parks, argued that the bail of $500,000 for each of the two capital murder cases was excessive and should be lowered. He contended that Darlie would not be a flight risk. He requested the bail be lowered to $50,000 per case.

For the first time, Darin Routier admitted that he and his wife had been having financial difficulties. He squirmed uneasily as he outlined in court financial liabilities that included two mortgages on the two-story Eagle Drive home, totaling about $130,000. The couple owed about $12,000 in credit card debt and about $10,000 in 1995 back taxes to the Internal Revenue Service. Darin, who normally bragged about his financial success, was dispirited at having to admit publicly that he was in financial difficulty.

Darlie pursed her lips and rubbed her forehead throughout the hearing. She smiled broadly when her lawyer, Parks, asked about their credit card debt, as though amused by the amount of charges they had incurred.

Darin estimated his personal debt at close to $200,000. His 1995 gross income had been $260,000, but now the couple had only about $2,000 in a business savings account and perhaps $1,200 "on hand."

"I haven't been able to make any money because I haven't been working," Darin said. But he also admitted that the debt existed before his sons were killed.

Under cross-examination Darin told prosecutors that he hadn't received any offers for movie deals. He was not asked if he had hired someone to look for a deal.

After hearing both the defense and prosecution arguments on bail reduction, Judge Tolle announced that the bail of one million dollars would remain in effect.

Darin Routier and Darlie Kee lowered their heads and dabbed their eyes after hearing Tolle's decision. They left the courtroom without speaking to reporters. Darlie was visibly shaken. Her hands trembled as she chewed on her nails. Tears, unseen during previous court appearances, welled in her eyes.

Darlie wasn't going home as she had hoped.

Eight-month-old Drake Routier was oblivious to his mother's courtroom plight. He was in court himself. During the temporary child custody hearing, Drake's father angrily criticized the supervised visitation he had been forced to endure since his only remaining son had been taken from him.

"I don't think I should have to go to a room with people looking at me through the glass in order to see Drake," Darin complained. He also told the court that Darlie was no threat to Drake and should be allowed to see him.

"I'm sure right now he [Drake] is feeling very irregular, very abnormal," Darin said, adding that Drake had never been away from his mother for more than 24 hours until the murders of his brothers.

"We are trying very hard to be sensitive," Margie Wright of CPS said. "This is a very difficult situation, and we don't want to add to the grief. There is a concern that he [Darin] would allow her [Darlie] to have access to the child if her visits were not supervised. The overriding concern has to be that this child is in a safe place."

The court appointed Mary Kay Garrett, a volunteer for Court Appointed Special Advocates, to offer an independent evaluation of the case. In the meantime, CPS recommended a psychological assessment of Darin to determine his ability to protect Drake.

Sarilda and Leonard Routier of Lubbock, Darin's parents, immediately petitioned the court for custody.

On July 10th, Darlie Routier's court-appointed attorney filed a motion for a change of venue, stating that the media attention given the Routier case could jeopardize his client's chance for a fair trial. Darlie Kee agreed, stating that the media had handled her daughter's predicament unfairly.

"It's been slapped on every channel and immortalized. I don't think it's being treated fair at all," Kee said. "The gag order has been a good thing."

Mama Darlie would later violate the very order she had validated.

"I cannot imagine a case of murder of a child under six that could be more grievous, more brutal than this case," First Assistant District Attorney Norman Kinne, said in an interview with the *Dallas Morning News*. Kinne had just announced that the Dallas County prosecutors would seek the death penalty against Darlie Routier.

"I honestly don't remember the last time we sought it against a woman," Kinne added. "I'm not sure we ever have."

Executions of women are extremely rare in Texas. The last woman was executed in 1863. Chipita Rodriguez was hanged for killing a horse trader and stealing $600. In 1985, then Governor Mark White pardoned Rodriguez after historical information was presented exonerating the Mexican woman of the crime.

Currently, only six women are on death row in Texas for their crimes, compared to 434 men. Prosecutors have

Five-year-old Damon Christian Routier. *(Photo courtesy of the Dallas County, Texas District Attorney's office)*

Devon Rush Routier was murdered eight days before his seventh birthday. *(Photo courtesy of the Dallas County, Texas District Attorney's office)*

Darlie Lynn Peck was a teenager when her mother introduced her to Darin Routier in 1985.

In 1986, Darin Routier graduated Cooper-Lubbock High School in Lubbock, Texas.

Darin Routier with his youngest son Drake, 14 months.

The Routier's former home on Eagle Drive in Rowlett, Texas.

The blood-soaked front and blood-spattered back of the t-shirt Darlie Routier wore on the night her sons were murdered.
(*Photo courtesy of the Dallas County, Texas District Attorney's office*)

The police were able to identify the bloody footprint found on the Routier's kitchen floor as Darlie Routier's.
(Photo courtesy of the Dallas County, Texas District Attorney's office)

A bloody knife was lying in plain view on the white countertop in the Routier's kitchen.
(Photo courtesy of the Dallas County, Texas District Attorney's office)

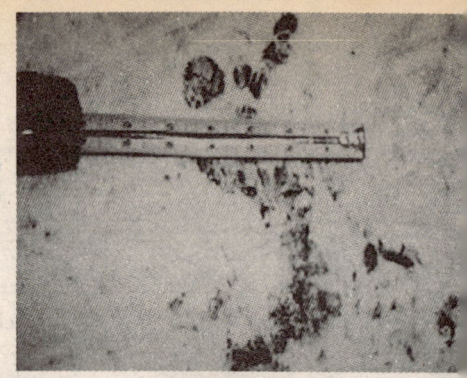

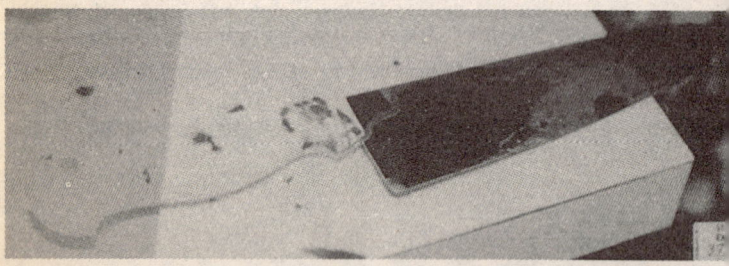

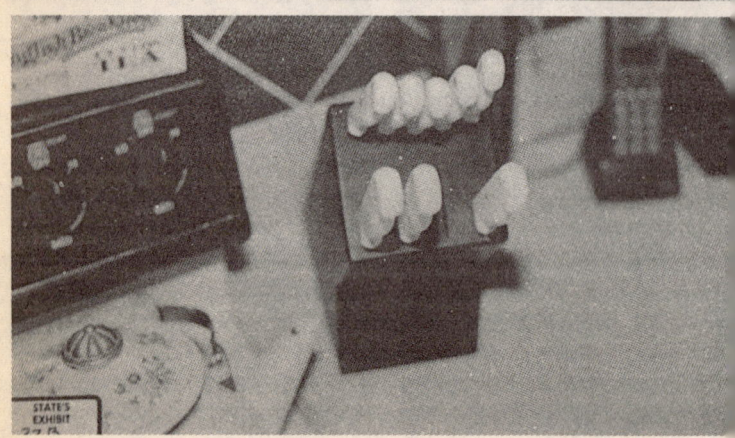

The wooden butcher block that had held the murder weapon was kept near the kitchen sink.
(Photo courtesy of the Dallas County, Texas District Attorney's office)

The garage window was open and its screen had been cut, but the dust on the windowsill had not been disturbed. *(Photo courtesy of the Dallas County, Texas District Attorney's office)*

Under the microscope, the fiber on the left from the cut screen was a match for the fiber on the right from the bread knife found in the butcher block in the Routier's kitchen. *(Photo courtesy of the Dallas County, Texas District Attorney's office)*

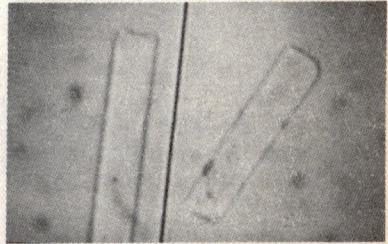

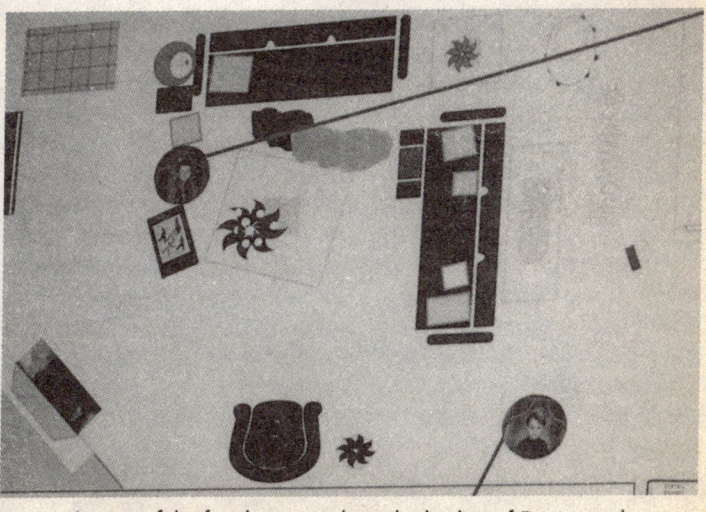

Layout of the family room where the bodies of Devon and Damon Routier were found.
(Photo courtesy of the Dallas County, Texas District Attorney's office)

Darlie Routier, 26, was arrested on June 19, 1996 for the murder of her two oldest sons. (*Photo courtesy of the Rowlett, Texas Police Department*)

The wounds to Darlie Routier's neck were stitched closed at the hospital. (*Photo courtesy of the Dallas County, Texas District Attorney's office*)

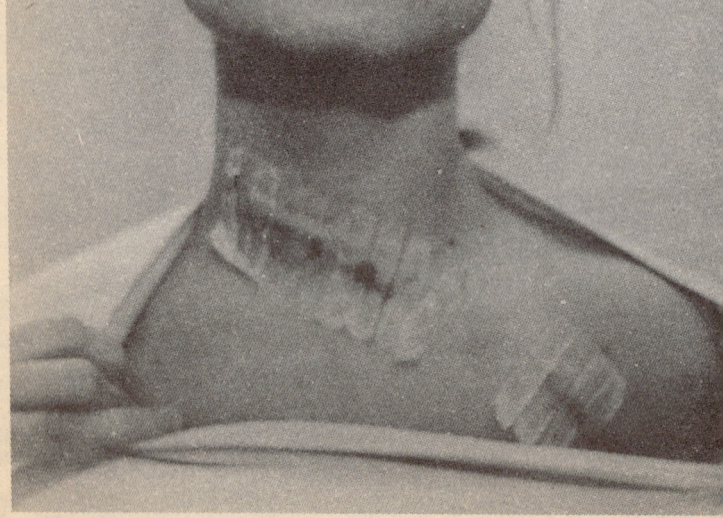

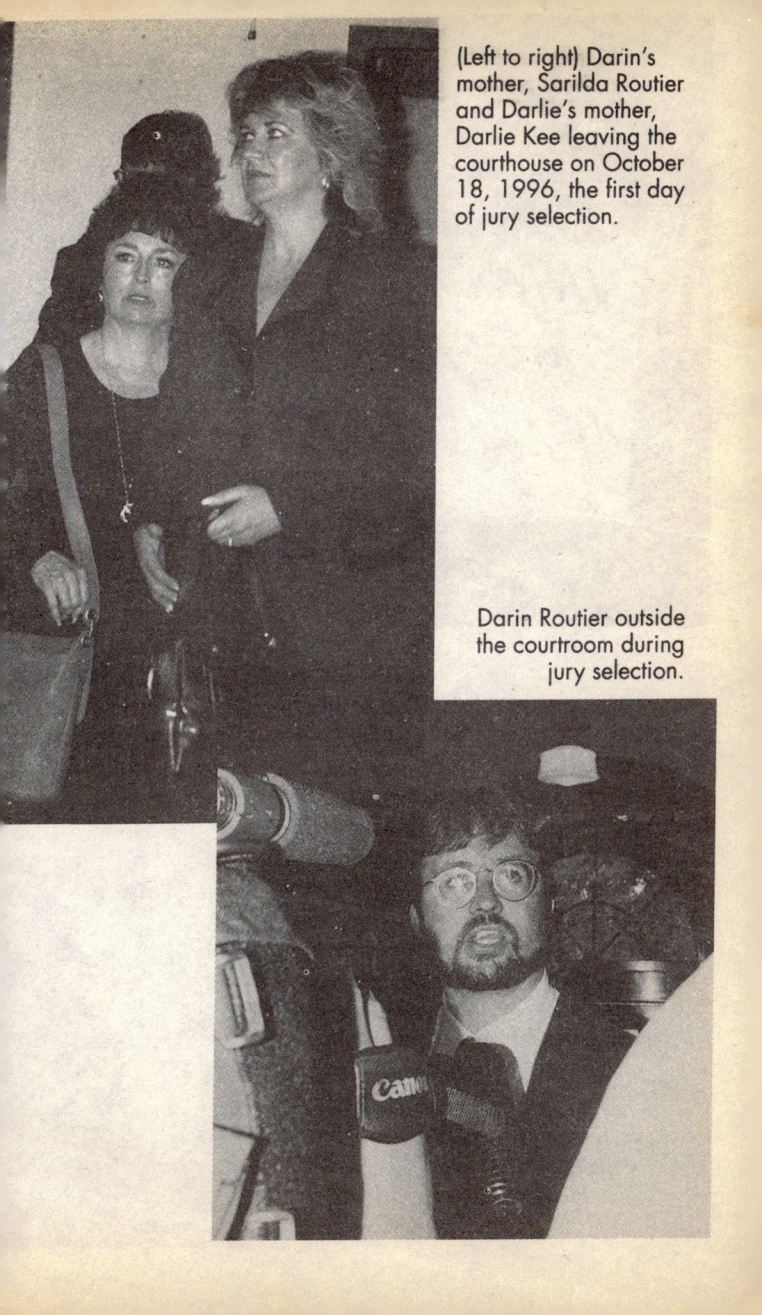

(Left to right) Darin's mother, Sarilda Routier and Darlie's mother, Darlie Kee leaving the courthouse on October 18, 1996, the first day of jury selection.

Darin Routier outside the courtroom during jury selection.

At the "Free Darlie" rally, Darin Routier's aunt, Sandy Aitken holds up a sign. She acted as spokesperson for the family during the trial.

Darin Routier held up a photo of their son Drake for Darlie to see as she waited in a holding cell at the Kerr County courthouse.

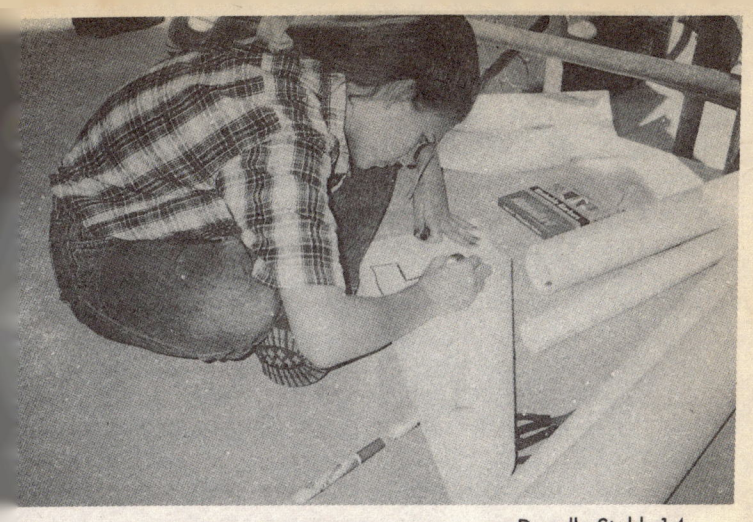

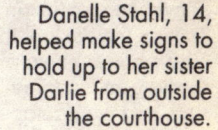

Danelle Stahl, 14, helped make signs to hold up to her sister Darlie from outside the courthouse.

Dana Stahl, 16, Darlie's sister, wore one of the t-shirts with a photo of Damon and Devon and the words "Forever In Our Hearts" on the front.

Darlie Routier's aunts, Lou Ann Black and Sherry Moses (left to right) inside the courthouse.

Shown here on Darin Routier, the back of the t-shirts had a photo of Darlie with her three sons and the passage from *Psalms* 120:2 "Save me, oh Lord, from lying lips and deceitful tongues."

While waiting for the verdict, Darin Routier and his mother Sarilda spoke to the press. Darin shaved off his full beard and bought a plain gold wedding band before testifying.

Defense attorney Doug "Maddog" Mulder led the team of five lawyers who defended Darlie Routier.

Defense attorney Richard Mosty.

Defense attorney John Hagler.

(Left to right) Assistant D.A. Toby Shook, lead prosecutor Greg Davis, and Assistant D.A. Sherri Wallace.

Police detective Jim Patterson.

Shawn Rabb of FOX 4 News/Dallas was one of the newsmen broadcasting from the courthouse lawn.

apparently been reluctant to seek the death penalty for women.

"The legislature passed this law," Kinne said of the 1993 expansion of the capital murder statute to include murder of a child under six. "If you're not going to use it in this case, when in hell are you going to use it?"

The decision by the prosecutor's office was expected by the Routier family.

"They can rot in hell as far as I'm concerned," Darlie Kee said of prosecutors. "They're trying to force her to confess and she'll never confess to something she didn't do."

Prosecutors, indeed, would have liked Darlie Routier to confess. But they knew a confession wasn't forthcoming. They began building a case based on strong circumstantial evidence—a case they were convinced they could win. If successful, Darlie Routier would die for the murders of her children—die for the ultimate betrayal of trust.

Chapter Sixteen

The phone lines at KRLD-AM radio in Arlington, Texas were jammed with callers. The station, located midway between Dallas and Fort Worth, featured morning talk show personality Rick Roberts.

Roberts, known for his outspoken conservative political views, hosted a program he boasted as "the court of public opinion." The law-and-order host featured a weekly Top Ten list of recently released sex offenders, and the addresses of those who currently lived in the metroplex. Roberts portrayed himself as a protector of children, a keeper of the key to decency and justice.

On July 25th, Roberts featured a 90-minute interview with Darin Routier and Darlie Kee. The husband and mother of the accused child-killer professed Darlie's innocence, disputing news reports about several aspects of the case.

Darlie Kee told listeners that entries in her daughter's diary had been taken out of context. On one page, Darlie expressed a need to be forgiven for something she was about to do. Kee explained that her daughter had written the diary entry as a letter to her children the previous winter, in reference to suicidal thoughts she was having after the birth of her third son, Drake. However, Kee failed to mention to the listening audience that the entry was actually dated May 3, 1996, a month before the murders.

In an attempt to discount allegations that her daughter's injuries were superficial, Kee read from a doctor's report that one of Darlie's wounds was extremely close to her carotid artery. No reference was made to statements made by Baylor attending physician, Dr. Alex Santos. His assessment that the wound, penetrating the carotid sheath but not the carotid artery, was merely superficial, was not addressed. In fact, Santos and the unnamed doctor Kee quoted both agreed that the cut was close to the carotid artery. Santos simply determined that close is not life threatening. Kee refused to release the doctor's report to journalists.

Roberts expressed his horror at the prospect that an innocent woman could be arrested, charged, and indicted for killing her own children. There was no one on the program representing the prosecution, no one to answer the Routier family's assault on law enforcement officials. Prosecutors were furious.

"Clearly, at the time of this interview, Mr. Routier and Ms. Kee knew they were prospective witnesses," Assistant District Attorney Greg Davis said.

Deputies for the Dallas County District Attorney's Office waited outside the KRLD studio for Darin Routier and Darlie Kee. As soon as they exited the facility, they were served with contempt citations for being in violation of the gag order.

"We did it purposely because we love DarLynn [Mrs. Routier's nickname] very much and we believe in her," Kee said. "Why aren't we allowed to say that? Do you think they are going to put grandma in jail, too?"

That is exactly what prosecutors had in mind.

"We're going to ask the judge to enforce his gag order—

whatever that might entail," First Assistant District Attorney Norman Kinne said. The possible penalties included up to six months in jail and a $500 fine.

"What are they going to do? Hang us on a cross for loving Darlie?" Darin asked. "We have a right to be angry."

Darin Routier had been working feverishly to raise $100,000, 10 percent of the one million dollar bond set by Judge Barker, and the amount required by most bail bondsmen. Once the money was raised, Darlie could go home. The family had been keeping her spirits up with letters of encouragement and assurances that she would soon be with them.

Darin kept his promise that he would sell everything he had to prove Darlie innocent. He held a garage sale and sold most of the couple's personal belongings. The antique furniture Darlie had diligently searched for; the china and crystal proudly displayed in the rosewood room; the toys, clothes, and even photographs of the dead Routier children. Material things no longer had a value to Darin Routier. He had lost everything that meant anything to him—Devon, Damon, Drake, and Darlie.

Proceeds from the garage sale, along with borrowed money from family and friends, was soon nearing the $100,000 mark. In a matter of days the appeals court was expected to rule on a defense request to have Darlie Routier's original one million dollar bail lowered to $100,000. Prosecutors were concerned. If Darin managed to secure the bail funds or if the appeals court lowered the bail and Darlie was released, would Drake be in danger? They had to take action.

On August 27th, prosecutors went back to court for the first day of a two-day hearing to ask that bail be revoked and Darlie Routier be held without bond.

Darlie entered the courtroom walking slowly, and very erect. She smiled sweetly at Darin, then gently slid into the chair next to Doug Parks, her attorney. Her over-bleached blonde hair was a startling contradiction to the three-inch roots of her natural brown coloring. Darlie was beginning to show the signs of stress.

Darin Routier, in a dark suit and short-sleeved wrinkled white shirt, sat next to Dana Stahl. The 16-year-old, red-headed, half-sister of Darlie supportively rubbed his neck, patted his knee, and hugged him during the proceedings.

Detective Patterson took the stand dressed in a gray suit, light blue shirt, and maroon and blue tie. His mustache was neatly trimmed, his dark hair combed straight back. He spoke clearly and knowledgeably about the evidence collected from the crime scene on Eagle Drive.

Patterson told the court of the inconsistencies in Darlie's story and the physical evidence found at the scene: The knife she said was dropped on the utility room floor—but no blood evidence to support that statement. The footprints between the sink and the family room—when Darlie initially denied being at the sink. The darkened security light when officers arrived. The injuries to Darlie—so inconsistent with the boys' injuries. The K-9 unit that didn't pick up a scent by the window with the cut screen. The lack of physical evidence that an intruder was on the premises. Probably the most damning statement Patterson made in the bond hearing was that Darlie Routier showed little apparent concern for her sons when police interviewed her at the hospital.

As Patterson spoke, Darlie rested her head on her hand, her elbow on the defense table. To some observers, she appeared bored.

Patterson explained Darin's demeanor and inappropriate behavior at the hospital. "He talked about the size of his wife's breasts," Patterson testified. "He never asked about the children. He laughed some. He cried some. He acted as if nothing serious had happened to his family."

Patterson concluded his testimony by stating that he

believed the murders had been planned in a few minutes, but not well planned.

Darlie Kee shook her head angrily.

Charles Linch, trace evidence expert from Southwest Institute of Forensic Science in Dallas, testified about the blood evidence. His overall opinion was that the scene had been deliberately tampered with.

"It appeared staged or altered to me," Linch said. For instance, the pattern of blood splotches on the kitchen floor did not match Mrs. Routier's account of an intruder running through the room with a blood-soaked knife. Instead, they suggested someone standing still, or walking slowly.

"Everything appeared to be happening in slow motion," Linch said. "Nobody's in a hurry."

Called by the prosecution, Darin Routier reluctantly took the stand. Assistant District Attorney Davis suggested to Darin that on the night of the killings Darlie had complained that she was left without transportation because the couple's Jaguar sedan needed repair. Davis further suggested that Darlie had been angry about what Davis called Mr. Routier's "flirting" with her sister, Dana.

Darin denied both suggestions. He admitted that he and Darlie had discussed problems with their cars and income from the family-owned business, but denied that the "discussions" had accelerated into an argument. He dismissd any improper relationship with his teenage sister-in-law, Dana Stahl.

During a court recess, reporters milled around discussing the attention Dana Stahl had been giving Darin during court. The implication by the prosecutor that Darin had been "flirting" with his wife's younger sister instantly became the object of courthouse gossip.

As court reconvened the following day, Davis tried to support the theory earlier presented by a medical examiner that Darlie's wounds could have been self-inflicted. Over the objections of the defense, Davis attempted to introduce

Darlie's 1992 breast-implant surgery through Darin's testimony. Davis claimed relevance based on the absence of wounds on her breasts, which Davis claimed suggested a deliberate effort to avoid injuring them. He reminded the court that Devon had been stabbed twice in the chest.

During cross examination, defense attorneys called no witnesses, but introduced the 911 recording made the morning of the murders.

"My babies are dying! Oh, my God! Oh, my God! My babies...." Darlie Routier's words reverberated throughout the courtroom.

Darlie sobbed. Her mother cried, along with most of the 13 supporters who had come to court to provide encouragement.

Prosecutors countered by presenting videotape of the gravesite Silly String party. "This is an example of the lack of remorse or grief at her sons's deaths," Davis said.

Defense attorneys urged State District Judge Paul Banner to deny the state's request. Parks called the state's motion "a cynical attack on the presumption of innocence."

Prosecutor Davis focused on the nature of the crime. "This was a very calculated killing," he said. "She butchered these two children with very deep, repeated stab wounds."

Judge Banner's decision favored the prosecution. Darlie Routier would remain in jail.

Routier's relatives sat in the courtroom in somber silence. Darin bowed his head. Darlie had been incarcerated in the Dallas County jail for two months. Darin had hoped Darlie would be coming home. He missed her. He needed her.

In a brief hearing the following week, courthouse gossip escalated as Darlie entered the courtroom and stared at

Darin sternly. Gone was the sweet smile and the mouthed expression of love.

Dana Stahl no longer sat with Darin, but arrived in court with a boyfriend no one had seen at previous hearings. The speculation from court regulars was that someone, perhaps Mama Darlie, had put an end to the affectionate show of support displayed by her middle daughter to Darlie's husband.

But anyone who knew Darin knew he loved Darlie.

"Me and her are soul mates. I do believe that God put us together for a reason," Darin told the *Dallas Morning News*. "People go through their whole lives wishing that they have the relationship that me and Darlie have."

Chapter Seventeen

Darlie Routier remained in the Dallas County Jail awaiting her capital murder trial. Visitations were allowed only twice a week. To keep in contact with the outside world, she talked with Darin, her mother, and other relatives and friends on a daily basis. The isolation was closing in. Darlie was bored. Restless.

Weary with a jail life of no TV and no music, Darlie wrote numerous letters to family and friends. Among them was Mary Cottey, a Rowlett woman who didn't know Darlie before the murders.

Cottey had met Darin Routier at the garage sale held to raise money for Darlie's defense. After visiting with Darin, she decided to write Darlie.

In the first letter to Cottey, Darlie blasted the Rowlett police. "They didn't know what they were doing—it's so sad and scary to know that is how the system works," she wrote. She added that investigators attempted to get her to pin the slayings on her husband, Darin.

In a second letter, Darlie wrote, "No one can imagine what Darin and I went through that night. A parent's worse nightmare and no one should be able to tell someone how they should have acted, my goodness we were in shock . . . let alone the fact that I was almost half gone myself."

Cottey believed Darlie was innocent.

"I cry for my babies all the time and it breaks my heart to know people are thinking I did this terrible thing—now that's crazy," Darlie wrote Cottey. "When we find the real killer, I bet I won't even get an apology!"

Jailers for Dallas County were puzzled at the anguish Darlie was showing in her corespondence. Their records indicated that Darlie had shown little grief or distress since her incarceration. A log book tracking Darlie's actions every 15 minutes, 24 hours a day, recorded Darlie talking on the phone, singing in her cell and in the shower, working crossword puzzles, reading, and napping. There were only three or four entries that indicated Darlie had been crying.

"What I see here is just about as strange as seeing a birthday party at a cemetery," reported Chief Knowles, Assistant Chief Deputy of the Dallas County Sheriff's Office. "What she described in her letters certainly isn't reflected in the log. She is certainly not what she is trying to make everybody think," Knowles added.

To some of the jailers Darlie appeared almost happy.

But Lou Ann Black, Darlie's aunt, disagreed. "She has a strong faith that God is going to take care of all this. She is going to be criticized no matter how she acts. How would you act if you were in prison or jail? Who is to say you would act a certain way?"

Darin Routier and Darlie Kee had raised $100,000, but they couldn't buy Darlie's freedom. The revocation of bond enraged the family. Darin and Mama Darlie felt more persecuted by the judicial system than ever.

Darlie's mother began to think of hiring a high-powered attorney for her daughter. Doug Parks, her court appointed attorney was a highly respected Dallas criminal defense lawyer, but Mama Darlie wanted the best.

In early September, well-known Dallas attorney Doug Mulder visited Darlie in the Dallas County jail. Speculation circulated through the legal community that he would soon be taking over the case. The question most often asked was if $100,000 would be enough to secure the high-profile attorney. Darlie Kee was convinced Mulder could free her daughter.

Doug "Maddog" Mulder, as he was known around the Dallas County courthouse, had a knack for drawing national attention to cases he litigated. As an assistant Dallas County prosecutor, Mulder tried and convicted Randall Dale Adams. Adams, found guilty of killing a Dallas police officer in 1976, claimed innocence but was sentenced to Texas's Death Row. The sentence was later commuted to life in prison.

After *The Thin Blue Line,* a 1988 documentary by New York film maker Errol Morris on the Adams case was released, Adams's conviction was set aside by the Texas Court of Criminal Appeals. Adams's defense alleged that the prosecution had improperly withheld information about some witnesses.

By the time Adams was being set free from the injustice, Mulder had been building a lucrative private criminal defense practice for several years. His successful defense of Reverend Walker Railey, accused of the attempted strangulation murder of his wife, also drew national recognition and controversy over his methods.

The last high-profile case Mulder defended was the capital murder case of Joy Davis Aylor. Aylor, charged with the murder-for-hire of her husband's girlfriend, fled to France where she lived for ten years before extradition. Mulder lost the fight and Joy Aylor was sentenced to life in prison.

The Routiers weren't interested in the accusations waged against Mulder, or Aylor's publicized contempt for her counsel. They were only interested in Mulder's reputation for coming out on top. The "Maddog" nickname was justly earned. Mulder was known as an attorney with tenacity and a no-holds-barred attitude. "I like to win," Mulder said in a *Dallas Morning News* interview. "And I like a decisive resolution of a case. And when I'm in the courtroom, I get one."

Whether it would be her court-appointed attorneys or Doug Mulder who defended Darlie Routier, the defense team would be traveling 300 miles to court.

Judge Mark Tolle granted the change of venue requested by Darlie's court-appointed attorneys and announced the trial would be moved to Kerrville, Texas.

"It wouldn't be a fair trial here because of the way things have been with the media," Darlie's aunt, Lou Ann Black, said, adding that the family was pleased with the decision.

But they would not be pleased for long. As soon as Doug Mulder finally took the helm of the Routier defense, he immediately asked that the trial be moved back to Dallas.

"It can be tried here, and it should be tried here," Mulder said. "I see no reason to waste the taxpayers' money when we can get a fair trial here."

But speculation was that Mulder didn't want the trial moved to Kerrville for one simple reason—conservative, law-and-order politics.

Kerr County had been a Republican threshold for decades. No Democrats currently held office. Dole-Kemp signs dotted lawns across Kerrville, a city with a population of about 17,000. A pickup spotted near the downtown area sported a bumper sticker that read, "Bill Clinton is a yellow-bellied draft dodger."

Mulder could see the writing on the wall—or in this case, on the bumper sticker.

The 1995 census estimated that the county was about 80% white, 16% Hispanic, and less than 30% black. Most of the county's population was over the age of 45, and most of the city's residents are over 65.

With the influx of wealthy, conservative retirees that had

moved to the beautiful, lush-green rolling hills of Kerr County, the *Wall Street Journal* labeled the town "the Palm Springs of Texas."

Kerr County juries were historically tough on crime. Three times in the previous two years, capital murder cases had been tried in Kerrville. They resulted in three convictions, three death sentences.

Mulder assembled a defense team that would come to be known as the Texas Dream Team. Mulder, as lead attorney, selected Curtis Glover, John Haggler, Richard Mosty, and S. Preston Douglas to fight for Darlie's life. Joining them in the effort was Lloyd Herrall, a former FBI agent turned private investigator.

But even with this highly regarded team of legal minds, Mulder was understandably concerned. He had to try to return the trial to Dallas.

Moments before jury selection began October 21, 1996, Mulder addressed the court in his usual confident manner. In his motion to reverse the change of venue, Mulder said the trial should be returned to Dallas because media coverage of the case had been balanced and not prejudicial toward either side. He ignored the Routier family's earlier comments against the media. He also said that a trial in Dallas would be more convenient for the dozens of witnesses who might be called to testify.

Judge Tolle didn't buy Mulder's argument, citing the defense's own insistence that the media had prejudiced the Dallas community in requesting the change of venue in the first place. In less than a minute Judge Tolle looked directly at Mulder and cut off the attorney's hopes of returning to Dallas with a curt, "Motion denied."

The Routier family couldn't sit idly by waiting for trial. They had to do something to help Darlie. The verdict would come from the court, but they could still influence public opinion, perhaps create reasonable doubt.

The first of two "Save Darlie" rallies was organized by Sandy Aitken, Darin Routier's aunt. According to family members, Aitken had been married to Sarilda Routier's brother, who had passed away several years earlier. Aitken had remarried, twice, and had lost contact with the Routier family. When she heard news of the boys' murders, Aitken, who had never met Darlie, gave up her job as an over-the-road, long-distance truck driver to take over the helm of the Routier publicity. She instantly became a self-professed family spokesperson.

Aunt Sandy, as she came to be known, made her first public appearance on KRLD-AM with Rick Roberts. At approximately eleven A.M. she announced a "Save Darlie" rally, scheduled for six P.M. in front of the Rowlett Police Department.

At the appointed time, news trucks, reporters, and a blaze of lights engulfed the front parking area of the Rowlett police station.

About a dozen picketers marched up and down the sidewalk between the parking area and the street, waving homemade poster board signs reading: "Free Darlie," "Let Drake Have His Mom Back," and "Admit Your Mistake Free Darlie."

An animated Sandy Aitken addressed reporters behind television cameras and radio microphones. When asked for her reaction to the number of people who attended the rally, a little more than a dozen outside the press, Aitken laughed and tossed her platinum-toned, bleached-blonde hair to one side. "I think it's great. Do you want a sign?"

"Why this rally? Why now?" a reporter asked.

"You know, Darlie is sitting in Kerrville where every single day they interview a prospective juror and they go through the entire description of death by lethal injection. That's pretty difficult to listen to. She needs to know there are people out here telling her she's not guilty. She has her family telling her everyday, but she needs to know everyone is out here saying she's not guilty," Aunt Sandy said.

But not everyone at the rally supported Darlie Routier. Not everyone thought she was innocent.

"She should burn in hell," Rita Adams told reporters, holding a sign declaring those sentiments. "She's guilty. Who did it, if she didn't do it?"

Adams, who worked in a building behind Routier's Testnec business, described Darlie Routier as a thoughtless mother. "The kids use to play out by that road," the young, dark-haired Adams said, speaking of a main street leading into downtown Rowlett. "Cars were going fifty and sixty miles an hour through there."

But Adams insisted that her guilty judgment was not based solely on her observations of an inattentive mother. She claimed she had read the evidence as outlined in the newspaper and had reached her decision.

A man with a sign reading, "Get A Rope," concurred with Adams.

Those ready to convict were far outnumbered by loyal supporters of Darlie Routier. But the supporters were all members of her family or close friends. None among those who marched in support, or opposition were Rowlett residents. None were the frightened neighbors from Eagle Drive.

For more than an hour picketers marched, Sandy Aitkens talked to reporters, and gawkers watched. Uniformed Rowlett officers stood on the front steps of the station staring at the spectacle. Their stares hid the anger inside. Investigators had done a good job. They were convinced they had arrested the killer. They looked forward to a Kerrville jury judging their work.

In Kerrville, jury selection was completd.

"I think we've got a good, solid jury," defense team member Richard Mosty, of Kerrville, said. "I'm pleased with the way it's turned out. The people we have are open-minded, objective, and they're going to require the state to prove its case."

Greg Davis said prosecutors were satisfied with the group of jurors selected.

Half of the panel members were 45 or older. The youngest was 24; the oldest 61. Four panel members had at least some college education. There were 11 whites and one Hispanic.

Promising jurors they wouldn't miss their Thanksgiving and Christmas holidays, Judge Tolle set January 6, 1997 as the first day of trial. Darlie Routier was transported back to the Dallas County jail.

Darlie was restless. She paced in her jail cell nervously. The trial was still six weeks away. For nearly five months she had been denied the opportunity to tell the public of her innocence. Gag order or no gag order, Darlie Routier decided it was time to speak out.

On November 5, 1996, Darlie phoned the Rick Roberts show on KRLD radio. She spoke very clearly. There was no emotion in her voice. Her words were precise.

Darlie began by telling listeners the obvious—prosecutors believed she had murdered her children. She instructed listeners that there was a big difference between thinking and knowing. She knew she didn't kill her children while prosecutors only thought she did.

Darlie warned the public that a tragedy such as the slayings of her children could happen at any time, to anyone. Nobody is immune, she warned, not even those who live in better neighborhoods.

"Do you know how hard it is to sit here and know you are innocent?" Darlie asked. She expressed her frustration at being falsely accused, wrongly judged.

Roberts asked what Darlie would like the public to know about her . . . about her as a mother.

"I'm not perfect," she said. "Nobody out there is perfect." Then Darlie set out to express her own agenda, ignoring Roberts question on her parenting.

Darlie talked about her life-long respect for the law, adding that officers are human and often make mistakes. She indicated this was one of those times when a hugh mistake had indeed been made.

When Roberts asked if she felt her case had been investigated the way it should have been, Darlie was quick to reply, "Absolutely not."

Roberts wondered out loud why his radio audience should believe Darlie. She told the talk-show host she wasn't asking for them to believe her, but to merely keep an open mind. She urged listeners not to rush to judgment based on what they had read in the newspaper or what they had seen on television, indicating that the media often put a spin on things to alter the original intention of a remark or an action.

Darlie ended her telephone on-air interview by saying she did not murder her children. She emphatically stated that she knew what happened in her house that fateful night. It was a declaration that would be used against her by Dallas prosecutors during her trial six weeks later.

Immediately after the Rick Roberts show, Darlie Routier lost one of her most important lifelines to the outside world. Based on violation of the court's gag order, Dallas County authorities took away her phone privileges.

Darlie's depression increased.

Darin Routier went to Lubbock where young Drake had been placed in foster care with Darin's parents, pending outcome of the trial. Relatives said Darlie was so infuriated that Darin left her in Dallas alone over the holiday weekend, that she forbid him to return to Lubbock for Christmas.

It had been a long six months for the Routier family. The day they had waited for since Darlie's indictment was fast approaching. They made plans to move, temporarily to Kerrville.

Darlie would at last have the opportunity she longed for . . . to tell her version of what happened in the early-morning hours of June 6, 1996. But with some eight different renditions of the story already told by Darlie, which rendering would it be?

Chapter Eighteen

As prosecutors drove into Kerrville, the county seat of Kerr County located 62 miles northwest of San Antonio, Texas, they saw magnificent rolling hills, the beautiful Guadalupe River, and picturesque oak, mountain cedar, and cypress trees. As they followed Highway 16 into downtown Kerrville, the charm of restored 19th-century storefronts, sprinkled between 20th-century progressive structures, lay before them.

In the center of town loomed the Kerr County Courthouse. Built in 1926, the two-storey stone structure had been the scene of many infamous murder trials. The founding fathers of Kerr County would have been dumbfounded by the half-dozen television trucks surrounding the old forum of justice, their satellite dishes rising high in the southwestern sky.

Greg Davis, lead prosecutor, and Assistant District Attorneys Toby Shook and Sherri Wallace had assembled more than 200 pieces of evidence to be presented to the jury. They had several heavy black notebooks containing the outline of the case, along with documents that would be presented to the court. Photos, display boards, a framed window unit, the rolled carpet from the Routier family room, even the kitchen sink, were all in tow. With the help of District Attorney investigators Mike Bosillo and Nita Kinne the prosecution team had everything they believed they needed for the conviction of Darlie Routier.

Davis, the father of a nine-year-old son, was on a mission. He would try Darlie Routier for the vindication of Devon and Damon. As a reminder of why he had been working so hard to prepare a convincing case, a black-and-white drawing of a hypodermic syringe, an emblem of the lethal injection Davis believed jurors would order for Routier, had been hanging on his office wall. Taped to the needle, as if to represent its deadly serum, were the smiling photos of Routier's slain sons.

Before the first day of court had even begun, raven-haired Sarilda Routier, Darin's mother, was mad. She and other family members had taken seats in the second row, then were told by the bailiff they would have to move. The seats had been reserved for members of the attorneys' families and staff. Sarilda complained to anyone who would listen.

"What about the family?" she asked. "Don't we get special seating?" But no arrangements had been made, and Sarilda, in her pink sweater, pink stirrup pants, and boots, was forced to scurry for a seat before court was called to order.

Judge Mark Tolle sat at the raised judge's bench in the center of the 71-year-old courtroom. Flanked on his right by the American flag and on his left by the Texas flag, Tolle's demeanor demonstrated his intention to control his court.

Greg Davis stood to read the charges against Darlie Routier. Under Texas law, the murder of a child under six was a capital offense, and could bring a death sentence to the

Rowlett homemaker. Prosecutors had opted to try Darlie only for the capital murder of Damon Routier. If they failed, or if she was given a life sentence, they could then try her a second time for the murder of the older boy, Devon.

Darlie was dressed in a red print dress with a large white Puritan-style collar. She had a cream-colored scarf tied at her throat. The dress fit tightly at the waist, emphasizing her silicone-enlarged breasts. Gone was the blonde bombshell image displayed in the Glamour shots that had adorned her home on Eagle Drive—the home she and Darin had prized—now repossessed by the bank for non-payment of mortgages.

Mulder wanted jurors to have the best impression possible of his client. He knew that if he presented Darlie in shackles, prison garb, and shuffling along in jailhouse slides, there would be a perception that she was a criminal before the trial even began. At Mulder's request, Judge Tolle had granted permission for Darlie to have a hairdresser color her hair. Her over-bleached locks were tinted a softer, light reddish-brown, but her dark roots were still visible. There was no style to her straight hair. It was parted on the right and hung below her shoulders. She wore no make-up.

As Davis finished reading the charges, Darlie Routier rose from her seat behind the defense table. In a loud and audible voice, she responded to the charge of murdering her son Damon with, "Not guilty."

The jury of 12 plus three alternates, nine women and seven men, filed into the courtroom. Visibly absent from the opening statements was Darin Routier.

Courtroom spectators waited with anticipation. No one knew the motive the assistant district attorney was going to give for the senseless slaying of two small children.

Greg Davis rose from the prosecution's table directly in front of Judge Tolle's bench and smiled a wry smile at the jury. The six-foot-plus attorney, dressed in a dark suit, white shirt, and conservative tie, strategically began to lay out his case.

"Evidence will show that Darlie Lynn Routier and no other person stabbed to death her own children," Davis told the jury. He characterized the petite homemaker as self-centered, materialistic, and cold-hearted. He praised Darin for being a hard worker.

"In 1992, they moved to . . . Eagle Drive. They began to buy things to show their success: a lighted fountain, a satellite dish. They spent the profits from their business on themselves. In 1995, they bought a nine thousand dollar spa, a twenty-four thousand dollar cabin cruiser. In 1996, things looked good on the surface. She had a new baby. The two older boys kept her busy. She could not lose the weight after Drake was born. The money train was beginning to peter out.

"June 5, 1996, the problems had worsened. The defendant had not lost the weight. She was taking diet pills. She was no longer the glamorous blonde who was the center of attention."

For the first time during Davis's opening statement Darlie Routier looked at the 45-year-old prosecutor. Her eyes narrowed and her lips tightened. Then suddenly a slight smirk appeared as she shook her head.

"Drake, Devon, and Damon were taking up more of her time," Davis continued. "She was angry that her lifestyle was starting to go away. By June 6, 1996, the Jaguar was not running. The boat was not running. There was trouble with the business. There was no savings. No retirement. Little money in the bank. They had under two thousand dollars available. June 1, 1996, the Routiers tried to borrow five thousand dollars. They were turned down."

Then Davis began to go over the tragic events of June 6, 1996. He explained that the boys were downstairs sleeping in the Roman room. Darin said he had gone to bed at 1:00 A.M., but that Darlie said she would stay downstairs with the boys.

"She claimed to be a light sleeper, that she was awakened by Drake turning over in his crib, and that is why she would stay with the boys," Davis explained.

Step-by-step, Davis walked the jury through the killings of Devon and Damon Routier. He characterized the two wounds in Devon's chest ... one through the pulmonary artery, penetrating his right lung, the other in his lower chest, piercing his liver. The jury remained stone-faced as he described Devon on the floor of the family room, faceup, his eyes open. Davis talked about the four stab wounds in Damon's back, one through his lungs, one through his liver.

With emphasis, Davis told the jury that Darlie Routier claimed to have been asleep on the sofa, within one foot of Devon and within four feet of Damon, when the murders of her children took place. Spectators whispered among themselves. How could that be? How could she have slept through the bloody carnage?

"Darlie Lynn Routier made no attempt to help her children," Davis said. "She never asked about their condition or where they were going. She gave different stories about what happened out there.

"The 911 call will be heard. You'll hear the defendant's voice. You'll hear her scream. You'll hear her say to them she woke up and saw her children had been stabbed. You'll hear her say she saw an intruder, that he had a knife. She chased him. She picked up the knife.

"Darlie Routier's focus turned from her children to herself."

Davis apologized for the physical and scientific evidence that jurors would be forced to see and listen to, mentioning the knives, Darlie's T-shirt, and the inconsistency of wounds sustained by the boys and Darlie.

"No intruder ever threw a knife down. No intruder ever left out that garage through a screen that had been cut. This defendant staged the crime scene to appear as if there was an intruder," Davis said, pointing to Darlie Routier.

"You will find the defendant guilty of the murder of five-year-old Damon Christian Routier."

Greg Davis returned to his chair beside Toby Shook at the prosecution table. The stage had been set. He had told the jury the motive for Darlie Routier taking the lives of her sons. It may have appeared illogical to some, that a mother would kill her children because she was self-centered, materialistic, and that the pressures of raising three boys had become too great, but it was the motive Davis felt most likely applied to Darlie Routier.

It was Doug Mulder's turn to address the jury. In an obviously expensive, well-tailored suit, he approached them. His salt-and-pepper hair curled at the nape of his neck, just above his collar. He spoke in a self-assured, almost cocky manner.

"First appearances are strong," Mulder said. "The state has to prove beyond a reasonable doubt that Darlie is guilty."

Mulder continued by telling jurors that Darlie was traumatized by witnessing the murders of her two children, and that she was being convicted on statements made while in that traumatized state.

The defense attorney then recapped the Routiers' life together. "They met in West Texas, in Lubbock. They were trying to get ahead. They moved to Rowlett, where they found success. Darin started a little business. They bought a nice house. They had two beautiful children, then they had another one. The house was decorated with Mickey Mouse stuff, child stuff. You'll see a family in an upscale house. You'll see attention to the children. Their lives focused around the children. Darlie helped her husband some in his business. Friends, family, and neighbors will say Darlie was a loving mother, a mother who was so concerned about her baby that if he even moved she knew."

Mulder then brought to the attention of the jury facts the prosecution had not mentioned in their opening remarks.

"The state didn't say there was a bloody sock found

seventy-five yards down the alleyway with her sons' blood on it. A description was given that night of a black car. By the time sirens were going off, that car was gone. That car is a mystery to this day," Mulder said.

"What happened is that by six o'clock A.M. Rowlett police had decided that Darlie Routier was guilty, and they never looked back. They developed tunnel vision. They focused on Darlie Routier, and never looked elsewhere. One of the things you'll see, as in a rifle scope, the state's theory has changed.

"Mr. Davis said that the mulch was not disturbed, but there was none outside the windows. He said there was no blood from the assailant through the kitchen and garage, but they would not expect to have much blood on him. They say she didn't try to help the child. Why didn't he (the Rowlett policeman) help the child? The officer says he knows she's guilty because there is no high-velocity blood. Well, no one would say there should be, because high velocity relates to gunshots. It means nothing. The prosecution says there was no dust disturbed on the windowsill. You could step over it. The dust means nothing. A hair found on the window was tested. It indicated it had been pulled out and was blonde, bleached. DNA tests say it belongs to a Rowlett police officer.

"The state has continued to go back and try to find something to prove Darlie Routier guilty. As late as last Friday, testing continued to be done. The rifle scope remains aimed at Darlie."

Mulder moved to the defense table and extended his arm, palm up, toward his client. "This lady is an American mother, like any other American mom. Not perfect. Not psychotic."

Mulder took his seat beside Darlie Routier.

The struggle between the state and the defense was set to begin.

Chapter Nineteen

The State of Texas versus Darlie Lynn Routier began with Dr. Joanie McClain, then Dr. Janice Townsend-Parchman, Dallas County medical examiners. McClain had performed the autopsy on Damon Routier, Townsend-Parchman had autopsied Devon, as well as examined Darlie at Baylor Hospital.

Neither physician could conclusively identify the white-handled butcher knife Greg Davis held up in court as the murder weapon. Both agreed that it could have been used to kill the two small boys. But under cross-examination Townsend-Parchman stated that she couldn't tell if the weapon had been serrated, the width or the depth of the instrument, or if more than one knife had been used to kill Damon Routier. She couldn't tell the number of assailants.

Davis walked along the jurors box holding up first photos of Devon, then later Damon laying on the cold autopsy tables—their small bodies riddled with punctures. The panel stared intently at the pictures. Then their gazes automatically drifted to the accused killer . . . the boys' mother.

Darlie doodled on a notepad, showing no emotion.

Davis asked Townsend-Parchman to step to the defense table to identify the wounds of Darlie Routier. The same wounds the doctor had seen on the afternoon of June 6th.

Darlie stood and removed the tan scarf from her neck.

"Could Darlie Routier's injuries possibly have been self-inflicted?" Davis asked.

"Yes. It could be possible they were self-inflicted. It is also possible that someone else did it," the medical examiner answered.

Returning to the witness box and to the discussion of Damon's wounds, Townsend-Parchman explained that the nature of Damon's injuries to the lung and liver rapidly oozed, until he lost enough blood to lose consciousness. He could have made noise.

Speculative whispers filled the courtroom. Had Damon Routier called out? Had he named his killer?

Both doctors indicated that the boys had been in good health, had good hygiene, and were not abused. They were in good health . . . except for the stab wounds.

During Townsend-Parchman's cross-examination, Mulder casually leaned on Judge Tolle's bench as he asked questions. Twice, during the cross Judge Tolle interrupted. "Quit leaning on the bench, Mr. Mulder," Tolle reprimanded.

The second time the judge spoke with a touch of irritability in his voice. "Mr. Mulder, don't lean on the bench! If you do it again, you'll be back to sitting down!"

The jury was losing interest in Mulder's cross-examination. They were becoming frustrated with his disorganization and time lost while Mulder flipped through the state's exhibits trying to find a photo of Darlie taken in her hospital room.

"Did you notice any bruising on Darlie's right arm?" Mulder asked, as he continued to search the exhibits.

"No. There was no bruising on Darlie's arms," the doctor said.

A sharp exchange between the judge, Davis, and Mulder

about the exhibits and Mulder's inability to find the photo prompted Judge Tolle to call for a 10-minute recess. "I want to see you in chambers," Judge Tolle demanded of Mulder.

As jurors reentered the courtroom, Mulder sat behind the defense table, apparently ordered to do so by the court. He remained seated for the remainder of the questioning of Dr. Townsend-Parchman.

At the morning break reporters talked among themselves, commenting on Doug Mulder's sense of disorganization.

"I've never seen him like this," one reporter remarked.

"I've seen Mulder in court a number of times," Bill Brown of Channel 8, ABC, said. "He usually comes into court and takes over. Controls the court. Judge Tolle isn't allowing him to do that. He's frustrated."

William Gorsuch, an engineer with Rockwell International, and a neighbor of the Routiers, took the stand for the prosecution. The burly, bearded engineer explained his activities and observations on June 6th in clear and concise detail.

"I left work at one twenty-five A.M. I called home first to say I was on my way. I called to make sure it was safe to go in. I have a handgun," Gorsuch said, softly laughing. Spectators and jurors laughed with him.

"I got home between one forty-five and one fifty and parked in front of the house. There were only two vehicles in the area.

"I looked around at the stars for three or four minutes. I checked the neighborhood, looking down both sides of the street, but I didn't see anything unusual. There were three floodlights on the Routier fountain and a street light on. Darin's dark green Pathfinder was parked in front of his house.

"I went in the house. I set the alarm, got a drink, and went to bed at two-oh-five or two ten. My bedroom windows, facing the Routier house, were open. I don't like airconditioning. I awoke from some loud noise. I can't identify what it was. Darin was running down the sidewalk yelling, 'Someone's stabbed my children and my wife.' He was yelling loudly. It was two forty because I looked at the clock. I looked out the window and saw Darin running across the lawn, even with the fountain. He only had on blue jeans. Then I saw the police coming up over the bank in the yard at the corner of the house. Darin ran over to meet the police, then went back in the house.

"I looked around and saw nothing. It occurred to me that maybe someone was around. I looked out in the alley. No one was there. I picked up my pistol and went downstairs and out the front door. More police, ambulances, and fire trucks arrived."

Gorsuch described the dark-colored car that had come into the neighborhood and the police search of the occupants and the vehicles as seen from his front porch.

"I went back in my house and put my gun away. I didn't think it was too smart to be around the police with a gun," Gorsuch said with a grin. Again, the spectators chuckled.

Mulder approached the witness with a confident air.

"Did you take any notes, Mr. Gorsuch?" Mulder asked in a condescending tone.

"No."

"You did that business with the stars and the moon, then went inside," Mulder began.

A juror in the back row rolled her eyes as Mulder talked down to the witness as he went over the aerial map of the neighborhood with Gorsuch. A female in the front row yawned. Mulder was losing the jurors' attention.

Mulder again insulted the witness about his star gazing.

Darlie smiled as though enjoying the sideshow Mulder was creating, and jotted down another note on her pad.

"I bet you put in your own alarm system," Mulder said smugly to Gorsuch.

"Yes, I did," Gorsuch said with pride.

If Mulder thought he was making points with the jury by ridiculing the meticulous engineer, he was wrong. His mind-control game wasn't paying in Kerrville.

On the second day of Darlie Routier's capital murder trial, Sarilda Routier slipped into the courtroom just before court began. Under subpoena to testify, Sarilda, along with most of the Routier family, were forced to sit out the trial in a designated area adjacent to the courtroom.

"I love you," Sarilda told Darlie, in a mother-to-child voice. Her dark eyes were sad, her mouth puckered in a pout.

"I love you," Darlie replied with a smile.

Hometown Kerrville court goers, along with veteran news personnel, were all asking the same question ... where was Darin Routier? Most of Darlie's family and a number of her friends sat diligently outside the court in silent support of Darlie. Darin's continued absence was glaring.

Officer David Waddell took the stand and told jurors of the bloody scene on Eagle Drive, of his fear that an intruder might still be in the house, and of Darlie's failure to help her children. He detailed his part in insuring the integrity of the crime scene. While Waddell talked, Davis walked in front of the jury showing them photos of Damon and Devon lying on the bloody white carpet.

Mulder was on his feet. "We weren't in the jury box and we were unable to see the photos being submitted, judge."

Davis turned the crime scene photos in view of the defense team. Darlie glanced up but showed no expression of emotions.

Before Waddell was excused for the day, the jurors heard for the first time the 911 tape of Darlie Routier begging for help for her dying sons.

Lou Ann Brown, the attractive, dark-haired mother-in-law of Darin's brother Deon, freely cried as she listened. Throughout the courtroom, spectators rummaged in their handbags and pockets for tissues.

As the jury listened to the young mother's cry for help, her claims of an intruder, and her admission that she'd picked up the knife, the jury watched her reactions closely. Except for a few swipes of her nose, Darlie showed little emotion. She dabbed at the corners of her eyes when she heard her voice say "Bye" at the end of the tape.

Jurors would be asked to answer the question: Were the cries for help sincere, as the defense contended, or staged as the prosecution asserted?

Court was dismissed early because of icy weather that had swept over the Texas hill county.

Sandy Aitken was stopped in the hall by a Dallas newsman. "Was it a good day for Darlie?" he asked.

"There aren't going to be any good days for Darlie for a long time," Aitken said solemnly. "Even when this is finished and she goes home, it's going to be a long time before there are any good days for Darlie."

The cold weather outside had chilled the air to below freezing. The cold accusations of the prosecutor had chilled the family's spirits.

Chapter Twenty

Darlie Kee, Sarilda Routier, and other family members sat outside the courtroom frustrated that they could not hear all the testimony in Darlie's case. Under law, witnesses subpoenaed to testify for either the defense or the prosecution are not allowed to hear what is said in court. This, in theory, protects their statements from being tainted.

The Routier family felt displaced. They were confined to the outer waiting area of the courtroom. Everyone going and coming from court, as well as courthouse employees, could see them and hear their conversations. On the other hand, prosecution witnesses were sequestered in a private room at the rear of the courtroom.

The family had a plan. While they waited outside the courtroom, Sandy Aitken took her place inside, playing recording secretary for the relatives and friends who could not attend the trial proceedings. "Aunt Sandy" carried a large spiral notebook in which she wrote down statements made by the State's witnesses. At each recess, or during the lunch break, she would scurry out to where the family waited and report her interpretation of how the witnesses's testimony was going.

Aitken's eyes would dance and sometimes she'd giggle as she told Mama Darlie and Sarilda about what she believed to be inconsistencies in the statements being made in court. Her "spin" on the testimony made the family feel optimistic. It gave them hope.

During a morning break on the second day of testimony, as Aitken reported to the family, prosecutors and the press gathered in the center of the courtroom. For the first time since lead prosecutor Greg Davis entered the courtroom January 6th, he allowed a slight smile to cross his face. The bricks were being laid. The wall Darlie Routier's attorneys would have to climb was growing taller.

Davis even allowed himself a little levity during a break in Barry Dickey's testimony. Dickey, a music recording producer, had been asked by the prosecution to filter and analyze the contents of the 911 tape.

The lead prosecutor was pleased. Dickey had explained that audio changes in the tape indicated Darlie was moving back and forth between the kitchen and the family room, from a vinyl surface to a carpeted surface.

Davis thought the point was important. He contended that Darlie was busy cleaning up blood, and covering up evidence.

"Greg, are you going to play the tape backward?" a reporter joked during the brief recess.

"Yeah, we'll probably hear John Lennon's voice in a demonic state," Davis said.

"You know what you hear when you play the latest Shaq backwards?" the reporter asked. "Perry Como."

The reporters surrounding Davis laughed. To many it may have seemed inappropriate, but it was a moment of lightness that made the otherwise appalling, unspeakable act they were covering tolerable.

Even Mama Darlie appeared to be in better spirits. She

was apparently viewing Sandy Aitken's courtroom reports in a favorable light.

"Yesterday was a bad day, but I feel much better today. Our faith and our family is getting us through this," she said, speaking softly to reporters.

Rumors had circulated around the courtroom that Mulder had instructed Darlie Kee to wear "conservative" clothing to court. In particular, she was to leave the short skirts at home and find something that fell just beneath the knee. If Mulder had talked to Mama Darlie about her clothing, it had no impact on what she was wearing.

As court resumed and Dickey's testimony concluded, the State asked that the 911 enhanced tape and coordinating transcript be admitted into evidence. The defense immediately objected, with Judge Tolle overruling the objection.

"Your Honor, we objected based on the fact that the tape is hearsay," Richard Mosty, a defense team attorney from Kerrville, repeated.

"Overruled," Judge Tolle said with authority. "Take it up on appeal."

Without hesitation, John Haggler, one of five attorneys on the "Texas Dream Team" defense, spoke. "We move for a mistrial, your Honor." Haggler, an appeals expert, served on the team for just such motions.

"Denied," Judge Tolle responded. Then he addressed the jury. "Please disregard my use of the word appeal."

Dr. Alex Santos, the emergency room doctor who treated Darlie, testified that she appeared emotionless during his hospital examinations.

"Most mothers, when they're made aware that their child has died, get hysterical," Dr. Santos told the jury under questioning by Assistant District Attorney Toby Shook. "They cry. They usually tell me that I'm wrong. They want to see the child and prove to me that the child is all right."

Darlie Routier, he said, sat calmly in her hospital bed and responded to his questions in a quiet monotone.

By day three it appeared Doug Mulder was taking on less of a high-profile role in the courtroom. Spectators and reporters theorized that it was because the jury didn't seem to relate to his sarcastic manner with witnesses. S. Preston Douglas, another Kerrville defense attorney, cross examined Dr. Santos.

Under questioning by Douglas, Dr. Santos said that trauma could cause memory loss of what occurred before and after an event. "The mind can compensate for the injury to protect the body," Santos explained.

Santos added that trauma with memory loss is usually a trauma to the head. Such as, a victim who has no idea how they got to the hospital. It's a form of amnesia, most commonly associated with a closed-head injury. Santos stated that there was no evidence of that type of trauma in Darlie Routier.

The physician told jurors that, at Darlie's request, he had ordered 25 milligrams of Demerol for pain and 1.5 milligrams of Xanix for anxiety. He did not believe she would have been groggy under those dosages.

Next, jurors heard from five Baylor Hospital nurses, Dr. Patrick Dillaw, and then a Baylor Hospital police officer.

The medical team testified to the flat affect of Darlie while in the hospital. Her lack of expression, lack of visible grief, seemed to baffle each of the medical personnel.

"The nurses cried more than Darlie did," Diane Hollon told jurors as she wept on the stand while testifying.

The nurses also told the jury a variety of statements about the attack—relating the varying and inconsistent statements Darlie had told them while a patient at Baylor.

Darlie gave Dr. Dillaw a very limited description of the intruder, saying she had only seen the man from the back. Prosecutors said that description was at odds with her accounts of having struggled with the man.

She told Rowlett detectives, in a conversation overheard

by Phyllis Jackson, a Baylor Hospital police officer, that she awoke with the attacker on top of her.

She told trauma unit coordinator Jodi Cotner that she had chased the intruder through the house and picked up the knife. She later told Cotner that she awoke when her younger son shook her, saying, "Mama, Mama." She told Cotner that she saw Damon was bleeding, got up, told the boy to lay down, and went to the kitchen.

She told intensive care nurse Paige Campbell that she awoke with a man standing over her trying to stab her. She also told Campbell she got several small cuts on her hands trying to defend herself.

"The police can remember things and give supplemental reports," Defense Attorney Douglas later told the press in a sarcastic tone, "but if Darlie remembers, adds things, she's guilty of killing two kids." He didn't bother to address the difference between "adding" information later and changing whole chunks of the story time and time again.

When questioned by the assistant district attorneys and the lawyers for the defense, each of the nurses and both doctors denied seeing any bruising on the underside of Darlie Routier's right arm.

Their statements were consistent. There was no discoloration. No redness, which might indicate a new bruise. No blackness. No yellowing of the skin.

In a June 10th photo taken by Rowlett police two days after her discharge from Baylor, a bruise from just above the right wrist and extending to Darlie's right armpit was visible. All the medical staff agreed . . . the bruise was not there when Darlie was a patient.

A variety of theories were batted about by the spectators. Had Darin beaten Darlie after she was released from the hospital? Had Darlie inflicted the blunt trauma injury to herself—at home, or possibly in the hospital? For what purpose? Had this been done to help convince police there had been an attack by an intruder?

During cross-examination, Defense Attorney Richard

Mosty asked several questions about amnesia, and whether the medical team thought she could have been so traumatized by the event that she sustained memory loss. Mosty was setting the stage. Traumatic amnesia would be Darlie Routier's defense.

When Sandy Aitken reported the medical staff's testimony to Darlie Kee, she was angry and more than ready to set the record straight.

"I have over forty people who were in that hospital . . . who saw the bruises while she was in that hospital. I will testify to what Dr. Santos told me, and eight other people, when I get on the stand," Darlie Kee said. Her voice was shaky. She was near tears.

The next morning, 15-month-old Drake Routier was brought to the Kerr County courthouse by Sarilda Routier. He waddled around the first floor, his wide brown eyes sparkling. He grinned for the cameras, blissfully unaware that inside the courtroom the mother he hadn't seen in seven months was on trial for her life.

Sarilda Routier had taken Drake to the courthouse in hopes she would be able to slip him into the courtroom, for Darlie to get just a quick glance at him. But officials refused to let her take the baby inside.

As cameras encircled the baby, jockeying for shots they could use on their next scheduled newscast, Drake's court-appointed advocate and a CASA employee conferred with Sarilda. In the best interest of Drake, they told Sarilda that she was not to bring him to court again.

Day by day, the circus-type atmosphere taking shape outside the courtroom escalated.

As testimony continued inside the courtroom, tears flowed freely—more from the witnesses and courtroom spectators than from the defendant.

As paramedic Jack Kolbye recounted watching Damon Routier take his last breath, fresh tears filled the eyes of the paramedic, spectators, and jurors alike.

"He gasped for air, and that was the final time that he breathed," Kolbye said. "His eyes were open, and there was still a light of life in his eyes. As I was with him, it slowly faded."

Finally, Darlie Routier turned her face away from the jury and appeared to wipe away her own tears.

It had been a hard and bitter week for the Routier family. Regardless of what Mulder did in the courtroom, they seemed to feel like they had to fight back. Before and after the day's testimony, and during breaks, they took every opportunity to vent their frustration, their anger. In often unexpected and frequently alienating ways, they attacked what was being said inside the courtroom and what was being written about them in the newspapers. The family's bizarre behavior escalated throughout the remainder of the trial.

Desperate to convince him that Darlie was indeed a remorseful mother, Sarilda Routier dogged Dr. Santos from the courthouse to his car. Dressed in her familiar style of leggings, big sweater, and short boots, Sarilda chatted passionately. All the way, the belabored doctor did his best to smile and nod and calm the overwrought woman. To the press, Sarilda and other family members criticized the professionalism of the medical staff who treated Darlie. If anyone spoke against "our dear Darlie," as Sarilda often called her daughter-in-law, they were instantly condemned.

Family members confronted newspaper reporters about articles they had written, circling paragraphs they disagreed with and arguing about the way information had been presented. When prosecutors gave statements to the press, either in the corridor of the courthouse or outside on the front steps, Mama Darlie, Dana Stahl, and other family members and supporters would often interrupt their interviews by yelling out, "Liars!"

The angry antics of the family did little to enhance the image defense attorneys were trying to portray of Darlie Routier. Courtroom observers and reporters shook their heads and talked among themselves, commenting on the rude, and often crude conduct of Darlie's family. But public opinion of their actions didn't deter them from their goal. They continued to seek out reporters to get their story told.

"I know what I saw. I know what my family saw, and I know what we heard," Sandy Aitken protested angrily. "We saw a very distraught young woman. All of a sudden, now people are saying she never shed a tear, she never used a Kleenex. Well, let's just call it what it is . . . it's a lie!"

Chapter Twenty-One

Due to freezing weather, the seventh day of Darlie Routier's capital murder trial began late.

The icy wind that blew leaves from the trees outside was comparable to the icy stares Routier family members gave jovial court "groupies" as they filed by to take their seats in the courtroom.

Officer David Mayne presented documents that helped to establish the motive prosecutors had outlined in their opening remarks a week earlier. The documents included renewal forms for $5,000 insurance policies for each of the boys, a $50,000 policy for Darlie Routier, and a $200,000 policy for Darin Routier. Other papers found at the crime scene were handwritten notes naming Leonard and Sarilda Routier as the boys's guardians, and how the family's possessions should be distributed.

"Was there any other evidence found?" Prosecutor Davis asked.

"Yes," Mayne answered promptly. "Marijuana."

Mulder was on his feet in a flash. His face was deep

red and he spoke angrily. "It was only two grams. This is deliberate misconduct. I move for a mistrial."

Mayne's statement violated a pretrial ruling by Judge Tolle that prosecutors could not present testimony concerning drugs or sexual paraphernalia found in the Routier home. Such testimony would be considered prejudicial against the defendant.

Judge Tolle denied the motion for mistrial and ordered the prosecution to continue with their questioning. He instructed jurors to disregard the comment concerning marijuana. But the damage was done. The idea of marijuana in the Routier home had been planted in the jury's mind.

Prosecutors ignored Mayne's slip of the tongue and concentrated on the documents found in the family room.

"I think what it shows is that Darlie Routier was making preparations for a very important event that night," Prosecutor Davis told reporters at the end of court. "It's a bit more than coincidental that all of these papers were within two feet of Devon Routier at the time of his death."

Officer Mayne took a beating under cross-examination by Defense Attorney Mosty. Mosty raised several questions about the officer's evidence collection techniques, his photographing and logging of photos at the crime scene, and the tagging of evidence.

The officer conceded that he left Darlie Routier's nightshirt, still wet with blood, wadded up in a paper sack rather than hanging it to dry. He further admitted that the mistake could have allowed blood from one part of the shirt to soak through to another area and would probably not be considered good police work.

Prosecutors introduced testimony to show a financial motive for Darlie Routier to kill her children.

Okie Williams, a Bank One employee, told the jury that the bank had denied Darin Routier's application for a $5,000 loan on June 3rd, just three days before the murders.

At the end of the morning court session, Sandy Aitken told reporters that there would be more questions raised about the police department's handling of the evidence. The Routier family had been publicly critical of the police department's evidence gathering and continued to cast doubt on Rowlett officers' competency.

"You're just seeing the tip of the iceberg," Aunt Sandy said.

Members of Darlie's family quickly dismissed the report of marijuana found at the Routier's house. Others believed the idea of marijuana in the Routier house was ridiculous. Also dismissed was the idea that Darlie had been distraught over being turned down for a bank loan.

The family explained that the loan had been for Dana Stahl to buy a pickup truck. Darlie Kee was unable to acquire a loan for her daughter's vehicle because she had filed bankruptcy the previous year. Darin had offered to take out a loan himself.

"Children are costly. Children demand attention, they demand money," Davis told reporters after court was dismissed. "If you eliminate those children, you eliminate that demand."

The comments by Davis angered Sarilda Routier. "You kill the little lights of your life because they cost you money? The man has got a screw loose."

As word spread throughout Kerrville about the murder trial, more local residents were in attendance. Most cited curiosity as the primary reason for being in the courtroom. Most agreed they couldn't understand how or why a mother would kill her kids.

Public opinion was split. Some thought the 27-year-old mother was guilty. Others believed in her innocence. Diana Howard, a local hairdresser and mother of two, had been attending the trial with her mother. Howard couldn't believe Darlie could have killed the adorable boys shown in photographs during court. Her heart went out to the family.

Howard offered to fix Mama Darlie's hair for court, as well as her younger daughter Dana's.

While court testimony continued, Mama Darlie and Dana walked into The Cutters beauty shop. Dana was dressed in a short knit miniskirt and a crop top with no bra. The teenager sat in the black chair, lifting her right leg high in the air before crossing her legs at the knee.

"Dana!" Mama Darlie yelled. Then in more hushed tones, "I told you to wear underpants."

Dana tossed her head back with a laugh. "You know I don't ever wear panties," she said.

Noticing the frog tattoo on Dana's right ankle, Howard asked if she had any other tattoos. Dana said she had one on her right hip, and pointed out tattooed ivy winding from her left toe up to her ankle.

The perky teen bounded about the beauty shop, breasts bouncing under her knit top. Diana Howard carefully observed the reaction of the 78-year-old male barber as he watched Dana. *He might have a stroke,* Howard thought.

Mama Darlie pulled photos of Darlie from her handbag. Proudly she showed the Kerrville hairdresser pictures of her daughter in a variety of wigs. "Little Darlie loves hair pieces," she said. In one photo Darlie wore a cascade of curls, sewn into a straw hat, that fell past her waist. It was a "Daisy Mae" look.

"She wears them all the time," Mama Darlie said with a smile.

"How are all of you holding up?" Howard asked.

"Since Darlie's arrest we are all on anti-depressants—even little Dana," Mama Darlie said.

As Diana washed, curled, and combed Mama Darlie's hair, she continued to talk. She explained that Darlie's father lived in Pennsylvania, that he never paid child support, and that he had been very abusive to her during their marriage. She stated that Larry Peck had seen his daughter once since her arrest, but that he sent money regularly for her defense.

"Darlie was a good mom," Mama Darlie said, adding that it was more likely that someone would have accused her of such a heinous crime. "I was a bad mother. I drank and partied. Not Darlie."

Mama Darlie talked about Mulder and the frustration she had every time she talked to him. She commented that he always seemed to have his hand out, wanting more money.

Mama Darlie remarked that the prosecutors had a vendetta against Darlie, but gave no explanation why.

"Those boys were my life. I only had girls and I always wanted boys," Mama Darlie said sadly. "I have asked Darlie point blank if she did it. She said no. They [the prosecutors] are trying to make her out to be sane and a cold-blooded killer."

When Darlie and Dana were ready to leave the salon Diana Howard told them there was no charge—her gift to them for the stress they were facing. But Mama Darlie insisted in paying. "We won't take handouts," she said.

The afternoon session began with the most damning evidence against Darlie Routier.

James Cron, a 39-year veteran of law enforcement and a highly regarded crime scene investigator, took the stand. Among Cron's accomplishments were numerous published articles in technical journals, 150 awards, and the Governor's Achievement Award. He told the court he had taken part in more than 21,000 investigations, including more than 4,000 deaths. His credentials were impeccable.

Under the questioning of Assistant District Attorney Greg Davis, Cron began to lay out for the jury his observations at the crime scene on Eagle Drive. He took them step-by-step through each piece of evidence that was found. He also related what he didn't find.

Cron found no blood on the garage floor. He saw no blood on either side of the backyard fence, and no scuff marks suggesting that someone climbed over it. There were no signs of an attempted forced entry through the home's front window, the overhead garage door or a rear slidingglass door. A flower arrangement near the overturned coffee table was undamaged and without bloodstains. A lamp shade that had fallen from a floor lamp appeared otherwise undamaged and unstained.

"I was beginning to have some feelings about the offense," Cron testified, "that there had not been an intruder that had come through the window."

Cron explained the basic procedures, the common sense approach, to the homicide investigation.

"These procedures date back to the forties," Cron said. "You walk through to plan your action. You record everything with photos, notes, and sketches. You take care of the fragile evidence. You handle moveable objects. The scene is inspected, objects are moved, then more photos are taken to record what was under the objects. And finally you do another walk-through to make sure nothing has been overlooked."

Doug Mulder was ready to attack Cron's testimony, but it would have to wait until the next day. Cron and Mulder had been good friends for many years. Cron had testified for Mulder on many occasions while Mulder was an assistant district attorney. It would be interesting to see if Mulder would attempt to discredit his old friend as he had done with the Rowlett police.

Chapter Twenty-Two

On the seventh day of the Routier trial, Lou Ann Black and Sherry Moses arrived at the Kerr County Courthouse dressed in special attire. The T-shirts the women wore were in support of their niece, Darlie Routier. On the front of the white knit shirts was a photo of Damon and Devon. Under the picture of the two smiling children was the caption: Forever in our Hearts.

Black turned her back for television cameras to give them a shot of a picture of Darlie with her three boys, Devon on her right, Damon on her left, and clutching baby Drake in her arms. "Save me, Oh Lord, from lying lips and deceitful tongue. Psalms 120:2" was inscribed under the photo of the happy faces.

Black and Moses, along with Darlie Kee and other family members believed the deceitful tongues were wagged by the prosecutors . . . and by James Cron. The two Pennsylvania women clutched their Bibles tightly under their arms as they climbed the stairs to the second floor courtroom.

As James Cron took the stand for cross-examination by

the defense, the courtroom crowd anticipated a dog fight between the two crafty old friends, turned adversaries.

Mulder began his cross with questions about the vacuum cleaner. Cron held steadfast that the vacuum had been placed over the broken glass and bloody footprint—a footprint he identified as belonging to Darlie Routier. "The smears of blood on the handle were consistent with someone holding the handle with a bloody hand, not being knocked over during a struggle," Cron said. He added that the blood on the top of the bag, the corner of the base, and on the side of the vacuum near the cord were round droplets, indicating straight line drops.

"The vacuum was out of the ordinary," Cron said. "It was upside down with blood on it—that's unusual." He reiterated that the placing of an object over something like a footprint was normally associated with someone trying to "cover up" evidence. He compared it to the small bloody handprint on the carpet, concealed by a blanket.

Piece-by-piece, Mulder went over each of the items Cron discussed in his direct examination. Cron emphasized again that blood on the floor was inconsistent with someone running through the area. "A slow-moving individual left that blood," Cron testified.

In one of the more dramatic moments of the trial, a mock-up of the garage window was rolled into court. Detective Chris Frosch, who Darlie had identified as the same size as the intruder, was asked to step through the window. Three times Frosch went through the framed window, three times he did not disturb the dust on the windowsill. The defense had won a small victory.

"You'll notice that the detective touched the window in exactly the same spot where unidentified fingerprints were found at the Routier house," Mulder pointed out to the jury. No one knew if jurors remembered that the fingerprint expert had testified that the prints were the size and shape of a small child's.

Cron attempted to discredit the foiled demonstration

by saying that an intruder would have been running, and in a hurry to escape. He would not have been as careful as the detective. Cron stuck steadfastly by his theory that no intruder went through the garage window.

Unable to shake Cron, or his belief that there was not an intruder in the Routier house at the time of the murders, Mulder began his attack on the Cron's credibility.

"You're really a print [fingerprint] man, aren't you?" Mulder asked smugly.

"No, I'm a certified crime scene investigator," Cron said irritably. "I don't want to go through it again."

"Where did you say you went to college?" Mulder asked with a condescending air.

The jury shifted uneasily in their seats.

"I didn't go to college. I was trained by the Dallas Sheriff's Office."

Mulder had made a tactical error. Only four people who sat on the jury panel he was trying to win over to his side had even taken some college courses. These were honest, hardworking, blue collar-type people. They knew the value of hard work and experience. When Mulder put down Cron's lack of formal education, he was putting them down as well.

Cron completed his testimony by giving the court 16 factors in determining that an intruder was not present at the Eagle Drive residence on June 6, 1996.

1. There were no signs of entry or exit of someone coming in or out of the window.

2. The screen was cut when there were two latches at the bottom that would have released the screen easily.

3. A knife with screen fibers on it was found in the kitchen knife block. That was inconsistent with an intruder coming in.

4. Dust on the windowsill was undisturbed.

5. Lots of jewelry was found in plain sight.

6. Wounds of the boys were the same type.

7. Wounds on the victim were a different style.

8. The victim said the intruder did not say anything. Usually there is vulgarity or threats.

9. There was no cast-off blood found from Darlie's wounds.

10. The intruder was said to have gone from the family room to the kitchen to the utility room. There were no footprints other than the defendant's. Glass was placed on top of the bloody footprint that was found. There were no cuts on Darlie's Routier's feet. There was no bloody trail of footprints across the kitchen floor, where one would expect there to be.

11. There was some blood on the door leading to the garage.

12. The blood in the utility room was dropped, not splattered as would be expected if a knife were dropped.

13. The lack of any blood found in the garage.

14. The gate was difficult to open and shut. It was inconsistent for an intruder to close and latch the gate, especially if he had left a living witness behind that was armed.

15. He had never known an assailant to arm his victim.

16. The vacuum cleaner on top of the bloody footprint.

James Cron was dismissed.

Speaking to the press downstairs, Prosecutor Davis discounted the foiled window demonstration and concentrated on Cron's main theme.

"No intruder ever came in that house. The physical evidence is totally inconsistent with that story. There is no evidence whatsoever that there was an intruder, he [Cron] was looking hard for it, he just couldn't find it that day," Davis commented to the press, a small smile on his lips.

The defense seemed frustrated. They were unable to shake Cron's testimony inside the court. Outside, Richard Mosty, co-counsel, lashed out at Cron. "Mr. Cron missed his calling," Mosty said. "He should have been a psychic reader. He's out there twenty minutes and he's already solved the case."

FLESH AND BLOOD

* * *

Following the afternoon recess, an unidentified nun, dressed in a traditional black and white habit, walked to the witness stand. She was followed by an elderly, gray-haired woman. The older woman sat in the witness box, while the nun picked up a microphone from the court reporter's table in front of the judge's bench.

Courtroom spectators soon learned that the witness was Helena Czaban, the mother of Barbara Jovell. Occasionally she helped with the laundry and other housework at the Routier home.

A native of Poland, Czaban preferred to testify in Polish with Sister Krystyna Krawczyk acting as interpreter. The questions and answers being repeated in Polish and English soon became tedious for spectators, complicated by the thick accent of the nun herself.

Out of the jury's presence, Czaban told the court that the day before the murders she was helping Darlie Routier with routine household chores. According to Czaban, she asked Darlie three times where Drake was before noticing that Darlie was holding a tightly wrapped bundle in her arms. As soon as Czaban realized it was the baby she said, "Darlie, give me the baby!"

Darlie thrust the baby at Czaban and went upstairs.

The Polish housekeeper quickly unwrapped Drake from his swaddling cloths. His face was red, his lips light blue. Perspiration covered his forehead. Drake began to catch his breath. Slowly he began to cry.

Czaban cuddled the child close to her heavy frame. She was confused at Darlie's flip excuse that Drake liked his head to be covered. Then Czaban said Darlie Routier returned to the family room, carrying a large cherrywood box. She sat the box in the green leatherette side chair and opened the lid. Rows of rings, necklaces, and bracelets lined the interior.

"Come see what I have," Darlie said. She proudly took out one piece, then another, and showed them to Czaban.

"I need ten thousand dollars," Darlie said. She didn't mention selling the jewelry or how she intended to acquire the money.

Czaban smoothed her black-and-white polka-dot dress as she explained to the court that later in the day she had had to rush to catch Drake from falling into the glass-topped table, while Darlie sat on the sofa laughing at her. And, while Czaban was busy folding laundry, she heard Drake crying in the casual dining area. The child had slipped down in his seat and was hanging between the tray and the bottom of the chair. The inattentive young mother had gone back upstairs.

Czaban had been overwrought by the events of the day and as soon as her daughter arrived, she begged to go home.

Under cross-examination, Czaban told about seeing a black car parked in the alley behind the Routier house. She said she had seen the car around the Routier house on other occasions when she had been there.

Judge Tolle denied the admittance of Czaban's testimony, after defense attorneys objected that it was not relevant to whether Routier stabbed Devon and Damon. However, the judge left the door open for prosecutors when he said they could still use the testimony in an effort to rebut any assertions by the defense that Routier was a good mother.

Helena Czaban would eventually tell her story before the jury.

"This is ridiculous. We knew it was coming," Darlie Kee said outside to the television cameras. "I think she's trying to get even with Darin and Darlie because Darin fired her daughter. Drake, even now, likes to sleep with a blanket over his head. If we could do ours [presentation of evidence] at the same time, we could show you the truth.

The 43-year-old mother and grandmother was mad. She spoke sternly, her face hardened by her anger. The prosecution was taking much longer than expected. Darlie, her family, and her attorneys were ready to get on to their defense, get on to proving Darlie innocent.

On the last day of the second week of testimony, Barbara Jovell told jurors about her friendship with Darlie Routier. Their friendship was what had prompted Darlie to confide in her friend about a suicide attempt in May 1996.

"Darlie told me she was trying to commit suicide. She said she had all the pills out of the wrappers, was writing a note, then Darin came in. She had thrown the wrappers under the bed but Domain, her dog, had dragged them out. Darin found them," Jovell said.

"I told Darlie she needed to get help. She had beautiful children, a husband," she added.

But Darlie told her friend that things had gotten too much for her, that she wanted to end it all. She and Darin were planning a trip to Lubbock, and Sarilda was going to help with the kids. But Darlie still felt overwhelmed.

Jovell wiped tears from her eyes as she testified. Darlie avoided eye contact with her old friend. She chewed on her fingernails.

Had this been a serious suicide attempt, or was Darlie merely craving the attention of her husband?

Jovell said she was asked to go to the cemetery on June 14, 1996 to celebrate Devon's seventh birthday. Then the jury was shown the KXAS-TV "Silly String" tape.

Jurors were obviously moved emotionally by what they saw on the television screen. An older gray-haired juror in the first row stared at the screen with a look of disgust; another juror stared at Darlie Routier.

Darlie, who had smiled at various times during the initial

playing of the tape outside the presence of the jury, now appeared sad. She smiled only when she heard herself on tape saying that God's hot line was swamped, and that the boys called their home the *Home Alone* house.

There were no smiles from the jurors. One held a hand to her mouth in suppressed shock, another exhaled deeply while wiping her nose, a male juror wiped tears from his eyes.

"I don't think it's anything that won't be ultimately explained and well-received," Mulder later told reporters. But the images jurors saw on the courtroom television would stay with them forever.

After the playing of the videotape, Jovell told the court that she never saw Darlie cry at the cemetery and that the only time she carried the photos of Devon and Damon in her arms was when the television cameras were on her.

"Darlie had to make Darin spend time with the boys," Jovell said of her former boss. She also indicated that Darin Routier wasn't working very hard at his business, and that he was cheating clients by charging for tests that he had not performed. She indicated that, as bills mounted and the family business slumped in late 1995, Darlie grew increasingly nervous, depressed and angry.

As with other prosecution witnesses, the defense attempted to discredit Jovell. Richard Mosty hammered Jovell on her own history of depression and treatment.

A courtroom watcher leaned closer to the person next to them. "It takes one to know one. Who better to recognize if Darlie was depressed?" she said in hushed tones.

"Is it true that you told your doctor that you could fly?" Mosty asked.

"I used to dream a lot that I could fly—out of my body," Jovell said. "I enjoyed it too." Spectators chuckled.

After the lunch break Charles Linch of the Southwest Institute of Forensic Sciences (SWIFS) took the stand to deal the defense their worst blow. He testified that fibers found on the bread knife in the Routiers's own butcher block knife holder matched those from the cut screen. This was the defense's biggest problem. It didn't make sense that an intruder would break into the house, take the knife from the butcher block, cut the screen, return the knife to the block, and then flee.

Mulder later admitted, "I thought it was the most confusing piece of evidence. My biggest problem was that knife."

During his statements to the court, Linch described how an intruder would have had to hold onto the screen to make the second, downward slice. At the lunch break Martha Cammack, a Kerrville resident attending the trial, approached Assistant District Attorney Toby Shook.

"I don't want to insult your intelligence," Martha said, "and you've probably already thought of this, but we made an observation. Last week the doctor talked about the paper cut on her hands. Could that have been from Darlie holding the screen?"

"We hadn't thought of that. Thanks for the observation," Shook said before heading off to talk with prosecutor Greg Davis.

Each evening, court viewers grouped in twos or fours at local restaurants. They ate at historical-homes-turned-eateries, favorite Mexican restaurants, or fast-food getaways, but the topic of conversation was the same: Darlie Routier.

A petite lady in her seventies had been sitting in the back row of the courtroom since the trial began. She talked with a friend over her blue plate special at the cafe. "She's as guilty as can be," she declared.

Greg Davis had built the brick wall higher. And he wasn't finished.

After lunch, Richard Mosty continued his cross-examination of Charles Linch with technical information about diameters of Fiberglass rods, types of adhesives, and synthetic versus natural rubber products. A young pregnant juror in the front row stared at Mosty with open mouth, shaking her head. The juror, who spectators had dubbed "Lazyboy" because of his relaxed manner of reclining in his chair, put his left hand to his forehead and shook his head. The jury was lost.

Linch answered questions about a blonde hair found on the window screen. Because the hair was color-treated, at first it was thought to belong to Darlie Routier. Linch called the Rowlett Police Department. "Do you have a bleached blonde, that came in contact with that window?"

No, the department answered. Their officer was natural blonde. Linch asked for a hair sample and Officer Sarah Jones' secret was out. She color-treated her hair.

DNA tests confirmed the hair belonged to Sarah Jones.

While information about hair samples was being given to the jury, Darlie Routier pressed her lips firmly together, wrinkled her brow, and wiped her eyes, leaving many observers to ask why the show of emotion now when so little was shown during the descriptions of her sons' deaths?

From the type of cuts made on the nightshirt Darlie Routier was wearing the night of the murders, Linch concluded that the holes were made while holding the cloth away from her body. "You'd have to have tension on the shirt and make a short measured jab. These look like short little pokes," Linch said. "In sixteen years, I haven't seen a killer perform in that fashion."

As the evidence against Darlie Routier was heating up, exchanges outside the courtroom were igniting as well.

Norm Kinne, First Assistant District Attorney of Dallas County, told reporters that he believed the evidence proved there was no intruder in the home. He cited not only Cron's testimony, but the testimony of SWIFS blood experts that there was no evidence of a stranger's blood in the house. Darlie Kee could not hold back her hostility.

"That's a lie! You don't know what happened because you weren't in that house!" Kee said in a vicious tone.

Kinne and the prosecutors assigned to try Darlie Routier

had been the subjects of Routier family hostility for two months. During interviews the family shouted, "Liar!" They spoke of the prosecution in vicious and corrupt terms. Kinne was tired of the vocal criticism. He lost his composure.

"Do I have to interview in front of this trailer trash?" he asked the reporters gathered around him.

"You don't know my grandbabies," Kee shouted, and repeated that Kinne was not in the house when the killings took place.

"Well, neither were you," Kinne replied loudly. He then walked away.

Darlie Kee expressed shock at Kinne's remarks to the media.

"I just thought it was totally unprofessional of Norman Kinne to attack me when I'm a victim, too, of this whole tragedy," Kee said. "He's attacking me, just like he's attacking Darlie, just because I'm her mother."

Prosecutors elected not to compete with Darlie Kee, Sarilda Routier, Sandy Aitken, and the other family members for the media spotlight. The family gladly spoke to any member of the press in order to get out their own twist to the testimonies. They even sought out members of the press they thought would give them favorable coverage.

The media circus was escalating.

Chapter Twenty-Three

The capital murder trial of Darlie Lynn Routier was heading into the third week with the prosecution still at bat. Spectators thought it was time for them to leave the field. Many felt that they had successfully proven their contentions that Darlie Routier, not an unknown intruder, had killed her children. But prosecutors still had two heavy hitters to come to the plate.

Retired Oklahoma City police Captain Tom Bevel was the first up. His specialty: bloodstain pattern analysis. Bevel explained the three different kinds of blood splatters caused when blood separates due to a force.

"Low velocity bloodstain patterns are basically round, like a drop of blood from your finger," Bevel said. "Medium velocity bloodstain patterns are akin to swinging your hand with blood dropping from it. High velocity bloodstain patterns are more forceful, like your hands over your head coming down rapidly, or gunshots. The blood can back-splatter or forward-splatter."

Bevel added that low velocity blood travels at five feet per second, medium splatters at five to twenty-five feet per second, and high velocity splatters at one hundred feet per second.

From the prosecution table, Greg Davis picked up the white-handled butcher knife taken from the Routier home. He clasped the knife believed to be the murder weapon firmly in his right hand, dropped to one knee, and plunged the blade toward the courtroom carpet. Slowly he drew his arm back, then thrust it forward again, simulating how the murderer could have killed Devon and Damon Routier.

Jurors watched intently, some flinching with each downward stroke of the knife. One drew her hand to her mouth as Davis swung the knife in a killing motion. Another stood to look over the front row of fellow jurors for a better look.

The eerie scene depicted by the lead prosecutor had little effect on Darlie Routier, who sat quietly shaking her head in disagreement. She rolled her eyes as if to say, "no way."

Davis's dramatic demonstration was to show jurors how the blood drops of Devon and Damon Routier appeared on the back of their mother's nightshirt. According to the blood splatter expert, the cast-off blood adhered to the cotton shirt each time their mother drew the knife back over her head before plunging the next deadly thrust into each of her children.

"The stains are consistent with the defendant leaning over the child stabbing, withdrawing, and stabbing again," Bevel said.

Bevel addressed the knife dropped in the utility room by telling jurors of demonstrations he had conducted to simulate Routier's story of an intruder dropping the weapon.

"I took whole human blood, covered the knife on both sides, allowed the blood to stop dripping, and dropped the knife on the floor," Bevel said, explaining that the experiment had been conducted from varying heights and with varying motions. "The knife always bounced, creating outward blood splatters. The blood found on the utility room floor was inconsistent with dropping or throwing a knife."

Court adjourned for lunch.

* * *

While spectators, family, and the press waited in line to walk through the portable metal detector and to have their purses and briefcases searched by Kerr County deputies, about 50 high school students lined up to enter court. Jurors filed by, careful not to speak to anyone, as instructed by the judge.

"Give it to her," said a husky male voice from the high school contingent.

Inside the courtroom a stern Judge Tolle sat at the bench. "I want to welcome our high school students today," he said firmly. "But I want to warn you about making comments to jurors."

After another staunch warning from Tolle about proper conduct in court, Bevel continued his testimony.

The sock, one of the key pieces of defense evidence, contained only the blood of Devon and Damon. Bevel stated that if the intruder was wearing the sock on his hand, blood from all three victims would be expected to be found. And, because of the location and amount of blood, he discounted the possibility that the sock was being worn on a foot and covered by a shoe.

On cross-examination, Defense Counsel Mosty had Bevel acknowledge that he had once co-authored a textbook that said bloodstains found on objects that can be moved should be treated with suspicion. Mosty challenged Bevel, suggesting that the blood might have gotten on Routier's shirt as she rendered first aid to the boys, or that blood might have been sprayed onto her shirt by a paramedic removing rubber gloves.

"Darin said that Darlie was in the kitchen on the phone," Bevel said. "Darlie could not have gotten blood from the CPR splatters." Bevel did admit the rubber glove theory could be plausible, however, paramedics had testified that Darlie Routier had not come close to them as they worked and they had changed gloves to avoid contamination.

Tom Bevel was excused and court adjourned. The state had one last witness call.

The next morning, almost three full weeks into the trial, a tall, distinguished gray-haired man dressed in a dark suit entered the courtroom. He raised his right hand, pledged to tell the truth, and took his seat in the witness box.

"Please state your name," Prosecutor Greg Davis instructed.

"Allen Brantley."

"Please tell the court your occupation."

"I am a special agent for the Federal Bureau of Investigation," Brantley said.

Whispers filled the packed courtroom. "They've brought in a big gun," a reporter was heard to say. "The D.A. must really want to make sure he gets this conviction."

Defense Attorney Richard Mosty immediately objected, arguing with Judge Tolle on the admissibility of Brantley as an expert witness.

Out of the presence of the jury, Brantley told the court that he had been an FBI agent for 13 1/2 years, specializing in crime scene analysis. In June 1996 he was in the Dallas office of the FBI on an unrelated case, when the offense occurred. September 20, 1996, he was assigned the case. He was provided with photos, video, autopsy reports, sketches, medical reports, investigative reports, forensic reports, court documents, media accounts, the 911 transcript, witness statements, and he conferred with the medical examiners, Tom Bevel and Charles Linch.

"In my opinion, this crime scene was staged. The victims were killed by someone they knew and knew very well," Brantley said.

Defense Counsel John Haggler was on his feet. "I object, your Honor."

Judge Tolle smiled. He knew the appeals specialist, who had objected with regularity throughout the trial, would be citing a rule of order to substantiate his objection. He waited.

"Your Honor, there is no adequate and reliable evidentiary base for this testimony. The testimony is unestablished and unreliable," Haggler argued.

Sandy Aitken quickly stood and hurried from the courtroom to report the arrival of the unexpected witness to the family waiting out in the hall.

"Overruled," Judge Tolle said. "The court believes the benefits of the testimony will outweigh the prejudicial value."

The defense asked for a 45 minute recess to review the case materials Brantley provided to the court. When the Dream Team returned to the courtroom, Haggler said, "Let me make an objection."

"Oh yes, by all means," Judge Tolle said with a grin.

Defense attorneys and their client laughed at the judge's flip response.

Again, the objection was overruled, and Brantley's testimony was heard by the jury. He listed his credentials, including his years as a psychologist at a maximum-security prison facility in North Carolina.

"Humans commit crimes and human behavior can be analyzed," Brantley explained. "In my opinion, the crime scene was staged. Altered. Things were moved and disturbed."

Supporting Brantley's findings were his education, training, experience, and work with hundreds of violent crimes annually, along with interviews with hundreds of violent criminals.

"It's almost as if the offender had no regard for the children but had some attachment to items of property in the house," Brantley said. "I certainly would expect to see much more in the way of disruption or damage."

The FBI agent testified that several "risk factors" probably would have kept an intruder from breaking into the Routier home. For instance, the house was not situated off any major thoroughfares that would provide an easy getaway. Lights were turned on downstairs. A large animal cage was next to the garage window. "These are factors criminals have told me they look for," Brantley said. He added that although the attack was directed toward the boys, there was nothing in their lifestyle that would give a stranger a motive to kill them.

"At this stage of their lives," Brantley said, "their activities consist of playing with their friends and going to school. They're not going to high-crime areas at night, buying drugs. They're not going to bars. They're not picking people up for one-night stands."

Brantley echoed the conclusions of Rowlett investigators, James Cron, and Charles Linch. He added, "Most moms fight for not only their lives but those of their children."

Darlie Routier, sitting at the defense table, mouthed, "That's what I was trying to do."

Mulder's cross-examination began with a belligerent attitude. He accused the FBI agent of tailoring his opinion to fit the prosecution's theory. "You started with the answer and worked backward, didn't you?" Mulder asked with sarcasm.

When Brantley told Mulder he had not prepared any notes, Mulder retorted sarcastically, "Mr. Hoover doesn't give you-all typewriters anymore?"

Darlie Routier smiled, but most of the 150 spectators were silent, astounded that the experienced defender would stoop to such demeaning potshots. Mulder was alienating the jury with subtle actions such as calling the special agent "professor" when addressing him, a remark aimed at Brantley's positions on the faculty of the FBI Academy as well as the University of Virginia. It was as if he did not want to emphasize the FBI Special Agent title to the jury.

The State's case was complete. Greg Davis stood tall before the court. With a confident air he announced, "Your Honor, the State rests."

Chapter Twenty-Four

Finally, the day the Routier family had been waiting for arrived. At last they would be able to tell what they believed to be the truth—Darlie Lynn was innocent.

Doug Mulder began with a contingent of family members and close friends. They each spoke of Darlie as a good and loving mother, a generous person, a good friend, and a grieving parent.

Each testified that they saw the large bruise on Darlie's right arm while visiting her in the hospital. None, however, called the unsightly bruise to the attention of a nurse or a doctor.

"Do you recognize the blonde in the red sweater?" Assistant District Attorney Greg Davis asked Sherry Moses, Darlie's aunt, during her cross-examination. "She's been in the courtroom everyday taking notes. You've known just about all the testimony, haven't you?"

"Yes," Moses replied.

"Did the attorneys tell you about the rule of evidence?" Davis asked.

"I haven't talked with them."

"They didn't tell you weren't suppose to know what was being said in court?"

"No, sir."

Most of the defense witnesses were asked the same question, leading to courtroom speculation that Sandy Aitken's reporting could somehow have tainted the defense witnesses' testimonies. They knew about the bruises, about the accusation of inappropriate grieving, about the prosecution's allegation that Darlie Routier was depressed at the time of the murders. Each witness refuted each of those charges.

During the first recess, Aitken rushed out into the hall to talk with the family. "They kept turning to me, pointing and saying, 'That blonde'," Aitken said with a giggle. She appeared to bask in the attention she had drawn from the prosecution.

Like the others, Pastor David Rogers discounted claims that Darlie's grieving was inappropriate. He saw Darlie as a heartbroken, anguishing mother who cried openly over the loss of her boys.

The raven-haired Assistant District Attorney Sherri Wallace cross-examined Rogers, only the second witness she questioned during the trial.

She established that Rogers's church had 80 to 100 members, he sold computers and software on the side, and that his wife was employed by Darin Routier.

"You have established a strong relationship with the defendant, haven't you?" Wallace asked.

Rogers explained that he had not met Darlie Routier until after the murders, but had spoken to her on several occasions.

"In fact," Wallace said, looking at a piece of paper, "you have visited Darlie Routier fifty-one times in the Dallas County jail and one time in the Kerrville jail, is that about right?"

Rogers blinked and shifted his weight in the witness chair. "I don't know how often I visited her."

"Fifty-one times in six months," Wallace said.

Murmurs of conjecture filled the courtroom, along with a few raised eyebrows and several smirks. Had David Rogers taken a "special" interest in Darlie Routier?

"In all those times you visited with the defendant, what did she tell you about the offense?" Wallace asked.

Darlie shot an anxious look at Mulder and squirmed in her chair.

The defense immediately objected, claiming minister/parishioner privilege. Pastor Rogers was excused.

When Lou Ann Black, Darlie Kee's second sister, took the stand, she admitted that she had been keeping up with everything going on in the courtroom, including Darlie's bruised arm.

"It was the worst bruise I've ever seen," Black said. "I didn't ask her how she got it. I assumed it was during the attack. She didn't have to tell us, we knew she had been attacked."

Black continued her testimony by telling the jury that Darlie was not depressed, but had been looking forward to a 50th wedding anniversary celebration of Black's parents to be held on June 15th. "The whole family planned on coming up. Darlie was looking forward to attending," Black said.

Greg Davis stiffened slightly as Black later told the court, "Damon saved her [Darlie's] life. He leaned against her and woke her up."

Lou Ann Black was excused and Karen Neal was called to the stand. After reviewing the events of June 6th with Neal, Davis entered into evidence the lyrics to *Gangsta's Paradise* by Coolio.

There was no objection by the defense—"if Toby [Shook] would sing." Attorneys, Judge Tolle, the jury, and spectators joined in laughter at the request.

Davis read the words to the popular rap song, reciting rhythmic lyrics that referred to dying, lying in chalk, anger, and lives out of luck.

Spectators whispered to one another, focusing on the same lyrics that had shocked police detectives at the Routier boys's funeral. They wondered if the words to the rap song foreshadowed the events preceding Devon's and Damon's murders. Words about power and money, about watching television too much, and knowing that your luck has run out.

But the lyric that left the gallery with a bitter taste in their mouths was the last one Davis read. A line about how people are too blind to realize hurting other people hurts themselves, too.

Jurors listened with intensity as Davis read the song played at the funeral of Devon and Damon Routier. One shook her head disbelieving, another frowned with wrinkled brow. There were no smiles. No signs of understanding why the song had been played at the slain children's funeral.

Court was dismissed for the day, leaving one question in everyone's mind: Would Darlie Routier testify the next day?

The following morning the line to enter the Kerr County courthouse was twice as long as usual. Curious townspeople who had closely followed the trial in the news wanted to get a glimpse of Darlie Routier. Regular attendees who were concerned that they might not get a seat had left cushions, coats, or tote bags in their courtroom chairs overnight to insure their places. Apparently, everyone wanted to hear Darlie Routier explain what happened on the morning of June 6, 1996.

The courtroom addicts would have to wait, for it was not Darlie Routier who was called to the stand but Jim Patterson, lead detective for the Rowlett Police Department. It was an unusual move for the defense to call the police officer in charge of a case but the prosecution had chosen not to put Patterson on the stand. Mulder himself had wondered if it was because Patterson had been such a poor witness in pretrial hearings. The defense was anxious to ask Patterson some questions. But why?

Doug Mulder's questions began routinely, covering what time Patterson arrived at the crime scene, his conversations with officers, paramedics, and neighbors, and his initial meetings with Darin and Darlie Routier at Baylor University Hospital.

As Mulder flipped through a large spiral notebook of reports prepared by Patterson, Mulder asked if he could take out Darlie Routier's written statement. Prosecutor Davis interrupted, "I have the original. It has state's exhibit thirty-two on it. I'll just submit it."

"If you don't mind," Mulder snapped, "I'll submit the evidence."

"Just move it along," Judge Tolle said to the defense attorney.

"Judge, I'm peddlin' as fast as I can," Mulder said.

"And we appreciate the effort," Judge Tolle said, smiling.

The cutting exchange, which had become familiar to courtroom observers, drew a laugh from the defendant.

But Darlie Routier's laughter soon turned to frowns of sorrow as Mulder read her written statement to the court.

"Did you tell her she was the prime suspect?" Mulder asked.

"No."

"Where you following up leads?"

"We were following the lead sheets, talking to a lot of people. Detective Needham was following up on reports of a black car," Patterson said.

As Patterson testified that he had attended the funeral of the slain boys, Darlie Routier stared at the detective with contempt.

The tedious morning testimony was interrupted by the

midday lunch break. But as soon as court resumed, fireworks exploded in the courtroom with a revelation no one knew about.

"Do you understand federal law concerning illegal wiretaps?" Mulder asked.

"If you are indicating I violated a law, then I refuse to answer," Patterson said.

More than 150 surprised faces were focused on Patterson. Wiretap? When? Where? On who?

Judge Tolle hastily advised Detective Patterson of his fifth amendment rights in regard to answering the defense's question. He did not have to answer the inquiry concerning electronic eavesdropping if it would incriminate him. He could consult with an attorney if he felt the need.

"No one read me a statement that I violated a law," Patterson finally responded.

Mulder altered his words and rephrased his question four different ways to Patterson. "Do you believe a suspect being questioned should have conversations recorded?" Mulder asked.

"As a NARC (narcotics officer) I recorded conversations," Patterson said.

Jurors and others soon learned that Rowlett police had planted a hidden microphone beside the gravesite of Damon and Devon Routier. Patterson told jurors that detectives had hoped the secret monitoring would help them identify the killer.

"In case someone went up there and made a confession about what happened," Patterson stated.

But as Mulder's questioning became more intense, Patterson refused to answer any additional questions.

"If you say I've violated some state or federal law, then I'm not going to say anything more until I have legal counsel," Patterson said.

Judge Tolle appointed attorneys to represent Patterson and Detective Chris Frosch. A hearing was set for the following morning to determine whether Patterson would continue to testify at the trial.

As Patterson was leaving the court and the next witness was being called, mumbling among the spectators grew louder. The investigation had taken an interesting turn. Outside the courtroom, at the end of the day, the wiretap issue was on everyone's mind.

The Routier family members were appalled by the police tactic. "Whether it's illegal or not, we don't know," Darin Routier said, "but it is unethical. It's wrong."

"I think it's just unconscionable," Mulder told reporters. "But it demonstrates the lengths to which they were willing to go in this case."

But the prosecutors gave the impression that the revelation of an electronic eavesdropping device at the grave site was no big deal. "We think it's a non-issue," Davis said. "I know why Mr. Mulder wants to make it an issue—because he has no other issues to work with."

Everyone attending the trial would have to wait until the next morning to see just how big a deal the wiretap issue was.

The next witness was called to give yet another spin to the intruder scenario.

Mary Angela Rickels lived several blocks from the Routiers. On the night of the murders, Rickels claimed that two men attempted to break into her house while her husband was away at work. Her description of the two men, one a stocky tall man in knit cap with blond hair and wearing a jogging suit, the other a tall thin man with dark hair, wearing cowboy clothes, did not match the description of the assailant Darlie Routier had described. However, Rickels said one of the men was carrying what looked like a knife or a screwdriver. She added that she saw a small, box-shaped, dark blue car in front of her house as the men ran from her door and away from the car. She saw the car again at 3:00 A.M. and at again at 7:30 A.M., when her husband was home.

Rickels claimed the men did not attempt to break into her house once, but twice on the same evening. Most astounding was the admission that she did not call the police nor her husband at the time to report the incidents.

Courtroom spectators whispered among themselves, asking why a woman who had two armed intruders breaking into her home would not have called police.

Under cross-examination, Ms. Rickels told the court she and her daughter had been watching a horror movie on the night of the attempted break-in, that she had experienced a similar incident in college, and that she was on several types of medication. A woman in her mid-to-late 30's Rickels suffered from poor health as a result of three heart attacks and one stroke. Her speech was slightly slurred and her movements slowed.

"I buried my baby brother on June third," Rickels told the court. "I take a lot of drugs. I take blood thinners, anti-depressants, and cardiac medications."

The witness was excused and a mid-afternoon recess was taken. Court observers watched in shock as Rickels, obviously in poor health, lit up a cigarette outside the courthouse doors.

As court resumed, a fiery Sarilda Routier took the stand. She was a woman on a mission. She smoothed the nap of her black suit as she began her recitation.

Sarilda Routier looked directly at the members of the jury and told them how much she loved her daughter-in-law. She told about spending holidays together and shopping together, how they were more like girlfriends than in-laws.

"She is a daughter-in-law everyone would love to have," Sarilda told the jury. "She's one who loves your son and lets him love you. She's never jealous. She loves you. She gives you beautiful grandchildren."

Darlie Routier watched her mother-in-law from the defense table, a cloth draped across the front so that jurors would not see the shackles around her ankles. She gazed at Sarilda with sad, puppy-dog eyes.

"I'm offended by anyone saying it [her grief] wasn't there. I was there and it was appropriate every step," Sarilda said with fury.

The witness was passed to the prosecution. Spectators drew a deep breath, expecting the impassioned little woman to come to verbal blows with the lead prosecutor. But in his relaxed, low-key style, Greg Davis looked into Sarilda Routier's eyes and said, "I'm sorry you had to come down here. I know you loved your grandchildren very much."

Chapter Twenty-Five

Darin Routier walked through the double wooden doors of the Kerr County courtroom with confidence. His shoulders back and head erect, he marched briskly to the witness stand. Darin had been a visible supporter of Darlie after the first week of his mysterious absence.

His conservative dark jacket, gray pants, white shirt, and multicolored tie was a contradiction to the T-shirts and faded blue jeans he had been wearing outside the courtroom in days leading to his testimony. His scruffy full beard had been shaved; only his mustache remained, setting off his wire-rimmed eyeglasses.

A sparkling gold wedding band adorned the third finger of his left hand, a band that he was reportedly told to buy by Mulder, in lieu of the ornate nugget ring that he normally wore. Darin Routier had been transformed from the flashy, young businessman to more of a conservative entrepreneur.

Darin and Darlie avoided eye contact.

As Darin's testimony began a faint sound could be heard just outside the doors to the courtroom. What was it? spectators sitting near the exit asked. Singing. While Darin sat in the witness box, his mother and other Routier family members softly sang *Amazing Grace*. They were praying for Darin and asking God to give him strength.

Darin's testimony began with how he met Darlie, his schooling, and the early beginnings of Testnec, his solely owned business. He stated that his 1995 tax return reflected earnings of more than $264,000. He netted just over $95,000.

Darin discounted accusations that they were having financial problems, stating that he had $78,000 in a business account, $64,000 in a personal account, and $18 to $20,000 in accounts receivable.

"I do business with a handshake. I do a lot of work for big companies like NASA, Lockheed, and the Air Force," Darin boasted.

Testnec had one full-time employee, Barbara Jovell. "She did a lot of the testing," Darin told jurors about his wife's onetime best friend. He sat casually with his left foot resting on his right knee. "She didn't get along well with people; she is very demanding. She became jealous of Darlie because of the time she was spending with the new baby, and I had to take over many of Darlie's responsibilities. She thought she should be making as much money as we were," he said, as though to discredit Jovell's earlier testimony. "I paid her ten dollars an hour."

Mulder broached the subject of Darlie's state of mind on May 3, 1996, the day she wrote a journal entry in her diary indicating thoughts of suicide.

"I was at work when Darlie called," Darin said. "She called at two-thirty or three o'clock. I could tell she was blue. She said, 'I need you to come home and help me with the kids.' I asked her what was wrong and she said she was feeling bad. I said, 'Baby, I'll see you when I get there at five o'clock.' I went home. Darlie was laying on the bed and Drake was in the crib. Darlie was writing in her journal and she was crying."

"Did you read your wife's diary?" Mulder asked.

"No, I never read the diary. It was private. We just sat and talked."

Darin went on to explain that he and Darlie talked about him needing to spend more time with the kids and that he didn't want to work like his father.

"She had some sleeping pills," Darin explained. "I didn't think she was serious about suicide. If I thought so, I would have gotten her help."

Darin indicated that the following day Darlie perked up and two days later she got her first menstrual period in a year, her cycle interrupted by the birth of Drake and breastfeeding. He said Darlie was generally upbeat, that she was the caretaker of the family.

Darin began talking about the evening of June 5th. and the events of June 6th. He left work at 5:30 P.M., taking Dana Stahl home with him. Barbara Jovell and her mother were at the house when they arrived. He parked the Pathfinder on the curve by the mailbox, in an effort to slow down cars that often sped by the house. He said a black car slowly drove by the house at about 30 or 35 miles per hour. Helena, Barbara's mother, told him about seeing a black car parked in the back earlier.

Darin talked about eating dinner and fixing the back fence because it was dragging. He said he began helping to get items ready for a garage sale. Darlie was working on tags and he was "looking through stuff to see what I wanted to keep, or at least hide," Darin said with a grin. Darlie laughed out loud.

Darin told the court that he got home from taking Dana home about 10:15 P.M. Darlie was watching TV. Devon was asleep in front of the big screen TV, and Damon was curled up with a kitty next to Devon. Darlie was watching HBO with the baby asleep on her chest.

As if to explain earlier testimony concerning blankets covering Drake's head, Darin stated that the baby grunted at night, wiggled and shook the bed. He liked to sleep under the blankets—he liked complete darkness, claimed the young father.

"It took me thirty minutes to get Drake to sleep. I watched the news and went downstairs. I talked to Darlie. Both boys were asleep. We talked about upcoming trips; Pennsylvania on June fourteenth, and Darlie was going to Cancun with friends. My ten-year reunion was coming up and my sister was getting married August twenty-sixth. Devon and Damon were going to be ring bearers. Darlie was making the pillows. We also discussed resaying our vows on our tenth anniversary."

Darin continued the story of June 6th by saying that he and Darlie talked until 1:00 A.M. He made a point of stating that Darlie had on a white T-shirt and panties. Panties that paramedics said she was not wearing when she was in the ambulance.

Darin's Aunt, Sandy Aitken cried loudly as he described his discovery of the boys bleeding in the family room. Judge Tolle gave her a harsh warning about disturbing the proceedings, then ordered that she move to the back of the courtroom.

Darin's testimony before the court differed from previous statements made to authorities when he told jurors that Darlie brought him wet towels and that she was standing over Devon while he was blowing air into his mouth. His new rendition curiously coincided with evidence presented in court by crime scene investigators and the blood splatter expert.

Darin further stated that Officer Waddell never drew his gun from his holster and that he refused to go into the garage, even after Darlie's urging. "We were all three in shock," Darin said.

He explained away Darlie's blood on the vacuum by telling jurors that he observed Darlie standing by the vacuum, holding onto it for support—a statement not heard before.

"I needed a ride to go to the hospital," Darin said. "I

only had on glasses and a pair of pants. Terry [Neal] got me a T-shirt. I thought I'd throw up. I washed the blood from my face, hands, chest, and glasses. I rinsed the iron taste from my mouth." As observers cringed at the thought of Darin's sons' blood inside his mouth, Sandy Aitken could be heard wailing in the back of the room.

Following a ten-minute recess, Darin's testimony continued with his contention that Darlie's grief was not inappropriate and that Darlie was incapable of holding Drake at the hospital because of tubes in her arm. He mentioned the bruising on his wife's arm, describing her appearance as "looking like a whipped little puppy."

Darin's attitude of compassion turned to contempt when Mulder asked questions about the Rowlett police.

"I feel like they lied to me," Darin said. "I never failed to cooperate."

Darin admitted that he had picked out the songs for the funeral, in particular *Gangsta's Paradise*. "It was the boys' favorite song. Whenever we were in the car, they'd say, 'Daddy, crank it up.'"

Darlie cried as Darin told the jury that the boys also loved to listen to their mommy sing.

Anger filled Darin Routier's voice as he described his loss. "Minutes of tragedy covered up four years of memories," Darin said, referring to the house on Eagle Drive. "There was fifteen to seventeen thousand dollars in damages to the house. We've never collected any insurance."

"We met on July first and again on September twelfth. You have shaved your beard and cut your hair. Is that a coincidence?" Davis asked, bringing to the jury's attention Darin's new traditional appearance.

Time had run out. Court was dismissed for the day. Darin would have to return to face the lead prosecutor again.

The next morning, Darin Routier arrived in court in an ill-fitting, shiny gray, velveteen suit. The fabric swished as he walked past the gallery to the witness stand. This was the suit that persons "in the know" indicated Mulder had specifically told Darin not to wear to court.

Prosecutor Greg Davis' questions to Darin Routier took a turn no one expected when he asked if the sock found down the alley was his. "I don't know," Darin answered.

"Didn't you tell Corrine Wells it was your sock?"

Darin shifted uneasily in his chair.

Davis informed Darin Routier that he knew he had gone to the home of Corrine Wells on Bond Street in Rowlett, on December 6, 1996, that Corrine Wells had bought the house from Darin and Darlie, and that Wells had caught Darin outside looking at the windows on that date.

"While you were at the house, you told Wells that the sock was yours," Davis said. "You also told Wells that if Darlie wanted to take that sock down the alley it would only take her twenty-seven seconds to do it."

Darin stared at Davis sternly.

"You told Wells you wanted to see if you had cut the screens at the house on Bond Street, right?

"Yes," Darin answered curtly.

"You were curious about screens on Bond Street, a house you hadn't lived in for three years?"

"Yes."

The line of questioning left more questions in the minds of observers than answers. Why did Darin go to the house to check the screens? Did he go to cut the screens himself? Why?

Darin's mood changed from angry to hostile when Davis switched to a discussion of the statements he had made to Jamie Johnson of Child Protective Services.

Davis reviewed discussions Darin had with Johnson regarding Darlie's emotional state, revealing that Darlie had been depressed, tired, and not herself. "You told Johnson that Darlie had said, 'I'm sick of everything. I'm having a hard time keeping the house clean.'" Davis said.

According to Davis, Darin had told Johnson that Darlie wanted everything perfect. She was a "cleanaholic." She would clean and clean, and the kids would come right behind her making bigger messes. He admitted to the case worker that Darlie's cleaning had become an obsession.

The disappointment that Drake was a boy and not a girl was felt by both parents, Darin had told Johnson. "Of course, we wanted a little girl. We still do," Darin said, as if Darlie would be home soon and their lives would be returned to normal.

Darin Routier grinned proudly as he discussed how beautiful Darlie was and how she took great pride in her appearance. The remarks also brought a smile to the lips of his wife across the room.

It would later be reported that Darin's own mother once remarked that Darlie had such a cute body that she should walk around naked all the time.

Darin's love for Darlie had obviously not diminished through the difficult times they faced. Their sex life had always been an important part of their lives, so important that when Darin was asked how he and Darlie got along, in preparation for Drake's custody hearing, his response was to tell the interviewer that their sex life was great. He added that they had sex "all the time" and slept in the nude. It was more than the interviewer had wanted to know.

Davis implied that Darlie was so obsessed with her looks that she spent $5,000 for breast implants. The remark brought an objection from the defense. The breast implants, like the marijuana, and the pornographic materials found in the Routier home, were not to be mentioned in court by order of the judge.

Darin admitted that he had not been concerned about the May 3rd suicide incident. "I just had a good cry with her, we woke up, and everything was fine," Darin said. Some observers felt that perhaps Darin didn't want to realize there was a real problem with his wife, his perfect mate.

Routier denied being two months behind on mortgage

payments for the couple's Rowlett home, even though Davis held a foreclosure letter from the mortgage company in his hand, but he acknowledged owing $10,000 in unpaid federal income tax and another $12,000 to credit card companies.

"You had a twenty-eight foot boat, a spa, and a two-door Jaguar, isn't that right?" Davis asked.

"That's part of living large," Darin replied smugly.

"Did you get in a situation where you were caught up in the material side of life?" Davis asked.

"Somewhat."

Darin denied telling a Rowlett woman that he and Darlie were planning to make money by selling the rights to their story, for Darlie to pen the work in order to cut out an author, and hold out for the big bucks.

"I told her that's how we were going to pay for these attorneys," Darin said, "but that was just hopeful thinking."

Davis returned to the murders. "She woke up every time that baby rolled over in bed. But Darlie was able to sleep while Devon was stabbed two times, and while Damon was stabbed four times in the back, and through her own stabbing, right?" Davis asked.

Darin looked at Davis through narrow, angry eyes.

"On September ninth [at a pretrial hearing], you didn't mention anything about Darlie bringing towels to Damon. You never told Jamie Johnson anything about Darlie going over to Devon," Davis said.

"I wish I'd never talked to Jamie Johnson," Darin said sharply.

Davis ended his cross-examination of Darin Routier with a dissertation that would not soon be forgotten.

"At the July 1, 1996 bond hearing you tried to show yourself as poor with only two thousand dollars in the bank. Now you are trying to paint your finances rosy.

"On June 6, 1996, there was a real lucky intruder. Lucky that the window was open. Lucky that the alarm system was off. Lucky that he happened to find a sock. Lucky enough to find a weapon. Lucky that your wife didn't wake up. Lucky enough that she didn't get a good look at him. Lucky enough to drop the knife and not have it used against him. Lucky that no blood was on the floor or window. Lucky enough to scale the fence without marking it, or go through the gate and latch the gate behind him."

Mulder ended with a lucky list of his own.

"Lucky enough they didn't pursue fingerprints. Lucky enough they didn't pursue the car information."

Chapter Twenty-Six

One surprise after another developed during the Darlie Routier murder trial. Just as prosecutors and the defense team were entering the courthouse on Tuesday, the day after Darin Routier's testimony, news broke that a subpoenaed witness for the defense had accused Mulder's team of trying to tamper with her testimony.

Mercedes Adams, a good friend of Darlie's and with whom she had been planning a trip to Cancun during the summer of 1996, told reporters a shocking story.

In a thick Mexican accent, the dark-haired, dark-eyed, Adams told reporters that an attorney for Routier was trying to shape her testimony.

"I told him Darlie had told me the attacker was on top of her, face to face, but he said, 'No, he was on Darlie's legs,'" Adams said. "I said no, he was on top of Darlie, and he said, 'No, he was on Darlie's legs.'"

Adams told reporters that she felt the attorneys wanted her to lie on the stand.

The allegation by the potential defense witness infuriated Richard Mosty. "That's ridiculous. We had a lot of people down here and we weren't going to put on eight different witnesses to say the same thing," Mosty said.

The Wednesday, January 29th court session began with a special 8:30 A.M. hearing called by Judge Tolle. Detectives Jim Patterson and Chris Frosch stood before the judge with two unidentified gentlemen in dark suits. Only a handful of observers heard the proceedings, as most were unaware of the special session.

The subject of the hearing was the hidden microphone at the Rockwell cemetery—a microphone, it was later discovered, that was actually planted by Garland police officers. Patterson and Frosch, with Kerrville attorneys assigned by Judge Tolle beside them, both exercised their rights under the fifth amendment.

Prosecutor Davis, out of the presence of the jury, asked the court not to go into the matter in open court. He made it clear that the state would not offer into evidence any reference to the gravesite.

Mosty argued that the central theme of the case was that Rowlett officers resorted to illegal activity to incriminate Darlie Routier. Pointing to the defendant, he said, "They wanted to indict her so bad they violated state and federal laws."

Judge Tolle ruled that, because the recordings were not admitted into evidence, the defense was not to go into the matter any further with witnesses on the stand.

The ruling enraged Mulder who paced angrily before the judge's bench. "Calm down, Mr. Mulder," the Judge warned.

"This undermines the whole defense," Mulder said bitterly.

People other than the prosecution and defense attorneys also debated the ethical issues concerning the bugging of the gravesite.

"It seems totally unethical to bug the private conversations that are made in a graveside service in a time of prayer and ministry to the family," Pastor David Rogers said. "People have a right to speak privately to their ministers without the state interfering."

But others disagreed with Rogers. "There is no right to privacy in an open, public cemetery," said Phillip Linder, criminal defense attorney and former Dallas County assistant district attorney. "If you're going to talk out loud and someone hears that, you're in a public place. Tough cookies."

The first of three witnesses to be called by the defense that day was Dr. Vincent Di Maio, medical examiner of Bexar County, with offices in San Antonio.

Dr. Di Maio stated that in his opinion the injuries incurred by Darlie Routier were obtained from an assault, not self-inflicted. The doctor's opinion was based on photographs of the wounds and medical records. Di Maio did not speak to Dr. Dillaw who initially examined Darlie, or to Dr. Santos who performed surgery on her.

"Wouldn't the surgeon be a better judge of the seriousness of her wounds?" Toby Shook asked on cross-examination.

The short, stocky doctor leaned back in his chair, and answered argumentatively, although laughing. With a nervous twist of his neck and raising of his eyebrows, Di Maio answered, "Yes. But based on the location, path, and nature of the wounds, it is most probable that they were inflicted by someone else."

To demonstrate, the doctor brandished a metal ruler at Defense Attorney Doug Mulder's throat, dragging the ruler's edge backhanded above Mulder's collar and across his necktie. Some members of the gallery chuckled at the mock attack on Mulder, but Darlie Routier was visibly shaken. Tearfully, she clasped her hands to her face.

* * *

"Traumatic amnesia" was the diagnosis Dr. Lisa Clayton, a Dallas psychiatrist, gave to Darlie Routier's lack of memory concerning her attack on June 6, 1996. Clayton told jurors she believed that Darlie had not slept through the attack as she had contended but rather had blocked out all memory of the attack.

The young, long-haired, attractive blonde first met Darlie Routier while treating her at the Dallas County jail. She took an instant liking to the young mother and believed her rendition of the June 6th attack. Sources close to the family said that Clayton told the Routier family she believed Darlie had not killed her children and, after a call from Doug Mulder, Clayton then became a paid consultant for the defense.

Clayton cited the six categories of women who kill their children as offered by psychiatrist, author, and leading authority in the field Dr. Philip Resnick as the basis for her findings. According to Resnick the categories of women who kill are (1) Battering/accidental—the child experiences abuse over a long period of time. (2) Retaliation/vengeance—mom's who are angry at the father and want to get even. (3) Mentally ill/psychotic—women who hear voices, are delusional, or paranoid. (4) Unwanted child—mostly teenage mothers who have a child out of wedlock. (5) Mercy/altruistic—the mother is suicidal but the child cannot live without her. (6) Neo-naticide—the child is killed within 24 hours of birth.

Based upon five or six visits with Darlie, a total of approximately 12 hours, listening to the 911 tape, and reading Darlie's written statement and her journal, as well as visits with Mama Darlie, Sarilda Routier, and Darin Routier in Dr. Clayton's expert opinion she did not believe Darlie Routier was capable of killing her children. Nor did she believe Darlie fell into any of Resnick's six categories.

Members of the gallery talked in hushed tones. "I put

her in at least two of the categories," an older female spectator said. "I see her in three," another commented. But none were trained psychiatrists. They were just everyday people who had sat through nearly four weeks of testimony.

Clayton told the jury that Darlie Routier's grief was not inappropriate, that she suffered from psychotic numbing, which would have rendered her emotionless. When Clayton informed the jury that in her opinion Darlie was not suicidal on May 3rd, but that she suffered from PMS, members of the jury rolled their eyes.

Dr. Clayton testified under cross-examination by Toby Shook that Demerol in conjunction with Femorin, the diet pills Darlie was taking, combined to produce a truth serum of sorts. "It is like someone who is drinking," Clayton said. "They are more likely to tell the truth."

"You're telling this jury that because she was on Demerol, she would have confessed?" Shook asked in astonishment.

"Yes, most criminals confess," Clayton responded.

"They do?"

"Yes."

"Well, they keep giving me the wrong cases," the good-looking assistant district attorney said, eliciting laughs from the crowd.

Chapter Twenty-Seven

Darlie Routier got up as usual the morning of January 29th, dressed in a seafoam green dress with white trim, combed her long, straight hair, and waited for the two deputies who had been driving her to the Kerr County courthouse for the past four weeks. But this day was different. This was the day that she would be given the opportunity to tell the jury and the press her memories of the deaths of her two precious babies.

Once Routier arrived at the courthouse she had to wait a few minutes longer, as her attorneys and the prosecutors argued before Judge Tolle. Two witnesses on the defense witness list, Arenda Routier and Lloyd Herrall, had been in court while testimony was presented. The judge was decisive. "Anyone who has been in the courtroom will not be allowed to testify." That included Herrall, Mulder's private investigator who had sat next to Darlie throughout the proceedings.

The courtroom was quickly cleared for a 10-minute recess. While the jury and spectators were out of the room, Darlie Routier was led to the witness box. It would have been prejudicial for the defendant, who celebrated her 27th birthday January 1st in the Kerrville jail, to be seen walking to the witness stand in shackles.

Sitting in the raised witness chair, Routier was the center of attention of the overflow crowd. She had her audience.

Just outside, her husband Darin sat on the dusty wooden floor, his ear pressed to the crack where the two doors met. Sarilda Routier, and Darlie's aunts, Lou Ann Black and Sherry Moses sat at the worn wooden table in the center of the hall, their Bibles open to selected verses as they read and prayed for Darlie.

Mama Darlie nervously stood in the far corner of the alcove, leaning near the door that led to the Kerr County district clerk's office. The gravity of the moment was etched on her distraught face.

The courtroom was silent. Everyone eagerly waited for Darlie to begin the fight for her life.

Darlie's initial testimony repetitively covered her childhood, her courtship and marriage to Darin, and the birth of her three children. She stressed to the jury, who she played to during her recollections, that she had no ill effects from the diet pills she was taking to lose the 15 pounds she needed to shed after the birth of her last baby.

Darlie admitted that in April and May of 1996, she began feeling unusually moody. She cried a lot. "I started a letter," she said, facing the jury. "I read it and realized how silly it was. I didn't really feel like I wanted to end my life. They were private thoughts. I did not attempt to take my life. I called Darin and told him I needed him to come home, that I wasn't feeling well." She added, "I'm really embarrassed about that," she said, lowering her hazel eyes for a moment.

Doug Mulder, asked her when she began her journal. Darlie explained that she started to write a journal at the suggestion of her grandmother. "It is important to reflect on what's important in your life," Darlie said. "It was not written for the public. I'm really embarrassed," she said again.

Mulder asked Darlie to read the first entry in the diary, dated September 7, 1995.

The defendant opened the small black book with gold trim and began to read. During the recitation, Darlie looked up occasionally at jury members as though she were reading them a bedtime story, or a scene from a one-act play. She wrote of dreams of death and knowing that she was not ready to leave her wonderful life. Jurors listened intently.

Mulder then asked Darlie to read the next entry, dated September 15, 1995.

". . . I don't understand why Denny did to me what he did, so it is very hard to try and forgive him," Darlie read.

Spectators looked at one another, wondering what meaning the entry held.

Darlie's soft voice went to a shrill pitch as she scrunched her eyes and sniffled. "When one of my babies are away I do not feel complete," she had written while Damon had been away at his grandmother's. She shed no tears.

Just beyond the courtroom doors, muffled songs could again be heard from the Routier family. *I Walk In The Garden Alone,* had been added to their repertoire which included *Amazing Grace.* If not singing, the family could be heard reciting Bible verses or what some called, chanting, or speaking in tongues. The family clung to their faith in God to get Darlie through her testimony.

The third entry, written October 1, 1995, brought tears to Darlie's eyes.

"Sometimes I feel I'm missing something . . . Maybe it's the excitement of when I was younger," Darlie said, tears filling her eyes. Rina Way, a dark-haired juror who sat nearest the witness stand, handed Darlie a tissue.

"I want to grow old with Darin but I don't want to feel as though part of me has to die to do it," Darlie read.

Had Darlie's despair, her depression, come from a sense of identity loss in her marriage?

As the defendant wiped her eyes, she began reading the April 21, 1996 journal entry. She spoke of the joy of having three wonderful, gorgeous, healthy children; of Dana, her 16-year-old sister, moving in with her boyfriend and planning marriage; and how she wanted people to remember her when she was gone.

Darlie's bangs, now grown out, hung loosely across her left eye as she read. Occasionally she would toss her head back so that the bangs would not obscure her vision.

"I often wonder what God's purpose is for me being here. I know my children, of course, but I really feel as though some way there is some meaningful importance that God expects us to figure out. What it is I do not yet know," Darlie read.

"I know sometimes God puts us through difficult trials in our lives and it is these trials that has made me such a strong and independent person," she continued to read.

Questions on the lips of observers were: what trials had Darlie faced at 26 that were so influential? And, what had they done to shape her personality?

"I pray for God to put his hand down upon my marriage. We need to be strong and help guide each other back to the right path."

The picture Darlie Routier was painting through her journal writings was of a young woman overwhelmed by the burden of three children and frustrated with her marriage.

Eight days after asking God's intervention in her marriage, Routier wrote an upbeat journal entry. She read her thoughts from April 29, 1996 to the jury.

"Today has been a pretty good day. This weekend was a little crazy but it was fun. We went to a wedding and it really made me realize how important marriage is, the commitment to one another. Darin and I have decided to renew our vows to one another on our tenth anniversary. So many things in our life has changed since we made our first commitment. Three children, two homes, a business and a lot of growing up."

Mulder asked his client to explain the plans she and Darin had made to renew their wedding vows.

"Darin asked me if I'd remarry him again. We began planning the wedding. We would renew our vows on our tenth wedding anniversary," Darlie said, smiling at the jurors. "The boys were going to be ring bearers. I had already bought the stuff to make pillows for the boys to carry. Drake was just going to sit in a tux."

Mumbles could be heard throughout the gallery as spectators began to mathematically calculate that the Routiers's 10th wedding anniversary was more than two years away at the time of the murders. What kind of elaborate event was Darlie Routier planning?

Before Darlie Routier began reading the final journal entry, she addressed the jury.

"I don't know why I wrote this. I'm embarrassed to have to sit up here and read this," she said in a tone that many later called whiny.

She turned the narrow pages until she came to the end of the book. Only five entries preceded her May 3rd thoughts, yet Routier had flipped to the last pages to begin that entry. Although Darlie had discounted the alleged suicide attempt, her diary reflected a woman who would no longer need pages in a journal. She had gone to the end.

"Devon, Damon, and Drake, I hope that one day you will forgive me for what I am about to do," Darlie read. "My life has been such a hard fight for a long time and I just cannot find the strength to keep fighting anymore. I love you three more than anything else in this world and I want all three of you to be healthy and happy. I don't want you to see a miserable person every time you look at me. Your dad loves you all very much and I know in my heart he will take care of my babies. Please do not hate me or think in any way that this is your fault. It's just that I . . ."

Darlie slowly closed the black bound book and looked sadly at the jury. Her defense attorney asked for an explanation.

"I called Darin. Drake was asleep in his crib. Damon was watching TV. I was laying on the bed crying, the journal closed on the bed. Darin came in and asked, 'What's wrong?' I told him I didn't like the way I was feeling. I was crying all the time. He read the journal and cried. We cried together for a couple of minutes. Darin asked me how I was going to do it and I told him I thought about taking pills. I already had sleeping pills in the house."

Darlie told the jury that she and Darin flushed the pills down the toilet, and she had felt much better. The next day Darin had told her to call him if she had any problems. Two days later she got her menstrual cycle and that had made a big difference in the way she felt.

Smiling, Darlie looked at jurors and described her home as a welcome house to all the neighborhood children. There were only two rules she had insisted upon—no shoes in the house and no food or drinks on the carpet.

She mentioned the black car Helena [Czaban] had seen the day before the murders and a number of hang-up phone calls she received in April and May, but admitted that she had considered them no cause for alarm.

On the night of June 5th, the Routier boys had been playing in the redwood spa. Their splashing and roughhousing had emptied half the water from the Fiberglass tub. The boys were in trouble with their mother, and Darlie refused to let Devon spend the night with a friend.

"Go upstairs and get dry clothes on," Darlie testified she told the boys, before vacuuming where they had dripped water on the family room carpet.

Darlie told jurors that Darin took Drake upstairs to feed him and to watch the news. "I don't like the news," Darlie said. "It is too negative."

She recalled wearing a T-shirt and panties.

Mulder asked that the 911 tape be played again. As Darlie sat slumped on the stand, sadness filled her eyes.

Jurors's eyes remained fixed on the transcription copies of the 911 tape provided by the court.

Darlie wiped tears from her eyes.

Prosecutor Davis leaned against the wall of the courtroom with his arms crossed, looking disgusted as Darlie's clear, audible voice on the tape says, "Someone walked in here and did it, Darin." Then her voice returned to high screeching cries and agonizing moans.

Darlie disagreed with one segment of the transcript. The transcript read, "I woke up ... I was fighting ... he ran out through the garage...."

"I said, 'frightened' not 'fighting'", Darlie said smiling. Mulder grinned at Mosty, sitting at the defense table.

Davis rolled his eyes, nodded his head, and let out a small "ha."

After the lunch break, Darlie resumed her testimony concerning the night of June 5th. She described Damon hitting her on the right shoulder, a man walking away from the couch, and hearing a glass break. Darlie told the jury that she put her hand out and told Damon to stay back. The man had gone into the utility room. The only light was from the glare of the television. Taking a couple of steps into the kitchen, she flipped on the lights. She realized there was blood on her, then saw a knife in the utility room. "It was instinct to pick up the knife" she said. She then put the knife on the kitchen counter and walked into the family room.

"I saw Devon was not moving. His eyes were open. He had cuts so big," the defendant said in a high-pitched voice. Her face was contorted, but there were no tears. She explained to jurors that she turned around and Damon was standing behind her. After turning him around she could see huge wounds on his back.

"I screamed, Darin! Devon!," Darlie said emotionally.

She related the efforts Darin made trying to save the boys as she called 911.

"I put a towel on Damon's back. I told him to hold on. 'Hold on, baby.' He said, 'Okay, mommy.' That was the last thing he said."

There were few dry eyes in the courtroom. But among those were Darlie Routier's.

"I went over to Darin. He was breathing into Devon. Blood was coming out of the wounds. I didn't know what to do. I just put a towel on him." Darlie continued her story of putting towels on Damon and screaming for Karen Neal across the street.

With sad eyes and passion in her voice, Darlie Routier looked at the jury and asked, "Can you imagine your babies are dying in front of you? What do you do?"

All but one male juror looked directly at Darlie during her plea.

Darlie's recollection of the events switched to the chaos of police and paramedics arriving, and Darin helping her onto the stretcher.

"Darin said, 'Your panties are gone'," Darlie said, helping to build the assumption that the intruder may have taken them.

"I realized my arms were bruised in the hospital. I didn't know I had been beaten. I didn't realize they were from blunt trauma. My mouth was very sore and raw. I think the man had his hand over my mouth while attacking me."

Darlie justified the birthday party at the cemetery as a celebration for Devon. "He wanted nothing more than to be seven." The eyes of a few spectators closed, perhaps thinking that the boy's wish had been snatched from him so violently.

"For two weeks he'd ask, 'Mommy, am I seven yet'? I loved those children more than my life. I did not stab those children, nor did I try to stab myself," Darlie told the jury in a definitive manner.

In a surprise move by the prosecution, Toby Shook took

charge of the cross-examination of Darlie Routier. Some speculated it was because of the mutual contempt Davis and Routier had for one another. Others theorized that Darlie would be more receptive to the younger, good-looking Shook.

Shook addressed the defendant's diary, in particular the May 3, 1996, entry.

"I hope one day you'll forgive me for what I'm about to do," Shook read from the book. "You had no traumatic amnesia at that point," he said when he finished the passage.

Shook had Darlie admit that the sleeping pills she planned to use that day had been in the house for some time prior to May 3rd. He reminded her, however, that she had told Dr. Lisa Clayton that she thought about suicide, bought the pills, and called Darin.

Shook shifted to Darlie's claim of molestation by her stepfather.

"When did Denny Stahl molest you?" Shook asked

"I was eight years old the first time," Darlie said.

Shook had Darlie confirm that the police were never called on the molestation and that her mother did not divorce Denny Stahl for nearly 10 years after the alleged incident. It was an admission that puzzled spectators and had them asking why a woman would stay with a man after her daughter accused him of violating her.

But Shook had a question of his own: Why would the defendant let her sons spend the day with an accused child molester?

On Mother's Day, 1996, Darlie allowed both Devon and Damon to spend the day with her former stepfather and accused molester, Denny Stahl, who had maintaind contact with the family over the years. Darlie justified her decision by saying that one of her sisters, Stahl's natural child, had gone with the boys. She told the court that she hadn't been concerned. Shook asked if that was the same sister who Darlie had wanted to protect from Stahl when she was younger. Darlie had no response.

Shook began attacking Darlie's claim of traumatic amnesia. During the Silly String tape Darlie had said, "This killer went to the children first, then came to me." If unable to remember details of the incident, how could she know that? Shook wanted to know.

"I assumed that. I figured that's what happened," Darlie responded.

"Do you think you slept through your boys getting killed?" Shook asked.

"I don't know."

"Devon was within one foot of you. Do you think you could have slept through it?"

"I cannot answer that, I don't remember," Darlie said. "I have no idea what happened that night."

"Don't you think you would wake up if he cut your throat?" Shook continued.

"I don't know what happened," Darlie repeated.

Shook reviewed the description of the intruder Darlie had given authorities. A tall man, built somewhat like Detective Frosch, with long, dark hair.

"Do you know Glen Mize?" Shook asked, referring to a man who had been in the Routiers's shop on several occasions and who Darlie had told police may have been the intruder.

"Yes, he would come in the shop and say things to Barbara," Darlie said, insinuating that Mize had made advances toward her friend. Darlie told the court that she had called Mize's wife and told her about the incidents, and that Mize once threatened her over the phone.

"You told the police the intruder might be Glen Mize, didn't you? Well, let's just see if it could be Glen Mize," Shook said, turning to the back of the room and nodding to an officer stationed by the witness room door.

As Glen Mize stepped through the door, followed closely by Detective Chris Frosch, mouth open and eyes wide,

Darlie Routier appeared stunned. Frosch and Mize walked through the swinging half-door that led into the "bull pen" area of the courtroom and stopped before Darlie Routier.

Mize, significantly shorter than Frosch, also weighed a good 50 pounds more than the well-built detective. Indeed, Mize's hair was long; not just below the collar as the defendant had described her assailant's hair, but more than halfway down his broad back.

"They don't have the same build, do they?" Shook asked with a smirk.

"No, sir," Darlie replied, lowering her head and speaking softly.

"We can rule out Glen Mize?" Shook asked.

"Yes, sir." Darlie was visibly shaken by the surprise appearance of the man she had once accused of murdering her two sons.

Diana Howard had been in the courtroom through most of Darlie's testimony. She was tired. There were no seats in the overcrowded room and she had been forced to stand against the wall. The Kerrville hairdresser decided to take a break.

As Howard walked out the double doors into the hall she was immediately accosted by Sarilda Routier. "How do you think it's going?" Routier asked in her usual rapid-fire manner.

"I'm the wrong one to ask," Howard said, trying to avoid being the bearer of bad news.

"What do you think?" Routier persisted.

"Well, I think if they had to decide right now they would find her guilty," Howard finally said.

Sarilda Routier grabbed the cross around her neck and began to shake. "Evil! Evil! Evil!" she yelled, picking up her Bible and reading verses rapidly.

* * *

While Diana Howard was being forced to answer Sarlida Routier's inquiry outside, Darlie Routier was forced to continue answering Toby Shook's questions from the witness stand.

Darlie told Shook that during Bill Parker's questioning at the Rowlett Police Department he did not show her her voluntary statement, did not ask her to read it, and did not ask her if her statements were true and correct.

"Bill Parker asked you six times during his interview if you killed your kids and you answered, 'If I did, I don't remember,'" Shook said.

"I never said that," Darlie said curtly, her eyes narrowed in anger.

"In your ten-page statement you never mentioned going to the kitchen sink or wetting towels," Shook told Darlie.

"No," she said flatly.

"You didn't mention wet towels until you knew the police had taken the kitchen sink."

"I didn't think any of that stuff was important."

"You didn't mention the vacuum in your statement, did you?"

"No."

"You didn't know your blood was found on the vacuum, did you?"

"No."

Shook emphasized that she could not help Damon because she was busy holding a towel to her own neck.

The prosecutor stressed to the jury that if Darlie had been fighting with the man as she said on the 911 tape, she would have known what was going on. If she could tell paramedics what happened inside the house, she indeed remembered. And if she could tell Paige Campbell at Baylor Hospital that she tried to grab the knife

FLESH AND BLOOD

from the man, she did not suffer from traumatic amnesia.

Darlie sat expressionless while Shook tore apart her defense.

During a 10-minute recess, Doug Mulder strolled to the front row of the spectators's gallery where his old friend Norm Kinne was sitting. "She's a cold bitch, isn't she?" Mulder said with a smile as he leaned toward his old friend. A Dallas television reporter standing to the left of Kinne was shocked by the comment spoken in a loud whisper.

With the jury out of the courtroom, Mulder next quietly approached his client. Spectators mulled around, talking among themselves, unaware of the attorney and his client.

Mulder leaned forward, pressing his face very close to Darlie Routier's. "You're on trial for your life, let's see some Goddamn tears!"

Immediately, Darlie began to cry. The crying continued while Shook resumed his questioning.

"Do you remember calling KRLD and talking to Rick Roberts?" Shook asked. "You said, 'I know what happened in that house that night'." Darlie gave no response as she wiped tears from her eyes.

Shook reminded Darlie and the jury that from the courtroom demonstration it could be safely assumed that Glen Mize was not the man who attacked Darlie Routier on June 6th.

The assistant prosecutor began reading portions of letters written by Darlie Routier while being held in the Dallas County jail. In a letter to Sandy Aitken, dated November 1, 1996, Darlie had written about Glen Mize, "We believe we know who did it. We already have so much on him. I know it's him."

To Karen Neal, Darlie wrote, "I know who did it. I can't write it down, they read my mail but I know." And in another letter to Neal, "I believe Glen did it. Mom and Darin can give you all the details."

As Shook read excerpts from Darlie's jail letters, the young mother began to cry almost uncontrollably.

"I would like to know where you're getting all those letters," Darlie demanded.

"From the central jail file," Shook said.

"Isn't that illegal?" Darlie barked.

The comment drew some suppressed chuckles from the gallery.

Shook continued to read portions of the letters written by Darlie Routier to members of her family and a number of friends. She continued to accuse Glen Mize and added a neighbor as a possible suspect.

"He fits the description," she wrote about her neighbor. "He has wide arms, wide around the middle, and across the back. This man could be on his balcony and see in our hot tub. He could be watching me at any time."

"There is no house that has a balcony that could see in your backyard," Shook said. "That's a lie."

Darlie Routier was sobbing as Shook read from one final letter. "I guess by now you must know they found a small amount of the boys's blood on my gown. It must have been Damon's. I tried to help Damon."

With Darlie crying unrestrained, Shook passed the witness back to the defense for re-direct examination.

"Why did you write them [family and friends] about those suspects?" Mulder asked.

Darlie explained that the information about possible suspects that she put in the letters came from private investigators working for the court-appointed defense attorneys who were originally assigned to defend her. She simply relayed the information to family and friends because she was eager to believe it herself.

Mulder had no more questions for his client.

Shook wanted the jury to hear one more time that Darlie Routier had falsely accused Glen Mize, and that she did not suffer from traumatic amnesia. "You wrote, 'I know it's him, I saw him and I know it's him'. That's a pretty

FLESH AND BLOOD

positive statement, isn't it?" Shook asked as he sat down between Davis and Wallace at the prosecution table.

Darlie did not answer.

"The defendant will rest her case," Mulder said, with Darlie Routier still crying in the witness chair.

Chapter Twenty-Eight

"I know Darlie's innocent," Darin Routier said after his wife's testimony. "I'd bet my life on it."

Routier had bet everything else he owned on his wife's innocence, and in the process had lost his house, his prized material possessions, and his only remaining child. He would have to wait a little longer to see if his wager paid off.

While Darin Routier, Mama Darlie, and the other Routier family members's responses to recent testimony were uncharacteristically low-key, the prosecution took pleasure in what most spectators perceived as a courtroom victory.

"She [Darlie] apparently doesn't take to coaching very well. I don't think she made a very good witness for herself," Daivs said, holding back a boyish grin. "She seems to have one of the most selective memories I've seen in a long time."

On the other side of the case, Mosty spoke to the press in hollow tones. "This isn't a case of how Darlie Routier performed on the witness stand. This is a case of if the state proved their case beyond a reasonable doubt," Mosty said solemnly, adding, "Darlie was overmatched in the courtroom by an experienced district attorney."

Many courtroom spectators agreed. They felt Darlie had hurt herself by testifying and had given the State a big boost.

The stress of the four-week ordeal was showing on Doug Mulder's face. Not only had he been forced to contend with a conservative law-and-order jury, and what seemed to be insurmountable evidence, but with a defendant's family of newshounds as well. He had asked them to avoid the media spotlight. Few had complied.

"This case is not a real difficult one," Mulder said. "It's been unduly complicated by some of the friends and family. They've been, in all candor, somewhat difficult to control. Everyone wants to be a star."

Courtroom "junkies" who usually arrived at the Kerr County courthouse between 7:30 and 8:00 A.M. each morning for the Darlie Routier trial, began arriving between 5:30 and 6:00 the morning of closing arguments. Court was scheduled for 9:00 A.M. No one wanted to miss the final showdown.

The rumor had circulated that only 50 courtroom seats would be available for spectators, the remaining 100 reserved for the Routier family, family and friends of both the prosecution and defense teams, a section for members of the Rowlett Police Department, and a number of seats for the press. Anxious spectators crammed into the hallway, waiting to pass through the free-standing metal detector, and waiting to see if they would be one of the 50 allowed inside.

Tension ran high. Tempers became sharp. Observers who had become fast friends over the four-week trial suddenly became competitors—vying for a seat in what had become the Super Bowl of Texas murder trials.

Susie McDaniel, the mother of hairdresser Diana Howard, was a courtroom veteran. She had attended numerous trials in the past and had been used as an expert witness in several. The attractive, middle-aged blonde with a great sense of humor felt the anguish building.

"Okay," McDaniel said in a loud voice, standing at the front of the long line. "The metal detectors are broken. We're going to have to do a strip search. Men on the left. Women on the right. Take off all your clothes."

The anxious crowd stood speechless for a moment, then in unison broke into hilarious laughter. Susie McDaniel had successfully eased the tension.

Inside, a reporter looked for a seat and made a humorous comment about the overcrowded conditions. A minister, who had come from Dallas as a favor to a friend to comfort the Routier family, found the reporter's sense of humor to be distasteful.

"Would you please be quiet and have a little respect for the family?" he snapped.

The reporter was quick to respond. "Excuse me. I've sat here for four weeks. I've seen crime scene photos, I've heard autopsy reports, and I've seen grown men cry on the stand. It's been difficult. Laughter is a release. Besides, that family didn't have any respect when they shot Silly String all over the boys's grave," she replied.

Some of the people around her were shocked at the sharp words, but all understood. It had indeed been a long, grueling four weeks, filled with death and tragedy.

Darin Routier sat next to his mother, holding hands. Darin was dressed in a shiny, charcoal gray velveteen suit, with a large silver cross hung around his neck. He breathed deeply as the judge took his position at the bench.

Finally, everyone was in place. It would be the last time prosecutors and defense attorneys would have to square off on the question of Darlie Routier's guilt or innocence.

Toby Shook spoke first.

"This has been a long and tedious trial," Shook began.

He thanked the jury for their service then got straight to the meat of his argument.

"The State had to prove Darlie Routier intentionally killed her sons with a knife. Everyone wants the reason. Sometimes that is apparent, and sometimes it's not. We may never know the real motive, but that doesn't change the evidence. We are not required to prove the motive," Shook told jurors.

The prosecutor asked the 12 members of the panel to use their God-given common sense in evaluating the evidence. He then reviewed, step-by-step, each piece of evidence placed into the court record. "It's like a jigsaw puzzle when it all fits," Shook said. Jurors appeared to listen intently.

Shook reemphasized the discrepancies in Darlie's stories.

Sarilda Routier leaned into her son, resting her head on his left shoulder.

"She killed those boys, then she faked that scene," Shook said with fire in his voice. "We don't know, she may have had to go back and finish Damon off." The words brought shivers to the spectators, along with a few gasps.

"She didn't cry until she was caught in a lie," Shook continued, referring to Darlie's own testimony. "That's when you saw real tears. Those are the ones you should have seen at the gravesite. You didn't see those tears because she didn't care for those boys."

Sarilda and Darin leaned even closer and began to cry.

Then Shook went in for the close. Greg Davis would wrap up the prosecution remarks after the defense had their say, but Shook wanted to make an impression on the jury that they would not soon forget.

"Little Damon moved," Shook said in a sympathetic tone. "That is the most frightening part of this case. You see, Damon was awake. His eyes were open. He saw his murderer. He saw his mother." Shook pointed to Darlie Routier, a scowl across his handsome face.

With narrowed, angry eyes, the defendant looked at Shook and said, "No."

As Shook returned to the prosecution table, heavy sighs rippled throughout the courtroom. Shook had seized the emotions of the spectators. No one could tell how his words affected the stone-faced jurors.

Curtis Glover was the first of three defense attorneys to address the jury. He attempted to discredit Jim Cron by saying that Cron waltzed through the house in 20 minutes, then secretly laid the groundwork to go after Darlie Routier. Glover accused the police and prosecutors of claiming the crime scene was staged whenever the scene became confusing, as with the existence of the sock.

And, he added, "I don't know what his [intruder's] intentions were. Her panties were gone."

Defense attorneys had alluded to the missing panties for weeks but had presented no evidence to support their inference that the intruder had made off with them. Nor had they presented evidence to support the idea that Darlie Routier was even wearing panties at the time of the murders.

During a brief recess, Darlie, sitting at the defense table, and Darin sitting in the family section of the gallery, shared a private moment. "I miss you," Darlie mouthed to her husband, a small smile on her lips. Darin responded in kind.

After the break, the second defense attorney, Richard Mosty, approached the jury. "I will never apologize for defending the woman I believe in," Mosty told jurors.

He attempted to discredit Jim Cron, the crime scene expert; Tom Bevel, the blood splatter expert; Charles Linch, the trace evidence expert; and Allen Brantley, the

FBI agent. He questioned their abilities as well as their motives.

"People want to know why this happened because it doesn't make sense," Mosty told the jury. "This woman turned from loving mother to killer, just doesn't make sense."

Mosty made reference to Bill Parker, the State's only rebuttal witness. "Mr. Parker, in that deep voice, said she didn't deny it," Mosty said. "She told you somebody else did it. Isn't that denial? And through everything else, they copy her jailhouse mail. Through all this, they don't get a confession. They never ever got what they wanted.

"It is important to go back and look at the evidence," Mosty instructed jurors. "The hard facts. The scientific facts. This isn't a coulda', shoulda', woulda' case."

Mosty, the most passionate of the defense attorneys, was finished. He had much more to say to the jury, much more he needed to say on behalf of his client, but his time had run out. Doug Mulder would close for the defense.

In a soft, sincere manner, Mulder thanked the jury for their time and attention. Then, as if shot out of a box, Mulder exploded. His voice reverberated throughout the courtroom. "Let me make one thing clear," he said, pointing to the jury. "You aren't down here to return a verdict to make me happy. And you aren't down here to return a verdict to make Greg Davis happy."

Jurors who had sat passively through Mosty's tiresome recap of witnesses suddenly sat at attention.

His voice returning to a more normal tone, Mulder continued the theme of conspiracy and mismanagement by the Rowlett police. The focus of his attention: the mysterious black car, a black car that no one could identify by make, model, or license plate.

"This was a normal family," said Mulder so softly that spectators strained to hear. "She doesn't just all of a sudden, out of the blue, go haywire. Who of us could withstand the scrutiny this woman has been put through?"

Then, in Mulder's familiar backhanded manner, he tried to destroy the validity of the prosecution's witnesses, just as the two attorneys before him had tried to do.

"Professor Brantley," Mulder said, referring to the FBI special agent, "said, 'I think it's someone who knew the boys very well'. Well, Professor Brantley, how long did it take to commit the murders and stage the scene?" Mulder next questioned if the window of opportunity had been large enough for the defendant to kill her children *and* stage the scene.

Mulder then attacked his old friend. "James Cron left the sheriff's office three years ago, grew a beard, and now calls himself a consultant," Mulder said.

He compared Bill Parker, interrogating detective, to a used car salesman closing a sale.

Darlie watched her attorney's performance from the sideline, resting her chin on her hand, a smile that some later called "smug" on her face.

"I've done all I can," Mulder said, a hint of frustration in his voice. "You've been most attentive. This lady is simply not guilty." He walked back to the defense table, a much more subdued stroll than the strut he had exhibited on the first day of court, four weeks earlier.

Mosty stood before the court and asked Judge Tolle to grant the defense an additional five minutes of argument. Once granted, Mosty hammered at the sequence of events.

"At two twenty-nine the 911 call starts. At two thirty-seven, the 911 tape ends. At two thirty-eight paramedics arrive. At two thirty-nine, Damon is dead," Mosty told jurors. "If the State's theory is to be true, all this has to happen in two to three minutes. She stabs the kids, gets a smidgen of blood of each, runs into the ally, comes back into the house, picks up the knife, cuts herself five times. She had to lay her head on the pillow, she lays down the knife carefully, she has to leave a blood trail to the utility room, she goes to the sink, she goes to the children, she has to knock over the coffee table, she has to walk through the house, she has to pick up the knife off the carpet, and she has to get to the vacuum cleaner. She has to do all that in two to three minutes."

As Mosty took his place at the defense table, spectators quickly calculated the timetable Mosty had proposed. The question on their lips was: who said the murders took place only moments before the 911 call or that the other events occurred in the order Mosty listed?

Medical examiners testified the boys could have lived five to ten minutes—enough time to kill and stage the scene.

Greg Davis stood and walked over to the jury box. Spectators knew this was the finale. Closure to an emotion-driven month.

"I'm the last lawyer talking to you. I know that's probably a relief," Davis said with a crooked grin. "There's been an overall effort to show you the truth. I'm not going to apologize for representing the good people of Texas. I'm very proud to be the voice of Devon and Damon Routier. These two little boys don't have voices anymore," Davis said, holding photos of the two slain children for jurors to see. "I'm going to use my voice to speak for them."

In the gallery, Deon Routier, younger brother of Darin, sobbed. His wife Dana consoled him while wiping away her own tears.

"There is a distinct difference between good and bad," Davis continued. "What does a guilty woman do when she comes to trial? She alters her appearance. Poor me, I'm the victim."

Davis reminded jurors of the number of people Darlie Routier accused of killing her children: Glen Mize, until he appeared in court; a neighbor; a man in a dark cap; and, finally, a drug-crazed maniac.

"They blame the police," Davis said. "That's the oldest, most regularly used defense." But Davis countered the charge by reminding jurors that Charles Hamilton spent five hours lifting prints from the house when he could have said they were all Darlie Routier's, that police called in James Cron, a seasoned, highly respected crime scene analyst, and Charles Linch for blood evidence. Davis asked jurors why Rowlett investigators would have done that if they had already made up their minds?

Darlie Kee sat in the family section of the courtroom, anger painted across her face. As Davis reputed each statement made by the defense, Kee shook her head and whispered, "Liar."

Addressing the sock found 75 yards down the alley, Davis said Darlie Routier had tried to disassociate the sock from the house. But evidence showed fibers on the sock were consistent with Darin's shoe, and Darin's own testimony that the sock was his connected the sock to the Routier household, not to an intruder.

"She claims amnesia," Davis said. "The I-can't-remember, or I-won't-remember defense. Ask yourself, do innocent women sleep through the stabbing of a child five feet away, one foot away, or sleep through their own attack? Does she give eight accounts of the incident?

"This one right here is not an innocent woman," Davis said, pointing to Darlie Routier. "She killed her two children. The evidence points to one person. Only God and she know exactly why she did it.

"I never had the pleasure of meeting them [Devon and Damon]. They were ours too. Our future. They looked up with open eyes and the last thing they saw was their killer," Davis said as he approached the defense table for the third time and gestured toward Darlie.

"Liar!" Darlie hissed. "You're lying! I didn't kill my kids!"

Davis paused, then said, "Now she says I'm a liar. They saw this woman in a rage, coming down on them with a knife."

The emotional argument by Davis brought tears to several of the normally expressionless jurors.

* * *

After the closing arguments, people gathered outside. Standing in front of the Kerr County courthouse, Sarilda Routier spoke to the press. "We've just got to keep our hopes up. It's good against evil, truth against evil, truth against lies, and we believe truth wins and lies will be dispelled."

Shaun Rabb, reporter for FOX 4 News, stood on the lawn of the courthouse for his six o'clock newscast.

"Beginning this afternoon twelve men and women will be asked to decide if Darlie Routier is good—or evil. Twelve jurors will decide which version of what happened June 6th they believe is most correct . . . In Kerrville, Shaun Rabb, Fox 4, Texas."

Prosecutors exited the courthouse through the sallyport of the old county jail. They had taken the new path in recent days to avoid confrontation with members of Routier's family. The press spotted them and rushed toward them for interviews.

"To prosecute someone like this woman, this evil, it is a pleasure to work this hard on this case," said Sherri Wallace, assistant district attorney.

When asked how he felt when called a liar by the defendant, Davis smiled and said, "The only other person who said that to me was Juan Chevez, a man convicted of killing twelve people."

While prosecutors were giving statements to the press, the sheriff's car carrying Darlie Routier back to the Kerr County Jail, passed through the sallyport. Darlie appeared optimistic, flashing a smile and a victory sign to the media.

During deliberations, jurors sent two notes out to the judge. The first was a request to review testimony of Darin Routier about whether he locked the door between the utility room and the garage. Darin had told jurors that he did not lock the door, but on cross-examination he said he had testified in another hearing that he had locked all the doors before retiring.

The second note asked to review comparisons of the knife wounds inflicted on the boys to the injuries suffered by Darlie Routier.

After six hours of deliberations jurors retired to their hotel rooms for the night. It had been an emotionally exhausting day.

The next morning family members of Darlie Routier arrived at the courthouse wearing the familiar T-shirts with photos of Devon and Damon on the front and Darlie and her children on the back.

With television trucks from San Antonio joining those from Dallas in the front parking lot of the Kerr County courthouse, reporters from Dallas, Fort Worth, Houston, and San Antonio combined with journalists from New York to create a media feeding-frenzy. The scene was a scaled-down version of media day at the Super Bowl.

Family members were dotted across the lawn giving interviews to any member of the press who asked. Occasionally a member of the defense team would appear to give their prognostication of the verdict. Gregory Conlin, one of five courtroom artists working the trial for various television stations, sat at a picnic table giving finishing touches to an amazing likeness of Darlie Routier. Danelle Stahl, Darlie's youngest sister, sat on the cold concrete walkway and scribbled out messages on paper to hold up to Darlie who waited in her holding cell on the second floor of the courthouse annex.

Darin Routier raised a photo of the couple's youngest son Drake over his head as Darlie stared through the glass-enclosed mesh wiring. The husband of the accused killer stared through binoculars or gazed through a high-powered photographer's lens to get a better look at his young wife.

He mouthed, "I love you." Darlie cried and mouthed, "I love you, too."

Darin lifted the sleeve of his cotton T-shirt for photographers, proudly exposing his right bicep. "My love for the boys somehow blossomed and I had this done," he said with a coy grin. The images of Devon and Damon were tattooed on his arm.

Tattoo artist Todd Hlavaty had put the boys' likeness on Darin's arm sometime before Christmas 1996. Hlavaty would later tell reporters that he found Darin's manner odd.

"He was so convinced that everything was going to turn out A-OK, and they were going to get all this money from a movie," Hlavaty said. "The focus of the conversation was more on the fame and the mistakes the D.A. made, instead of on whoever the intruder was."

Hlavaty added that Darin seemed more concerned about his wife being in jail than the boys' deaths.

"He said, 'Keep this hush-hush until after the trial.' This will be your most famous tattoo." Indeed, Hlavaty's work had drawn the attention of state and national reporters covering the Routier trial.

When asked about his wife calling the lead prosecutor a liar during closing arguments, Darin Routier angrily responded, "It took every bit of energy we had just to sit there. If she hadn't done it, I would have."

"He's a liar," Sarilda Routier chimed in, referring to Davis.

Shortly before noon Darlie Routier looked out the window of the holding cell. With tears streaming down her colorless cheeks, she shook her head. No one knew the hidden meaning of her gesture.

Moments later, defense attorneys filed into the courthouse. "This must be it," a newsman yelled to his camera man.

Suddenly the quiet spectators standing idley in the courthouse foyer tossed their Soda cans in the trash, grabbed their coats, and rushed to claim their seats inside the courtroom. Two bailiffs, five Kerr County deputies, and one plainclothes constable lined the walls inside the courtroom. If there was trouble after the verdict was announced, they were ready.

Darlie Routier sat crying at the defense table. She lifted her face to the ceiling and wiped away tears with trembling fingers. There was no question in the minds of spectators, as there had been during her testimony—Darlie Routier was crying real tears.

Mulder leaned to his left and talked to Darlie and his investigator, Lloyd Herrall, in hushed tones. The attorney who the Routier family had placed their money and their faith in looked sadly at Darin and Mama Darlie, slowly making a thumbs down motion with his right hand.

Darin leaned forward in his gallery seat and wept. Mama Darlie remained silent and dry-eyed. Darlie's sisters, Dana and Danelle Stahl, sobbed loudly. Darlie's family entwined arms and braced themselves for the verdict Mulder had so bluntly revealed to them.

Jurors entered the courtroom with the same expressionless faces they had maintained throughout most of the long, tedious trial. Noticing the stacks of evidence used by prosecutors had been removed from the courtroom, the jury gave the court reporter verbal instructions. Sandra Halsey, official court reporter for Criminal District Court Number Three, then placed the smiling photos of Devon and Damon Routier so they would be facing the defendant. The jurors wanted Darlie to be looking at her children when she heard their verdict.

Some of Darlie's relatives sobbed as the guilty verdict was announced. Others yelled condemnations at prosecutors.

"They're all lying!" Danelle Stahl shouted. "Greg Davis is a killer!"

Darlie's young sister next aimed her venom at the jury. "You'll burn!" she screamed as jurors filed in. "How can you live with yourselves?"

The short, fiery mother-in-law of the convicted killer climbed up on one of the gallery seats. "Greg Davis, you look at me! You look me in my eyes," Sarilda Routier shouted. "I have a right for you to look in my eyes. God will forgive you, but I won't! How dare you! How dare you!"

Downstairs, Mama Darlie and her two youngest daughters, Dana and Danelle, were making their way to the side doors, pushing newsmen and cameras out of their way.

"Guys, get out of my face!" Dana Stahl yelled. "This is not the time!" She pushed the glass doors open with such force that they banged against the brick wall behind them. Outside, she slumped on a picnic bench on the courthouse lawn and wailed.

With Danelle clinging to her arm, Mama Darlie made her way through the excited crowd of reporters. The pain of her sister's conviction contorted Danelle's young face. "Goddamn killers!" she screamed. Mama Darlie remained stoic. No tears stained her face. No color blushed her cheeks. She stared straight ahead as if in another place—another time.

Lou Ann Brown, the attractive mother-in-law of Darin's brother, spoke to the press for the first time. The dark-haired woman talked calmly, with great compassion and dignity. "I don't think you believe it until you hear it," Brown said. "I don't think Darlie was prepared. She was always encouraged, always in high spirits. Darin isn't doing very well at all."

While Brown commented on Darin Routier's response to the guilty verdict he appeared in the doorway behind her. The young husband appeared stunned. Supported by his cousin Randy Reagan on his left and Pastor David Rogers on his right, he began to make his way toward the crowd. As the trio stepped through the interior doorway toward waiting reporters, Mulder stepped up to the microphones. "Wait," Darin said, taking a step backward, as if waiting for his turn at the mike.

"You heard the verdict," Mulder said. "We are obviously disappointed. There's not much we can do at this stage. I don't know of anything I'd do differently. It's hard to say if Darlie's testimony helped or hurt. I can't second-guess it."

It was obvious to observers that the "Mulder magic" hadn't worked.

"When a person is obviously guilty," Prosecutor Cecil Emerson said, "there's not a thing that ten Doug Mulders or Johnnie Cochrans can do about it."

Of course the Routier family disagreed.

"They have facts, physical evidence, fingerprints, etc., that shows somebody was in there," Randy Reagan said. "If that's not reasonable doubt, I don't know what is."

"They decided within twenty minutes that she was the one," Darlie's aunt, Lou Ann Black, said. "Darlie Lynn knows and God knows that she is innocent."

For Darlie Routier's family, the battle was far from over. "As long as Darlie is alive and breathing, we will have to keep fighting," Darin Routier declared.

After Mama Darlie survived the initial shock that her oldest daughter had been convicted of murder, she spoke to the press. "We will continue to fight," Mama Darlie said, her voice filled with bitterness. Her eyes narrowed in an angry glare. "Our judicial system is one step away from being criminal. It is a total shock to your system when you know there is much more than reasonable doubt. I hope Greg Davis realizes when he goes to sleep at night, he has an innocent woman in jail. My daughter's blood will be on his hands when this is done."

The seething comments from the convicted killer's mother did little to deter Davis from the remainder of his mission. "I've never been verbally attacked like that before by a family," Davis said. "I've never seen anything like it." But the prosecutor remained determined to make Darlie Routier the seventh woman sentenced to Texas's Death Row.

"My only regret is that I can't bring those boys back," Davis told reporters. "We'll seek the death penalty. Anyone who could take the lives of two innocent boys is a threat to society."

Chapter Twenty-Nine

Darlie Routier laid her head against the backseat of the Kerr County sheriff's car and sobbed. Gone was her zestful optimism displayed the day before the verdict was announced. All that was left were tears, sorrow, and disbelief.

"She is very upset. She just can't believe that the verdict came out this way," her mother said the day after jurors found her daughter guilty of capital murder. "She just didn't know how she could continue. I told her to do it day by day."

Mama Darlie and Darin Routier had been to the Kerr County jail to visit Darlie. It was the first time they had spoken since the verdict was read by Judge Tolle.

Mama Darlie and Darin sat at a picnic table on the banks of the picturesque Guadeloupe River and talked with reporters. The stress of 19 days of testimony and two days of deliberations showed on their faces. They were exhausted, disappointed, and shocked. Most of all, they were afraid for Darlie.

"What's the difference in life in prison and lethal injection?" Mama Darlie asked, referring to the options the jury would face in sentencing Darlie. "There's not much difference except for the appeals." She lowered her head but kept her tears locked inside.

"Now they're trying to kill Darlie," Darin said emotionally. "They're trying to take a person who was a victim herself and try to kill her for absolutely no reason." Darin held his head up, and with a mixture of pride and sadness, he told reporters, "I had the most perfect wife, perfect kids, living in a nice big house with a booming business, and now all I have is hope. We are going to keep on fighting," he added.

Their fight would continue the next day—back inside the courtroom. Prosecutors would be fighting to send 27-year-old Darlie Routier to Texas's death chamber. Darlie and her attorneys would be fighting for her life.

Like a quake rumbling beneath the surface of the earth, the news of Darlie Routier's conviction could be felt 300 miles away in her home of Rowlett. Neighbors met curb side to discuss the tragic events of June 6th and comment on the conviction of a woman who they all knew.

"They saw the evidence, I didn't," Mary Inman said. "I'm sure they made the right decision. I'm just glad it's over. Now we can all go on."

Many neighbors echoed Inman's sentiments. It was time to go on, time to put the tragedy behind them.

Sergeant Dean Poos of the Rowlett police expressed the feelings of the community. "There are no winners in this case. Two little boys are dead. A family has been destroyed."

The boys would be missed.

"Sometimes I can still hear them [the boys], especially if I'm mowin' out in the yard," Brownie Sherril, the Routiers's backdoor neighbor, said. The hint of a reminiscent smile was on his lips.

FLESH AND BLOOD

Devon and Damon had not only been taken from the family, but from the neighborhood as well. Now they hoped peace could be restored to the small community.

Monday, February 3rd, the hallways of the Kerr County courthouse were once again packed with spectators hoping to get a seat for the grand finale of the Darlie Routier murder trial.

Susie McDaniel resumed keeping the crowd entertained and contented while waiting for their turn to pass through the metal archway.

"Look, y'all," McDaniel instructed. "Can y'all guess what Rick looks like?" Rick was one of two Kerr County sheriff's deputies who had been assigned to search persons entering the courtroom. The tall, ultra-slim, middle-aged man stared at McDaniel questioningly. His face was overshadowed by a large brimmed western hat perched on his small head.

Everyone stared at Rick. His pale cheeks turned pink, then changed to bright red as McDaniel said, "A thumbtack," and everyone laughed. Rick laughed with them.

Inside the courtroom, Davis and the other Dallas County prosecutors were seriously preparing for the sentencing phase of the Routier trial. Davis wanted Darlie Routier to die for killing her children. Legal experts believed he had a high mountain to climb in order to get a death sentence.

Nationally, 113 women have been sentenced to death since 1973, when the U.S. Supreme Court reinstated the death penalty. Only one death sentence against a woman had been carried out.

Extenuating circumstances typically keep parents, especially mothers, from being sentenced to death for killing a child. But Darlie Routier's case was different. Because she had not confessed and her attorneys had not portrayed her as a woman with severe psychological problems, the possibility of a death sentence was unpredictable.

Jurors could send Darlie Routier to prison for 40 years (the equivalent of a life sentence), or send her to Death Row.

The prosecution's first witness was the teenage stepdaughter of Glen Mize, the man once falsely accused by Darlie Routier of being the unknown intruder. The girl told jurors that Darlie Routier rarely paid any attention to her sons, then ages three and five, and that she let them roam free in the front yard. She also testified that her 16-year-old girlfriend frequently babysat for the Routiers and that Darlie gave the underaged girl cigarettes, alcohol, and marijuana.

"You don't like Darlie, do you?" Defense Attorney Mosty asked.

"Not especially," she replied.

Next, Eileen Schimer, a Routier neighbor, was called by the prosecution. She also told stories of how Devon and Damon Routier roamed the neighborhood unsupervised, that on a boating trip the Routier children, who could not swim, were not instructed to wear life vests, and of an incident at Devon's fifth birthday party when the defendant's volatile temper brought the party to a standstill.

Schimer testified that Darlie Routier had called a halt to a water fight between adults and kids at Devon's party. But Devon had squirted his mother again, enraging the young mother.

"She immediately grabbed a piece of birthday cake off the table and shoved it in his face," Schimer said. "Everybody stopped laughing and stared at her and at Devon. She told him that he was warned to stop and that he got what he deserved."

A hush fell over the courtroom. Spectators visualized the fun-loving, freckled-face little boy embarrassed in front of his friends.

"Devon stared at her. He was angry," Schimer said. "Later, Darlie told Devon not to try it again or try to get even with her. She said it under her breath and through her teeth."

Next was Kay Norris, the State's witness, was a former employee of American Pawn Shop. Norris described Darlie Routier as a tacky dresser who never wore a bra, a woman usually clad in a big T-shirt and shorts. Norris considered the defendant to be rude, often grabbing jewelry items from her hands while she waited on her. She admitted that, in spite of her rudeness, most employees wanted to assist Darlie Routier because she always bought something and employees were paid on commission.

"If she wanted something and Darin said no, she would curse him and say, 'I want it now!' She usually got it," Norris said.

Norris told jurors that Darlie once shouted at her sons to stop playing on exercise equipment near the jewelry counter.

"The first time she told them to get their asses over there," Norris said. "And when they didn't pay any attention, she told them to get the fuck over there." Norris claimed Darin said nothing, but continued to look in the jewelry case. The four-letter word seemed to offend many of the jurors, a number of whom blushed and wrinkled their brows.

Following Norris, Nelda Watts, a neighbor of the Routiers's, recounted for jurors the morning of June 18th, the morning Darlie Routier was arrested. She told the story of Darlie and Darin pitching stuffed bears taken from funeral wreaths on the front lawn of their Rowlett home, and tossing them into the family Pathfinder. Watts described the fun the couple appeared to be having, as Darlie jumped up and down, clapping her hands as Darin pitched the toys into the vehicle.

At the end of Watts's testimony, Judge Tolle slammed his gavel onto the desk. He announced a lunch break. Court would resume in just over an hour.

The five witnesses for the State had done little to convince spectators that Darlie Routier was much more than a flawed, indifferent mother. To get the death sentence they hoped to receive, the prosecutors would have to present evidence that she was a future threat.

After lunch, the first witness they called gave the State the ammunition they needed.

Helena Czaban, whose testimony was not permissible in the guilt/innocence phase of the trial, was now allowed to tell jurors the story of finding eight-month-old Drake Routier wrapped head-to-toe in a blanket and gasping for breath the day before his older brothers were killed.

Female jurors stared at Darlie Routier during Czaban's testimony, disbelief covering their faces.

But even more damaging was Czaban's statement that, at the funeral of Devon and Damon, she approached Darlie saying in her broken Polish accent, "Darlie, I am so sorry what happened. You have many problems, now these expenses. I'm very, very sorry."

"'I'm not worried'," Czaban testified Darlie had said, "'because I'll get five thousand dollars apiece'. The day before she told me she needed money. She needed ten thousand dollars."

The young pregnant juror in the front row looked directly at Darlie with a scowl on her face and exhaled deeply. A male juror rested his head in his hand and shook his head. Spectators whispered among themselves. Was money the real motive behind the murder of the two little boys?

"The State rests, your Honor," Greg Davis told the court. Judge Tolle immediately called for a 10-minute recess.

After the break, Dana Routier, wife of Darin's brother Deon, walked slowly to the witness box. The pretty blonde shook slightly. She was scared, scared she would say something that would further harm her sister-in-law, Darlie.

She spoke in a quivering voice, breaking into sobs as she talked about Devon and Damon and the closeness she had felt with the two little boys. Dana told jurors she had never seen Darlie be violent with the children and thought that Darlie had been a giving, caring, and loving mother. Dana Routier denied knowing of any emotional problems Darlie was having in April and May of 1996. Dana was excused.

On cross-examination by prosecutors, Melanie Waits told jurors that she, Darlie Routier, and several friends had thrown themselves a party on the Saturday night before Mother's Day in both 1994 and 1995. A male stripper had provided the entertainment at the Routier home in 1994, and in 1995 the group had stayed overnight at the Wyndham Anatole Hotel and partied at a male strip club known as La Bare. Wait described the event as an "adult slumber party."

According to Wait, guests included herself, Mama Darlie, Darlie Routier, Michele Ramsey, Barbara Jovell, and Darlie's two younger sisters, Dana and Danelle Stahl, 15 and 13, respectively, at the time.

Deon Routier reiterated his wife's statements of his sister-in-law as a loving and devoted mother. The grieving uncle cried when he told jurors, "I loved those boys, I still do."

The next defense witness entered the courtroom garbed in tennis shoes, jeans, and a red T-shirt adorned with Sylvester the Cat and Tweety Bird on the pocket. Twelve-year-old Rebecca Neal sat in the witness chair nervously popping her knuckles and crying.

"You would think they could have had her wear a dress," a spectator was overheard saying.

The young preteen was unable to control her crying to answer defense questions. Mulder finally asked the court if the girl's father could be seated in court, in an effort to calm her.

Terry Neal, Darin Routier's friend and neighbor, entered the courtroom clad in a green T-shirt, green nylon pants, and black laced-up combat boots. The physically robust man gave the appearance of a storm trooper ready to take the hill. He sat quietly in the front row of the courtroom, his eyes focused on his daughter.

In a shaky voice Rebecca Neal told jurors that she was always welcomed in the Routier home and that Darlie had been like a mother to her. She refuted the accusations made by Helena Czaban. The youngster had been at the Routier house on the day in question and said that Drake had been laying on the floor, with a blanket only half-covering his head.

Finally, Rebecca Neal's questioning was over, a brief period of time that must have seemed like hours to the frightened child.

"The defense calls Darin Routier," Mulder said loudly.

Darin Routier walked into the courtroom like a man on a mission. His mission: to save the life of his wife.

One-by-one Darin began to tear down the prosecution witnesses. "Watts isn't very social," he said of the gray-haired, retired school teacher. He explained that it was his sister-in-law, Dana Stahl, who had helped him dismantle the memorial wreaths, and not Darlie.

Darin claimed that he did not know Kay Norris of American Pawn, and that he had never witnessed his wife snatch jewelry from any salesperson, never saw Darlie yell at the kids, and never heard her use bad language.

He smugly insinuated that Eileen Schimer was a "very protective" parent with her children. He claimed he never allowed Devon and Damon to ride in the street as Schimer had testified. He asserted that he looked after the children while on the boat, smiling broadly as he exclaimed, "I'm the captain." Of the cake in the face incident: Darin stated Darlie only smudged a bit of icing on the child's cheek.

None of the 12 jurors looked at Darin Routier during his testimony. They remained stone-faced, waiting for the witness to finish.

"Darlie is guilty," Davis said during cross-examination. "You have to accept that. Do you understand?"

"No, sir," Darin replied arrogantly. "I do not. I've lost everything."

In sharp contrast to the slow movement of Darin Routier leaving the stand, Darlie Kee came swiftly into the courtroom. Her posture was erect, her attitude defiant. Per what some family members said were Mulder's instructions, she wore a conservative navy blue dress, the hem a little longer, the skirt a little less tight than her usual attire. Her frosted hair was neatly arranged up, off her neck and large gold loop earrings framed her face.

Darlie Kee looked straight at the jurors as she spoke. "Darlie is a kind, sweet person. I don't agree with your verdict. We have not chosen Darlie over these two little boys," she said with passion in her voice. "I'm asking you, if you have any compassion, do not put her to death because she did not do this."

The defendant's mother portrayed her daughter as a loving and caring person, responsible for helping to raise her two younger sisters, while Kee was building her career.

As Darlie Routier's mother stepped down from the stand, her mother-in-law prepared to testify. Sarilda Routier walked quickly to the witness box. Darlie gave her mother-in-law the same warm smile she had given all the witnesses who had testified in her behalf.

Sarilda turned and faced the jury, ready to make her plea for Darlie's life.

"To be truthful, I'm still in shock," Sarilda began. "I didn't prepare myself for that [verdict]. I don't know how you came to that decision. You know you're wrong."

Spectators shifted uneasily in their seats. They expected Routier to plead for Darlie's life, not admonish the jury for their decision.

"My goodness, if you decide to put her to death, we might find this man and she may be gone," Sarilda said, as some members of the gallery rolled their eyes.

"This decision isn't just against Darlie. It is against all of us. Please don't do any more to us. My daughter is under sedation. My husband may have a heart attack. Dig down deep inside you and don't make it any worse."

Sarilda Routier attempted to put the jury's decision on a personal level, a place they could not emotionally afford to go.

Davis asked her one question before the defense rested. "Mrs. Routier, do you remember telling me once that whoever killed your grandsons deserved to die?"

Chapter Thirty

Tuesday, February 4, 1997 would be Darlie Routier's last day in court. All that was left for her attorneys to do was to plead for her life, to beg 12 men and women to spare Darlie Routier.

Court was scheduled to begin promptly at 9:00 A.M. Conspicuously absent was Darin Routier. Mumbles filled the courtroom. Where was Darin?

Family members paced in the aisle, wringing their hands and shrugging their shoulders. Deon Routier bolted from the courtroom in search of his missing brother. Fear etched the face of his wife Dana.

Darin had reportedly told family members he didn't want to live without Darlie. The vague mention of suicide now gave those close to Darin a reason to be concerned.

Richard Mosty asked the court to delay starting the proceedings until Darin Routier could be found.

"Overruled," Judge Tolle announced, giving the defense five minutes in which to locate the missing husband.

At 9:15, court was called in session. Darin was still absent.

Judge Tolle instructed the jury that, because they had found the defendant guilty, they must now decide punishment. The charge of capital murder brought a mandatory penalty of death or life imprisonment. He advised them that they were not to be swayed by sympathy, compassion, or sentiment.

There were two special issues that the jurors must consider. Judge Tolle read Special Issue number one.

"Do you find from the evidence a reasonable doubt that there is a probability that the defendant would commit criminal acts of violence that would constitute a continuing threat to society?"

If the answer to number one was yes, the jury then must proceed to answer Special Issue number two. Jurors looked solemnly at Judge Tolle as he read the second issue.

"Taking into consideration all of the evidence, including the circumstances of the offense, the defendant's character and background, and the personal moral culpability of the defendant, is there a sufficient mitigating circumstance or circumstances to warrant that a sentence of life imprisonment rather than a death sentence be imposed?"

The court advised jurors that they must deliberate and could not make their decision by the drawing of lots. With that statement, Judge Tolle turned the closing arguments over to Assistant District Attorney Sherri Wallace.

"On June 6, 1996, two precious children were forever silenced by their mother," Wallace began. "On their behalf I want to thank you for your wisdom and common sense. I know this case has been difficult. It has been difficult for all of us. I know you don't want to believe a mom killed her children. But the evidence is overwhelming. This woman over here," Wallace said pointing to Darlie Routier, "murdered her children. This family comes in here and tries to blame you for their hurting. She is to blame." Wallace's voice intensified.

"The court has asked you to answer two questions. The answers are so easy. Number one. Think about the crime.

See, folks, this isn't some crime where someone snapped. She planned this thing. She planned for a week. She had been sleeping downstairs for a week. She waited until her babies fell asleep. She walked into the kitchen. She stands at the butcher block. 'What weapon will I use to kill my children?' She pulls it out. She could have stopped there. She could have asked, what am I doing?

"She goes over to Devon, laying asleep. Is there anything more precious than a sleeping child? He is breathing heavy. He is in a deep sleep, exhausted from playing all day. She looks at him laying faceup. He's dreaming about riding bikes, licking popsicles. She plunges the knife in his chest," Wallace said in a loud voice. Then softer, "She could have stopped then. Surely she realizes she's wrong." Wallace's voice rises again. "She does it again, until he's dead. Then she goes over to Damon."

Wallace picked up a photo of five-year-old Damon Routier and showed it to the jury. "Look at those eyes. She could have stopped. She could have said, 'I can't do it to my child,' but she doesn't. These kids are nobody. She stabs Damon. It's hard. She had to go through bone, pull it out and do it again."

Spectators squirmed uncomfortably in their seats. The female prosecutor was painting a vivid picture of what the State believed happened on Eagle Drive on June 6th. Wallace made the scene real—too real.

"She goes off, flippin' stuff around. She stages that crime scene. We know from the blood trail that that little boy was trying to get out of there. He calls Mommy, as he's dying, looking up at her. She watched a little boy die," Wallace's voice trailed off into sadness.

"What did that mother do? Not one dad-gum thing. She held a towel to her own neck and asked when the ambulance would get there."

Darlie Routier sat placid through Wallace's dialogue. She showed no sadness, no anger, no emotions.

"She's a threat to anything that gets in her way. As long

as you don't cross her, she's fine. If you get in her way, God help you."

Wallace addressed the issue of question number two, mitigating circumstances, with an equal amount of passion.

"The family doesn't want to believe the truth," Wallace began. "You know the truth. They haven't been in this courtroom. They don't want to believe it. Who does? You may not want to kill her because she is a woman. Does that make those kids one bit less dead?

"If a stranger broke into that home and did this to two little boys, what would you do? You'd kill him in a heartbeat. Don't you know their mom doing this is so much worse? Take the fact that she is a woman out of the equation.

"Think about what she said on the Silly String tape. She has the gall to say those children had such rich and full lives. How can someone who had not gone to kindergarten have a rich and full life?

"Her mom asked you to have compassion. I ask you to have as much compassion for her as she did for her children.

"The most scary thing is she looks like us. She looks like a human being. She's not. She's not one thing like us.

"There are senseless crimes. They don't make sense, but they happened. The people who do them are so evil. We reserve the death penalty for those people. People like Darlie Routier."

The courtroom was silent, except for the forceful voice of Sherri Wallace. She had been quiet throughout most of the trial. She had sat at the prosecution table taking notes, whispering to her male counterparts, and trudging through law books. Many had thought Wallace was no more than a token woman on the prosecution team, a pawn to show that a woman could prosecute another woman and ask for the death penalty. But Wallace was proving she was no token. She was in command of the courtroom. All eyes were on the pretty prosecutor, an angel in a white business suit come to avenge the deaths of Devon and Damon Routier.

"You have a tremendous opportunity," Wallace said as she approached the jury. "There are juries all around the state making decisions. People don't hear about them. They'll hear about what you do. Tell this nation that in Texas we protect our children. If you harm our children, you will get the stiffest punishment of our laws.

"Think about all the times she could have stopped. Changed her mind. Think about the last few minutes of life. What did they say? 'Mommy, it hurts?' It hurt!" Wallace emphasized.

"You must all be in agreement. You must all agree to the verdict. Tell this nation, this world," Wallace said stepping toward the defense table. "Darlie Routier, we are not going to tolerate what you've done to our children. You are going to die," Wallace said loudly, looking Darlie Routier in the eye.

Jurors had hung on Wallace's every word. Spectators took deep breaths. The young prosecutor had ripped at their hearts. But Darlie stared at Wallace with a lack of expression.

Betty Mosty, the wife of Defense Attorney Richard Mosty, and their two teenaged daughters cried almost uncontrollably. Mosty believed in his client and his family shared his sentiment.

Darin Routier had slipped quietly into the courtroom during the last of Sherri Wallace's closing summation. He grinned at Darlie, held his palms together, and mouthed, "Home praying."

Mulder had a hard act to follow. Sherri Wallace had grabbed the emotions of not just the jury, but everyone in the courtroom. The seasoned attorney strolled to the jury box. He told jurors that he was disappointed in their verdict, but added that it was not his position to quarrel with them. Then the attorney began to tear down the State's witnesses. He discredited the stepdaughter of Glen

Mize because of that relationship, he called Eileen Schimer a "volunteer" witness who wanted to get in on the act, and claimed Nelda Watts suffered from a case of mistaken identity.

Just as in previous days, Mulder's slam-dunk tactics were not playing for the jury. Disgust crossed the faces of many. They seemed tired of hearing about the faults of the witnesses.

But Mulder continued. Of Kay Norris he said she did nothing more than disapprove of Darlie's language. He saved his most biting comments for Helena Czaban. "She is traceable back to Basha (Barbara Jovell, her daughter)," Mulder said. "And the apple doesn't fall far from the tree," making reference to the mental problems of Barbara Jovell which had been exposed in court.

Then Mulder began a rambling that few in the courtroom understood. He began rehashing all the evidence presented in the guilt/innocence phase of the trial. The blood evidence, fingerprints, the defense expert who claimed Darlie's wounds were self-inflicted, Dr. Lisa Clayton who said she lacked the psychological makeup of a woman who kills her children, the medical examiner who testified that the boys would have lasted only eight or nine minutes, and blood splatters on her T-shirt, which Mulder claimed would have had the same chance of being found as in hitting the lottery.

Mulder was attempting to reinstill reasonable doubt, an issue jurors had already resolved.

"I've never seen a situation where all the victims's relations have rallied around the defendant. Obviously, they know her better than we do. They believe she is incapable of any act of violence of this magnitude," Mulder said.

He suggested that there would be a common thread, a history if Darlie Routier had been the killer. But he stressed there was nothing to suggest that Darlie was a devious person.

"I suggest you still don't know how or why it happened,

or the time restraints. The proof is not so positive as not to be infallible."

As Mulder sat down at the defense table, another defense attorney, Curtis Glover took over the helm. Like Mulder, he challenged the evidence in the case, in particular the time line.

In Glover's short summation, he told jurors that Davis would say that society needed to be vindicated. He argued that society did not need to be vindicated and that the family could only be further wounded by a death penalty verdict. Glover closed by asking one question. "In your heart of hearts, can you destroy this woman?"

Next up for the defense was S. Preston Douglas.

"The media will go on to other stories," the attorney said. "They will forget the names of the lawyers and the judge. Not one of you will forget passing judgment on Darlie Routier. I'm proud, humble, and scared," Douglas told jurors. "I believe that life is worth saving. The law provides enough punishment. That's life [in prison]."

During a break in closing arguments, a producer for the *Maury Povich Show* got the attention of Darlie Routier. He gave a thumbs-up sign and flashed her a smile.

This unidentified man had been sitting with the Routier family during closing arguments. Courtroom observers had been speculating on his identify. From the designer jeans, worn with loafers and a pullover v-necked sweater, the sleeves pushed up to his elbows, he was obviously not a Texan. He appeared out of place in the small country town nestled in the Texas hill country.

When everyone had regained their seats, Mostly addressed the jury. "This is the last place I want to be today," he said with sadness in his voice. "This is the only place I can be because I'm going to stand beside her no matter what."

Mosty stood behind Darlie Routier, his hands on her shoulders. Darlie cried softly as Mosty spoke. "By your verdict you've said something beyond our understanding has happened. Some set of circumstances came together. Some course of events came about where this young girl did something contrary to anything done in her whole life. Something no one can understand, define. Something happened completely different than this young girl sitting here.

"If you sentence her to life, that set of circumstances, events, chain of action, can never happen again. She won't be a continued threat to society. You know that whatever happened that night was a one time event, beyond explanation," Mosty rationalized. He did not move from behind Darlie Routier.

Newsmen in the audience shook their heads and wrote feverishly in their notepads. Why would Mosty imply that June 6th was a one-time event if Darlie Routier was innocent, as he claimed?

Mosty went on to say that the prosecutions hatred of the family was amazing to him. He praised the family for their support and asked the jury if they thought they could get a courtroom full of supporters.

"If there's anything we've learned from the New Testament, it is the story of forgiveness," Mosty said. "Every human being has value, has worth. I'm telling you there's a lot more to her than the State can muster."

Mosty had tears in his eyes as he continued to hold on to his client and beg the jury to spare her life.

"Mr. Davis said only Darlie and God know. If God only knows—I say leave the judgement to God. I beseech you in the name of God. Think that you may be mistaken."

Mosty sat next to his client. He was tired, drained emotionally. There was nothing left that he could do for Darlie Routier.

Defense attorneys had spent most of the time they were allotted to plea for Darlie's life by attempting to retry the case—a case in which the question of guilt had already been answered. The last lawyer to speak would be Assistant District Attorney **Greg Davis**. He would not retry the evidence, he would ask the 12 men and women to put Darlie Routier to death.

"If there was no evil in the world, there would be no need for the death penalty," Davis began. "Today that evil goes by the name of Darlie Routier."

Davis assured the jury that, regardless of the implications by the defense attorneys, they were not mistaken in their guilty verdict. He added that the prosecutors did not hate Darlie Lynn Routier, but hated what she did to those two children.

"We now know exactly what happened on June sixth. This case, on the facts alone, calls for the death penalty," Davis said.

"On June fourteenth Darin Routier said, 'a wolf came in and took the lives of two helpless sheep'. In this case, that wolf paraded around like a shepherd," Davis said, casting a glare at the defendant. Davis reminded the jury that both Darin and Sarilda Routier had commented before Darlie was arrested that whoever killed Devon and Damon should die for what they did.

"This case calls out for death," Davis said. "She rammed that knife in five inches deep, two inches deep. She rammed it in his [Damon's] body four times. Is there one of us that would have said this case deserves the minimum?

"This is the kind of woman capable of the barbaric," Davis said picking up photos of Damon Routier. "She is capable of turning this," he said, holding up the posed, angelic picture of the small boy, "into this." Then he raised the autopsy photo of the slain child.

Muffled gasps could be heard from the gallery. Davis had certainly created a dramatic moment—a frightening visual of death.

"As her attorneys ask for mercy, that night she acted as judge, jury, and executioner. Their crime was acting like boys. Their sentence was death. The execution, a knife plunged in their bodies.

"Send a signal to the defendant and those like her who

would think of hurting children. You cannot hurt our children. We will come after you. These children deserved peace and happiness. They deserved justice on June sixth and today they get it. Say, 'when you take the life of a child in Texas, you better get ready to pay the price'."

Davis returned to the prosecution table. There was no more to be said. All he could do was wait, wait for the jury's verdict.

With tears in his eyes, Darin Routier looked at his wife and mouthed, "I love you." Darlie mouthed, "I love you, too."

Darlie Kee left the courtroom with tears in her eyes. It was one of the few times she had allowed herself to show sensitive emotion.

The always vocal Sarilda Routier had stayed away from court. She had returned to her home in Lubbock with baby Drake. She'd decided not to listen to the State ask jurors to kill her favorite daughter-in-law—her friend.

Spectators mulled around the courthouse. No one could guess how long it would take for the verdict to come back. For sure, no one wanted to miss the moment of reckoning for Darlie Routier.

Just four hours after the 12 jurors retired to deliberate, they emerged with a verdict. Everyone was shocked at the speed in which they had made their decision. Some spectators thought the fast verdict meant that there was no way they would sentence the woman to die, while others thought the quick decision meant certain death for Darlie.

Again, law enforcement personnel lined the interior walls of the Kerr County courtroom in case there was disorder when the verdict was read. Dana and Deon Routier entered the room holding hands. Darin Routier leaned forward, resting his head on the back of the seat in front of him. Tears ran down his whisker-stubbled cheeks.

"This has been a lengthy and vigorously contested trial,"

Judge Tolle said somberly. "This can be an emotional time. If anyone feels they can't stand this verdict, now is the time to leave. No one will think less of you."

Lou Ann Brown, Dana Routier's mother, wiped tears from her reddened eyes.

The jury marched into the courtroom for the final time. They seemed weary, emotionally depleted. Some showed the telltale signs of crying.

Judge Tolle addressed the foreman. "Mr. Walker, on special issue number one, how do you find?"

"Yes, your Honor." The jury believed Darlie Routier would be a continuing threat to society.

"On special issue number two, how do you find?"

"No, your Honor." The jury found no mitigating circumstances in Darlie's favor.

Darlie Routier had been given the death penalty.

Darin Routier sobbed, his head still resting on the seat in front of him. Dana Routier cried on her husband's shoulder.

There was no visible reaction from Darlie Kee and other members of the family. They appeared to be confused or in shock.

Darlie Routier stood, dry-eyed, and faced the judge.

"Darlie Routier, the jury having found you guilty, it is the duty of the court to access the punishment of death," Judge Tolle said.

Darlie Routier was taken back to the Kerr County jail to wait for transport to the women's correctional facility in Gatesville, Texas. There she would join six other women on Death Row. Betty Lou Beets, the oldest at 59, convicted of shooting her fifth husband to death. Cathy Lynn Henderson, convicted in the abduction and slaying of a three-month old boy she had been babysitting. Frances Elaine Newton, convicted in the shooting deaths of her husband and two children. Pamela Lynn Perillo, convicted in the robbery/slaying of a Houston man. Erica Yvonne Sheppard, the youngest at 23, convicted in a robbery/carjacking/murder. Karla Faye Tucker, convicted in the pickax slaying of a Houston man.

Mosty left the courthouse in tears. A man strongly opposed to the death penalty, the courtroom defeat weighed heavily on his shoulders.

"I told Darlie she should prepare herself for a death sentence because I thought the handwriting was on the wall," Mosty told reporters.

"If somebody killed me, this is where I'd want them prosecuted," Doug Mulder stated, referring to the law-and-order justice of Kerr County.

Tight-liped, Darin Routier and Mama Darlie left the courthouse arm-in-arm without comment.

Dallas prosecutors had won an enormous victory. A victory that was bittersweet.

"This was a fairly quick return on a verdict today," Davis said. "I think it sent a very strong, clear message to her [Darlie] and to others like her. This will not be tolerated."

The long, burdensome trial had been taxing on everyone, attorneys, prosecutors, and media personnel alike. Darlie Routier appeared emotionally depleted.

"She's not going to give anybody the satisfaction of a reaction," Toby Shook told reporters when asked about the defendant's lack of response. "I doubt if it even got her heart rate up."

By his own admission, Darin Routier had been living in a world of denial. Refusing to let himself believe otherwise, he'd believed that Darlie would be coming home. Now, finally facing the fact that his wife would not be going home, he vowed to continue the fight.

"A world without Darlie wouldn't be the same. The sky wouldn't be as blue. The sun wouldn't be as bright," Darin said. "I told her, as long as she can fight, I would fight for her. And that's what we'll do. We'll keep on."

All Darin Routier would now be able to do was visit his

wife once a week for a maximum of two hours. There would be no physical contact between them. The majority of Death Row inmates are abandoned by family and friends after incarceration, even by the most supportive families. Only time will tell if Darlie Routier will be one of them.

And only time will tell whether Darlie Routier will pay the ultimate price . . . her own life for killing her own flesh and blood.

Epilogue

Like a ripple created from a stone tossed into Lake Ray Hubbard lapping to the shores of Rowlett, the deaths of Devon and Damon Routier affected everyone touched by them.

Lives have been forever altered.

DARLIE ROUTIER: Darlie resides on Texas's Death Row for women in Gatesville, Texas. In sharp contrast to her once opulent lifestyle, her six-foot-by-nine-foot single cell is sparsely furnished with a stainless steel sink/toilet combination which hangs on one wall, a small cot, and a built-in desk with attached stool. She walks in a narrow exercise yard surrounded by a chain-link fence topped with razor wire.

Darlie has returned to the glamous look she enjoyed prior to her arrest. She colors and curls her hair, and wears the heavy makeup that was once her trademark.

It was revealed after her trial that her court-appointed attorneys arranged for her take a polygraph test in October 1996. The results were kept secret. Legal experts interpret the act of withholding the polygraph results as a sign that Darlie Routier did not do well.

Still craving attention, Darlie grants interviews to national television shows such as *Prime Time Live, Hard Copy,* and the *Maury Povich Show*. Her message is always the same—"I did not kill my children."

DARIN ROUTIER: Darin lives in Plano, Texas with his mother-in-law, Darlie Kee. He is attempting to rebuild his business, although insiders say he works only sporadically.

Darin has been observed sitting outside the Rowlett police station, glaring up at the second-floor windows where Detectives Patterson and Frosch are busy working on other cases. Sources close to him say he has purchased a bulletproof vest and a gun holster. "You don't know who you can trust," he told a friend.

Darin remains loyal to Darlie. He has confided in friends that the Saturday evening visits are becoming troublesome and he does not know how much longer he can keep up the weekly trips. It is also said that Darlie is upset that Darin's daily letters have dwindled to once a week.

A tattoo of Darlie has been etched above the images of Devon and Damon on Darin's arm—close to his heart.

DRAKE ROUTIER: Darin Routier, who cried outside the Kerr County courthouse that he had lost everything, relinquished parental rights to his youngest son, Drake, following the trial. In a custody hearing held March 5, 1997, Sarilda and Leonard Routier were awarded permanent custody of their grandson. Darin is not required to pay child support and has unlimited visitation rights.

When asked how he felt about his mother raising his only remaining son, with his typical broad grin Darin said, "She's a wonderful mother. Look how great I turned out."

Darin sees his son approximately twice a month.

FLESH AND BLOOD 305

DARLIE KEE: Mama Darlie has returned to her job as a secretary for a large telecommunications firm in Plano, Texas where she lives. She continues the fight for her daughter's freedom and her own media exposure by appearing on nationally syndicated talk shows and granting media interviews, including one for a German televison station arranged by Defense Attorney Mulder.

A bitter woman, Mama Darlie had announced that she will file suit against the City of Rowlett, the City of Garland, and Assistant District Attorney Greg Davis for the wiretap and surveillance filming at her grandsons' gravesite. Some report Mama Darlie also plans to sue the Kerr County jail for a fall she took on icy steps following a visit with her daughter.

SARILDA ROUTIER: Sarilda Routier and husband Lenny are raising their grandson Drake in their spacious, upscale home in Lubbock, Texas. Like Mama Darlie, Sarilda regularly appears on television and in the print media proclaiming Darlie's innocence. The Routier's have offered a $100,000 reward leading to the arrest and conviction of the person who killed their grandchildren. To date they have had no leads.

Sarilda takes Drake to visit his mother on Death Row, encouraging him to kiss the glass that separates them. The child will grow up never feeling the physical touch of his mother again.

Seemingly forgotten by Sarilda are her son Deon, his loving wife Dana, and their adorable son Dylan, as well as her own daughter, who is expecting her first child. Sarilda's life focuses on Darlie. Her energies are centered on helping "my sweet Darlie" come home.

Like Mama Darlie, Sarilda is bitter. She publicly ridicules the jurors, who she believes never listened to the family's cries of innocence. Some family members say she is also bitter that Darin, who is nearly penniless and in debt for Darlie's defense, has never paid her back for the funeral flowers for her grandsons.

OFFICER DAVID WADDELL: The first officer on the scene at the Routier home has left the Rowlett Police Department and taken a position with the Plano police.

SERGEANT MATT WALLING: Walling was promoted to lieutenant within the Rowlett P.D. On his way home from the crime scene June 6th, Walling felt like crying. He tried to cry. He couldn't. Not until Walling met with Rowlett paramedics for a debriefing later in the week did he let go of his feelings of despair, his feelings of helplessness for the loss of Devon and Damon.

DETECTIVE JIM PATTERSON: Patterson continues to investigate crimes against persons with the Rowlett P.D. He was awarded a police commendation for his work on the Darlie Routier murder case. Patterson is angry that he and his fellow officers were slammed to the mat by the Routier family after Darlie's arrest and continue to be ridiculed by them publicly. Patterson still sees the small faces of Devon and Damon Routier in his sleep.

DETECTIVE CHRIS FROSCH: Frosch has remained with the investigative division of the Rowlett P.D. Greatly disturbed by the accusation of illegal wiretapping and forced to invoke his Fifth Amendment right during the trial, Frosch had once considered leaving the force. Vindicated by Paul Coggins, U.S. Attorney General in Texas who stated that the surveillance measures enacted at the gravesite were not illegal, Frosch continues his work, as dedicated to law enforcement as ever. Frosch was given a Meritorious Service award for his work on the Routier case, along with

Crime Scene Tech Sarah Jones and Crime Scene Tech Charles Hamilton.

SERGEANT DAVID NABORS: Like Patterson, Nabors and CID Sergeant Lamar Evans received Police Commendations for their crime scene investigation at the Routier home. Feeling an enormous sense of loss, Nabors and his fellow officers who worked directly on the Routier case met for stress management counseling. They learned to manage their tears and their anger at the senseless slaying of the two little boys—emotions that still remain just beneath the surface. Even today, Nabors cannot look at the smiling faces in photos of Devon and Damon Routier without seeing them lying on the blood-soaked carpet of the Routier family room.

ROWLETT FIRE DEPARTMENT PARAMEDICS: Captain Dennis Vrava, Rick Coleman, Jack Kolbye, Bryan Kolshak, and Eric Zimmerman continue to serve the citizens of Rowlett. All these men have experienced post-traumatic stress disorder associated with the horrific slayings of Devon and Damon Routier. These big men, all over six-feet, with three more than six-feet-seven inches tall, have cried tears of sorrow for the loss of the lives they fought so hard to save. Some have experienced nightmares, sleepwalking, uncontrollable crying, and depression. All have participated in post-critical incident debriefings. Some continue to seek counseling. Some say no amount of counseling will erase the experience of peering into the lifeless eyes of Devon Routier, and watching the final light of life escape from Damon.

DEVON AND DAMON ROUTIER: For 10 months the gravesite of Devon and Damon Routier remained unadorned. Except for two small concrete angels and a few trinkets left by neighborhood children, no one would know that the unmarked grave was that of the two slain brothers. A grave marker now spans the Rockwell cemetery plot where the boys are buried.

With the family focusing on freeing the convicted killer of Devon and Damon Routier, the boys remain the forgotten victims.